One Lucky Hero

Also by Codi Gary

The Men in Uniform Series

I Need a Hero (a novella)

One Lucky Hero

The Rock Canyon, Idaho Series

Bad For Me

Return of the Bad Girl

Bad Girls Don't Marry Marines

Good Girls Don't Date Rock Stars

Things Good Girls Don't Do

The Trouble with Sexy (a novella)

One Lucky Hero

THE MEN IN UNIFORM SERIES

CODI GARY

EPub Edition JUNE 2016 ISBN: 9780062372253
Print Edition ISBN: 9780062372277

AM 10 9 8 7 6 5 4 3 2 1

For my sisters; Natalie, Nicole, Tina,
Jen, Erin, Tasha, Elaine.
Love you all!

Chapter One

Violet Douglas lifted her face to the bright sunlight beaming down from the clear August sky. Her large black sunglasses shaded her brown eyes from the harsh glare, but she closed them anyway, breathing in the scent of barbeque and beer. As she leaned back on her hands, scratchy blades of grass bit into her palms and made her bare legs itch, but she didn't care. It just felt so good to take a break from her life.

"Girl, are you sleeping?" Violet's best friend, Tracy Washington, sat next to her, and Violet turned her way when Tracy added, "We did not pay thirty dollars for these concert tickets so you could take a nap!"

No, they definitely hadn't, but they also weren't all that excited about the current band playing on the stage. While the majority of the park was set up with vendor's tents, the massive stage was supposed to have a host of acts each taking their turn. The concert had started earlier in the day, but Violet and Tracy had only arrived a little after four. There was no point waiting around in the heat for an artist they didn't like.

"I was just enjoying the fresh air."

"Shit, I don't know how fresh it is, but the scenery is fantastic."

Violet opened her eyes just as Tracy pulled her own dark sunglasses down her nose, obviously ogling a couple of shirtless guys in board shorts.

"Mmmm, I am telling you, some of these guys have got to be from the base. No gym rat could look that good."

"What are you talking about? All of them work out the exact same way. They lift weights and run for a ridiculous amount of time." Violet hated running personally and couldn't understand the appeal.

"No, military men don't run on a treadmill. Plus, they carry guns, and that's hot," Tracy said.

"So do cops and criminals." Violet nodded toward a couple of uniformed men walking through the crowds of people wandering around Discovery Park.

"Please, those are rent-a-cops, they barely have pepper spray." Tracy gathered her long black hair up off her neck and fanned herself. "Fuck, it is hot out here."

Of course it was hot. Sacramento, California, in the dead of summer felt like someone turned up a heat lamp and adjusted it to hit you right on the forehead. It was nearly six in the evening and still 104 degrees in the shade. Violet had lathered her pale skin with SPF 50 and had packed the bottle, a sweatshirt, and a blanket in her tote bag. Not that she really thought the heat would burn off tonight, but just in case, she didn't want to be caught without something.

Was that a sign that she was aging before her time? Being super prepared and sleepy at the thought of staying at the park until at least eleven? She was only twenty-four, and yet the drama that had taken over her life for the last ten years made her feel much older. Being the legal guardian of her brother and sister had definitely added to that. At her age, she should have been hitting bars and dating, but she had very little experience with either.

Not that she was a prude by any means, but after her mother had died and her dad's drug abuse worsened, she'd withdrawn from most of the kids in high school, and because she wasn't free to go out most weekends, guys had seemed to forget about her. At the time, she'd been too distracted to care, but now she was determined to make up for lost time. Especially with her sister, Daisy, leaving for Oregon State University in mid-September. Then she'd just have her brother, Casey, at home to worry about.

Of course, Casey hadn't exactly been easy to deal with for the last year. At first, Violet had just assumed her brother's moodiness was a side effect of puberty, but it had become more than that. He'd stopped going to his art classes at the youth center and started getting into trouble at school. It wasn't like him; Casey had been this unstoppable bundle of energy, until he wasn't. Now he hardly left the house, and when he did, half the time he came home in a foul mood, or worse, had another run-in with the cops and was brought home in a squad car. She'd grounded him, taken away privileges, and tried over and over to get him to talk to her, but he just kept saying he was fine. She desperately needed this break from trying to figure out what had happened to her little brother.

Just four more years and you can really focus on what you want. No one else.

"Oh, man, check out that guy," Tracy said. She adjusted her halter top, showing off another half inch of her cleavage.

Violet followed her gaze to two guys in cargo shorts and T-shirts about a hundred yards away, walking toward them. Violet's eyes passed right over the blond pretty boy and latched onto his tan, muscular friend. His dark hair was shaved close, and she couldn't tell what color his eyes were, but she was already dying to get a closer look.

"Which one?" Violet asked. *Don't pick mine. Don't pick mine.*

"The one who looks like a young Paul Walker. Damn, I could eat him up with a spoon."

"Gross, Trace." Violet stood up with a grin, pulling the hem of her shorts down. "Dibs on his friend."

"Oh, you're calling dibs, huh? What do you want him for?" Tracy rose to her feet, staring at the two men. "He looks like a dick."

"You can't tell that by looking at him. And as to what I want to do with him, I just want to have a good time." Well, maybe a little more than that. Over the last few months, Violet had been feeling rather restless. Was restless the right word? More like bored as fuck. It was the same thing every week: school, work, volunteer, cook, clean, drama, repeat. This was her first night out in months, and she wanted to take full advantage of her freedom.

"Your version of a good time or mine?" Tracy teased.

Violet laughed, remembering when Tracy had nearly been arrested for indecent exposure. She'd been drunk and getting it on with some guy in a club. The bouncer had threatened to call the cops if she didn't get her top back on and leave, and she'd actually flipped him off as she'd strutted out the door in her bra, the guy she'd been hooking up with following behind. There was no question that Tracy was crazy, but Violet loved her.

That didn't mean she was ready to become an exhibitionist, though.

"Somewhere in between, I think."

"Then let's go." Tracy took off, leaving Violet to grab her tote and catch up with a heavy sigh. Why was it that Tracy could never be subtle about anything, especially when it came to men?

Probably because she's never met a guy who's said no.

"Dude, you can't just walk up to them and be like, *What's up!*"

"Why not?" Tracy didn't slow down, but her tone sounded mildly puzzled.

"Because they might not be interested. They might have girlfriends. They might—"

"Will you shut up and follow my lead? If they don't take the bait, then we'll move on to hotter victims."

Violet wasn't sure how she felt about calling men *victims*. "Easy for you to say! Guys trip all over themselves to get with you."

Tracy tossed her hair and stared down her prey with laser focus, even as she hissed, "I swear to God, if you do not stop that shit, I will kick your ass. You are gorgeous. You look like freaking Julia Roberts in *Pretty Woman*, and I would kill for your long legs, so hush your butt and focus!"

About ten feet away, the Paul Walker look-alike glanced their way, started to turn back to his friend, and then did a double take. Violet caught Tracy's *come and get me, big boy* look and would have laughed, except that tall, dark, and potentially dickish followed his buddy's gaze. And when his eyes met hers—eyes like melted chocolate above a Roman nose and full lips—she swallowed hard.

But then his full lips pinched tightly in displeasure.

Violet's excitement shriveled like a popped water balloon.

"Hello, ladies." The blond flashed a million-watt smile at them, but Violet was immune. Maybe he was handsome in an obvious way, but she liked someone with more character to his face.

Too bad *that* guy seemed to be looking everywhere but at her. Did she have a booger on her face or something?

"Hey there." Tracy's voice had dropped two octaves and sounded like the purr of a cat.

"I'm Tyler."

"And I'm Tracy."

"Check that out, T and T. I guess that means we'd be dynamite together."

Tracy actually giggled. Violet snorted at the cheesy line, earning an elbow in her ribs from Tracy.

"This is my friend, Violet," Tracy said.

"Nice to meet you." Violet pushed her sunglasses on top of her head and held her hand out to Tyler.

"Nice to meet you, too. This is Dean."

Dean. She'd always liked that name. It wasn't a name used that often anymore, kind of like her own. She might have to use that little observation to break the ice, since his features were definitely schooled with a chilly edge.

She released Tyler's hand and held hers out to Dean, who took it reluctantly. His palm was warm, rough, and heat seared her skin as he squeezed gently. Violet's gaze shot up to meet his eyes, but he didn't seem affected by her at all.

"Hi, Dean."

"Hey." His voice was deep and gravelly, like Mathew MacFadyen without the accent. *Of course he would sound like Mr. Darcy...* His cool demeanor was definitely reminiscent of him.

He released her hand abruptly and wiped his along his shorts. Self-consciously she rubbed her finger across her palm, but it didn't feel sweaty.

What was his problem?

"So, where are you boys headed?" Tracy seemed oblivious to the tension between Violet and Dean, despite Violet's attempt at telepathy.

Come on, Trace, not these guys.

"To the beer garden. Wanna join us?" Tyler said.

Violet opened her mouth to say no, but Tracy jumped in. "We would love to."

So much for the best friend mind meld they always joked about. Disappointment threaded through Violet as she imagined how the rest of the night would go: awkward silence between her and Dean while Tracy and Tyler made out until Tyler asked her to come home with him.

Which pretty much meant Violet's night was going to be a total bust.

Tracy and Tyler fell into step beside each other, talking a mile a minute while Violet and Dean walked behind them. Violet kept glancing his way, hoping he'd say something, but he just stared straight ahead, his face blank.

It was really too bad he was being so standoffish. He really was hot.

Just talk to him. Maybe he's shy.

Violet didn't believe that for a second but tried anyway. "So, what do you do, Dean?"

"I'm a soldier."

"Like in the army?" It sounded stupid the minute it left her lips, but she couldn't take it back.

"Yes, soldiers are army." His tone was full of condescension, and Violet's muscles tensed, irritation prickling her skin.

So, Tracy really does have some kind of dick-radar.

"Sorry, just clarifying." *Why are you apologizing?* "I'm going to school for psychology."

Dean didn't say anything, and Violet's jaw clenched in frustration. "You're kind of taciturn, aren't you?"

"What's that mean?" he asked.

"Not very talkative," she said.

"I just don't have a lot to say."

This is NOT how I planned on spending my evening.

It was the first time in months that Violet hadn't needed to worry about her brother and sister, her classes, or her work schedule. Today was supposed to be about hanging with her best friend and doing something any normal twenty-four-year-old would enjoy.

Which meant she didn't need to tolerate hanging with a jerk who couldn't even make polite conversation. It wasn't like she was asking him to marry her or something. Just a little chitchat while their friends hooked up.

Instead, his attitude was threatening her good mood.

They showed their IDs at the beer garden and entered a large enclosed area with several beer vendors stationed around the perimeter. Tyler led the way to one of the bars and bought them each a beer. Violet took hers but didn't down it the way Tracy did. She didn't drink often and was afraid that if she drank too fast, she might not be walking out of here later.

"So, Tyler, what band are you here to see?" Violet figured it was probably one of the rock bands. They didn't look like the type to enjoy rap music or pop, but at a concert like this, where they had about eight artists from all different genres, it was hard to guess.

"Jimmy Eat World. How about you two?"

"Meghan Trainor," Violet and Tracy said together, laughing. The mind meld was back, apparently.

"You know, 'cause it's all about that bass." Tracy shook her ass as she danced around before taking a long pull from her plastic cup.

"I can appreciate that," Tyler said, his gaze glued to Tracy's ass.

Violet quickly disregarded her good intentions and drank her beer, narrowly avoiding rolling her eyes. If she had to listen to any more Cheese Whiz from Tyler, she was going to need a good buzz. She grimaced as the beer swirled around her taste buds. It was definitely not her drink of choice, especially when it wasn't even cold.

"Ugh, warm beer grosses me out." Violet spoke to no one in particular, she just couldn't help herself.

"If you don't like the taste of beer, then why drink it?" Dean asked suddenly.

Wow, some genuine interest. Shocking.

Violet glanced at Tyler, who was engrossed in conversation with Tracy. "Because it was free, and it would be rude to waste it."

She could have sworn his mouth twitched as if he was about to smile, but then it stopped. *Maybe it was a muscle spasm.*

"Are you always the epitome of good manners?"

Still a little stung by his previous rudeness, she said, "Indeed I am. Even when people don't show me the same courtesy."

This time, his cheeks flushed for sure. Vindicated, she downed the rest of her beer in a well-timed gulp.

That's right. Feel the shame, Mr. Jerk Face.

"If you're talking about me, I apologize," he said. "If I'm being brutally honest, I'm just not interested in women right now. I just wanted to get out of my apartment."

"Oh, well, if you're looking to experiment, I have a friend named Ian who would drool over you." Violet knew that wasn't what he meant but loved the way his eyes widened in panic.

"I didn't mean that. I'm not gay. I just meant that I'm not looking to date anyone."

"I know. I was just messing with you," she said.

His face darkened to an almost unhealthy shade of red. "I don't have a problem with people being gay, I'm just not."

"You know when you explain yourself, you only make things worse, right?" Man, did she love making him flustered. Especially since it wiped that stony look off his face.

His eyes narrowed and glittered. "You don't know me well enough to screw with me. I might be dangerous."

For a half a second, his words kick-started Violet's heart rate. He was right about that, and he definitely had the guns to twist her head off with one jerk.

"Are you?" she asked.

He leaned over her slowly, and she stiffened, her body screaming to step back.

"No, I'm not."

His soft words sank in, and she let out a huge breathless laugh. "That's not something you should joke about."

"Hey, you were messing with me first."

And now the heat radiating off his body was screwing with her senses, drawing her closer to him. The light scent of cologne drifted up, and she had the craziest urge to press her nose against his chest and get a better sniff. Violet caught herself in the nick of time, knowing that there was no coming back from that.

"I wasn't threatening and trying to intimidate you with my very presence. I don't know who told you that you were a funny guy, but you aren't. At all."

"You're right, it was a bad joke," he said. "I'm not really used to being around civilized company. Most days, I just hang with this guy"—Dean pointed at Tyler—"and a bunch of other dudes who think I'm hysterical."

"Are you the boss?" she asked.

"Yeah, why?"

"Then they really don't think you're funny, they are just lying because they don't want to get fired."

She said it all with a straight face and was secretly delighted when he chuckled. He was close enough still that the rise of his chest was only a few inches from her, and her gaze was drawn to the definition of his muscles through his T-shirt.

Geez, was she really so desperate that she was willing to hook up with a jerk with a weird sense of humor? She waited for her subconscious to give her a definite hell no, but apparently, the jury in her head was still deliberating.

"We don't really get fired from the military, unless we are suddenly unable to do the job."

"Well, regardless, if that's a sample of your humor, you need to watch some comedy. And not dark comedy like *The Cable Guy* or *The Ladykillers*." Violet glanced over at Tracy and Tyler, who were still nursing their beers. She was running out of witty things to say to Dean and wouldn't mind another drink in her system, but waiting on Tyler to buy another round was slow going.

Besides, it wasn't like she couldn't buy her own alcohol. Especially if it was something other than hops.

"I'm going to grab another drink. You want one?"

"I'll come with you and get one myself." He drained the remainder of his plastic cup, and she sighed in exasperation.

"It's a beer, not a proposal. You can grab the next round." Violet tapped Tracy and Tyler on the shoulders. "Another?"

"Sure, thanks," Tyler said.

Tracy nodded and mouthed, *Isn't he hot?*

Violet answered with a large smile, although he wasn't in her opinion. No, she preferred her men with dark eyes and no manners, apparently.

Except maybe the rudeness was an act. For a second there, she'd thought Dean might have a sense of humor. Granted, a dark and twisty sense of humor, but she liked that.

Liked him.

Maybe he wasn't a total loss. He might be suffering the effects of a bad breakup, and saw all women as the enemy.

Or you've been watching too many Hallmark Channel movies.

She could take the pressure off, give him notice that she wasn't looking for a boyfriend. Boyfriends were just one more thing to add to her ever-growing list of responsibilities; they were time consuming, needy, and the last thing she wanted was to put one more person's needs before her own.

As she grabbed their empty cups, saving Dean's for last, she looked up at him from beneath her lashes and went for broke.

"By the way…I wasn't looking for a date."

Chapter Two

DEAN SPARKS STARED after Violet, stunned silent by her bold admission.

Bullshit.

Dean had known the minute he saw her that she was the love, marriage, and baby carriage type. She wasn't dressed like some of the other women at the concert—hunting for some action—not in her tank top and shorts that were modest by comparison, but even before she'd lifted those bug-eyed sunglasses and flashed those deep brown eyes at him, he'd been struck by her sweet smile and entrancing voice. Then he'd touched her hand, and it was as if she'd burned him with just the heat of her palm. He hadn't meant to jerk away from her, but the sensation had been swift and intense, something unexpected.

Especially since he wasn't planning to stick around.

All he needed was for his pain-in-the-ass psychiatrist to sign off on his psych eval and he could get back to actually being a soldier, going where people needed him. Hadn't he been punished long enough? All because of one moment, one fraction of time in his ten years in the military, when he'd froze. When the bomb went off, he couldn't move, couldn't breathe. He'd just lain there, trapped under Private Hendrickson's body, his ears still ringing from the blast and impact as he'd hit the ground.

Once the ringing had stopped, the screams started. The cries for help, the moans of agony. Dean could still hear them, especially in the quiet.

Which was why he avoided it at all costs.

When he'd first been transferred to Sacramento and ordered to attend group therapy, he'd been numb. Matter-of-fact and detached. It wasn't until about three months after he'd settled in that the nightmares had started, but connecting with Oliver Martinez, Tyler Best, and Blake Kline had helped with that. They had all been ordered to attend group for different reasons, but Dean had found himself hitting Mick's with them a couple times a week to ease the loneliness of going back to his place.

It was all supposed to be temporary, even his friends. He'd figured six months tops, and he'd be cleared. Aside from the nightmares, he had adjusted to what happened. He was fine.

Instead, he'd been assigned as director of the new military outreach program, Alpha Dog Training Program. They were trying the community program out in the Sacramento area first, but the goal was to eventually have one in every city across the country. It was supposed to be a way to help kids who had gotten into trouble; instead of sending nonviolent offenders to juvie, they were sent to Alpha Dog to serve out their sentences. While there, the kids learned how to care for animals and train them in basic obedience. After their time at Alpha Dog was up, the program would assist them in finding part-time jobs with local animal shelters and veterinary hospitals or ROP programs to continue their education in Animal Health.

Dean was proud of the program, especially since it gave shelter dogs that wouldn't have been adopted otherwise a new lease on life. As the program's animal behavior expert, Best visited local shelters and evaluated dogs set to be euthanized, temperament testing them. If they passed, they found a new home at Alpha Dog, and once they went through basics with a kid, they would be put into a specialty program and trained by one of the experienced handlers. Right now the program focused on military, police, search and rescue, and therapy dogs, but they were hoping to expand the roles in the coming years.

As the director, Dean was in charge of the day-to-day operations and intakes, but some days it felt like he was just a glorified paper pusher. He didn't belong behind a desk; he needed to be back overseas. His father, grandfather, and great-grandfather had all been military, had worked their way up the ranks through blood, sweat, and tears, not by dealing with worried parents and angry teenagers.

He needed to prove that he could still do the job. That he wasn't donc. He wasn't ready to be finished with the field.

Still, it wasn't as if he didn't like Alpha Dog. He enjoyed working with the kids who came through and training the dogs. Hell, he wouldn't have his American pit bull terrier mix, Dilbert, if it wasn't for Alpha Dog, but that was supposed to have been a temporary placement, too. He was committed to finding Dilbert the perfect home before he left; he just hadn't found it yet.

The bottom line was he had never planned to stay this long.

Which was why he'd been steering clear of most women. He hadn't been living completely as a monk, but his hookups had been few and far between. The last thing he wanted was to lead a woman on only to bail as soon as he got his new orders.

Dean's gaze was drawn to Violet again, her gorgeous red hair flowing down her back as she laughed at something the bartender said. She was hot, with legs up to her chest and those perky tits under that blue tank top—but she wasn't hookup material.

And that was all he could offer right now.

She came walking back, juggling the four drinks in two hands. When she caught him looking at her, she flashed that wide, friendly smile again. It was like a ray of fucking sunshine, and damn if he didn't want to bask in it.

Before he even realized it, he was moving toward her. "Let me help you with those."

"I got them, but you can take yours." Violet held out the beer to him, and he took it, his fingers brushing against hers with a jolt.

Without asking again, he took another beer off her hands. "I'm trying to make up for being rude, but you gotta work with me."

Violet seemed to study him for a moment, as if evaluating his sincerity. "I appreciate the effort."

Her tone was soft and husky, and for just a moment, Dean couldn't look away from her eyes and was lost in their twinkly, dark depths. He half expected smoke to rise up between them the air was so charged, and a faint voice hollered deep inside him to look away, but he was too distracted by the soft sound of her breathing as her mouth opened a little. An unspoken invitation for him to come closer, to see if she tasted like her lips looked: sweetly tart, like sun-ripened raspberries.

"Yo, are you two gonna kiss or kill each other?"

Tracy's ill-timed joke broke the connection, and Dean turned from her, silently cursing himself as he brought the beer to Best. He sensed Violet beside him but couldn't look at her. What was wrong with him? Was it the fact that he was trying not to be attracted to her that made her more desirable?

"I come bearing libation." He glanced her way as she spoke, but she was giving Tracy an angry scowl and wasn't paying him any attention.

"I will accept your libation," Tracy said.

Dean held Best's beer out to him. "Here."

"Thanks, buddy. I love it when you serve me." Best took his cup and gave Dean a raised eyebrow as he took a drink of his beer, silently asking him what he thought of Violet.

Dean shook his head, and Best frowned, confusion muddying up his pretty face.

"Hey, Violet, thanks for the beer," Tyler called.

"Just returning the favor," she said.

"I like that. Most women wouldn't offer." Tyler grinned at Tracy, who tossed her hair.

"Are you assuming I'm one of those women?" Tracy asked.

"Shouldn't I?" he asked.

"Hell, yeah, you should." Tracy took a sip and shot him a wink, while he laughed.

During all the banter, Dean realized that Violet had made her way back to his side, her shoulder brushing his. The hairs on his arm stood up, and despite the heat, gooseflesh rose up over his skin.

"You aren't drinking your beer. Worried I slipped you a roofie?" she asked.

Dean released a startled laugh and then took a large gulp of his beer, holding it in his cheeks like a chipmunk. Violet giggled, and he swallowed, opening his mouth for her inspection. "There. Now I guess we just wait and see."

"Don't worry. If I wanted to have my way with you, I'd just go about it the old-fashioned way." She tipped her cup up to her lips and with only her eyes showing, wiggled her eyebrows.

Dean was intrigued, despite his best intentions. "And what is the old-fashioned way?"

Violet swallowed and stepped closer to him, laying her free hand against his chest. Dean stood frozen, holding his breath as she looked up at him from beneath the fan of her black lashes. Slowly, she stood up on her tiptoes and put her mouth next to his ear, her breath warming his ear and his cock stirred to life as he breathed her in.

"Well, I'd start by getting closer, giving you light, brief touches on your arm, hand"—she moved her hand lightly across his chest—"maybe even the front of your T-shirt."

God help him, where the hell had this come from? She couldn't have shocked him more if she'd stripped naked and danced around him. Maybe appearances were deceiving; she looked like she should be leading her church choir, not whispering sweet nothings to him in public.

She dropped back onto her feet, and Dean wanted badly to pull her back and press his aching hard-on against her.

He glanced toward Tyler, but he was back to being completely absorbed in Tracy.

"That... ahem... That's all it would take?" Dean asked.

"Well, I hope not. If you're that easy, then where is the fun?"

Dean choked, and Violet's laugh drew Tracy and Best's attention.

"What's so funny?" Tracy asked.

"Nothing, Dean and I were just getting to know each other. Right?"

Everyone was looking at him, but while Tracy and Tyler did so with curiosity, Violet's gaze held a definite challenge. Was she daring him to spill the beans or agree with her?

"We were just talking about the concert, and I told Violet that I was just glad I wouldn't have to sit through Gaga."

Tracy crossed her arms over her chest. "Okay, I know you're lying, 'cause Violet loves Lady Gaga and would never laugh at you dissing her."

"Actually, Trace, I have a confession..." Violet paused, and Dean saw Tracy's eyes narrow. "I actually hate Gaga. I just went to all those concerts to be a good friend."

Tracy put her hand to her forehead and pretended to faint. Best caught her in his arms, grinning at Violet and Dean. "Is she always this dramatic?"

"She was a double major at Sac State," Violet said. "English and theater."

Tracy blinked up at Best with a sigh. "Thank you for catching me."

"Anytime." Best almost sounded sincere, except Dean knew his buddy well. Tracy would be lucky to get a phone call after tonight.

Tracy looked at Violet with a grim expression. "I forgive you for this horrible betrayal."

"That's magnanimous of you," Violet said.

"One of my many qualities." Tracy fixed Best with a sly grin. "I'm also incredibly generous."

On that note... Now that their friends were distracted again, he asked Violet, "Do you really hate Gaga?"

"No, do you?"

"Yes."

Violet winked at him, the action comfortable and disarming. "I won't tell if you don't."

Damn, it was one thing to be attracted to her, but to actually like her and enjoy the way she surprised him made her hard to resist.

She raised her cup to her lips, her eyes closing. When she lowered it again, she licked her lips and sighed. "So much better."

"What did you get?" he asked.

"Wine. Want a sip?"

She held the cup out to him, and all he could do was shake his head. Why the hell couldn't he look away from the bridge of her nose, where a dozen or so small freckles kissed her skin? He had never thought freckles were sexy before, but on her they were irresistible.

She was getting to him. He had let his guard down, been charmed by her despite his reservations, and he was confused as hell. Was she just being an outrageous flirt? A tease?

He needed to put some distance between them. Because he wasn't sure letting her "have her way with him" was such a good idea.

"I've got to go," he said suddenly.

Dean almost missed the hurt in Violet's eyes, it was gone so fast. Best's glare, however, stayed firmly in place. Best was so chill, always the one to razz other people and give them shit. Rarely did he get angry about anything.

"Where?" Best asked.

"Bathroom."

"I'll go with you." Best gave the girls his classic player smile. "Don't go anywhere, ladies."

"Hey, you have ten minutes, and then no promises after that," Tracy said.

"Fair enough."

Dean looked toward Violet but she'd turned away, glancing around the beer garden as if searching for someone else to talk to. He couldn't blame her; he wasn't smooth with women when he tried, but he was an expert when it came to alienating them.

"Come on," Best said.

Dean walked alongside him, waiting for Best to blow up. Finally, when they were out of earshot, Best snapped, "What is your problem?"

Dean wasn't about to share his feelings with Best. They were buddies, but when it came to feelings, well…Best wasn't the most sensitive listener.

"I came to listen to music, not spend all night chasing girls," Dean said.

Best looked at him incredulously, almost bumping into a group of giggling teenagers. "Are you crazy? That is the *only* reason to go to a summer concert with another dude. You are my wingman; act like it."

"Fuck off. You don't need *my* help getting women." Which was really true. If Dean left right now, he didn't think it would take much for Best to take Tracy home.

And if Tracy went home with Best, what did that mean for Violet? Would she go home alone or look for someone else to pass the time with? The thought of her hooking up with another guy was like drinking his mother's old-school cold remedy; it left a rotten taste lingering in his mouth.

"Dude, did you just growl at me?" Best asked.

Dean flushed. He hadn't realized he'd made a sound. "Of course not, I was just clearing my throat."

"Good, 'cause you know I was just messing with you." His explanation was quickly followed by, "But you do need some action, because I gotta tell you, lately you have been acting like a real dick. And I mean, not your normal amount of dick, but a whole bucket of dicks, and I figure it's gotta be because you're backed up." Slapping Dean on the back, Best continued, "So why don't you take Violet home, clean out your pipes, and when you come into work on Monday, we'll see that frown turned upside down."

Dean shrugged off Best's hand, barely resisting the urge to twist it up behind his back until he screamed. Usually Best left him alone, preferring to torment their other friends, but tonight it was just the two of them, and Best's favorite pastime was being a wisecracking, annoying asshole.

"If I want to take a woman home, believe me, I don't need your permission," Dean said.

"It's not permission. I am *begging* you to take that beautiful, sexy woman home, bang the shit out of her, and then tell me all about it on Monday."

Dean knew Best was only messing with him. He might talk big and come off as obnoxious as possible, but he was a good guy deep down. Way, way deep down. Sometimes the guy loved a few too many women at once for Dean's comfort, but it seemed to work out well for him. Best looked like a surfer with blond hair, blue eyes, and golden brown skin, and his charm could disarm even the angriest woman. The guy had absolutely no issues with the opposite sex, whereas Dean, well…

Dean could be called brooding on a good day, and as Best put it, a dick the rest of the time.

Not that he cared, really. He needed to get his career back on track before he got involved with anyone seriously. Besides, some women were into assholes. He just had to keep things simple.

His reaction to Violet wasn't simple, though. Never before had he experienced a magnetic pull like this, an invisible force drawing him to her.

And he didn't like it. Not one bit.

"If you want me to be your wingman, then pick a girl whose friend doesn't look like she belongs in a poppy field or a church choir."

Best chuckled. "You afraid she's going to try to get her hooks into you?"

"I just thought it was going to be us drinking beer and hanging out," Dean said.

"Dude, I spend all week with you and most of my free time at Mick's. This is about hooking up with chicks in halters and bikinis—maybe both."

"Sorry, I guess I like girls who know the score. And that one isn't the type for a hookup and blow off. Maybe that kind of thing doesn't matter to you, but it does to me."

"Hey, I don't blow them off. I give them the best night of their lives and let them go without disappointing them. Besides, most women who hook up with a guy their first time meeting him *do* know the score. No matter how wholesome they may seem."

Dean thought about the things Violet had whispered to him. Could he have been wrong about her? Was she just looking to hook up?

"I don't think Violet is that way," he said. Think *being the operative term.*

"How do you know? You've hardly spoken to her, except for a few growls. From what I saw, she was more than happy to give you a little rubdown."

Dean downed his beer with a grimace and walked into the bathroom with Best behind him. Several urinals on the wall were already occupied, so they waited by the opening in silence.

Well, Dean was silent. Best wouldn't shut the fuck up.

"I know you want to get the hell out of here, man, but there's nothing wrong with finding someone to pass the time with."

"It's not fair to her." Dean saw a guy turn his way and gave him a hard look.

Nosy fucker.

"Whatever, all I'm saying is that if you screw me over by being an asshole, I'm gonna be pissed."

"Way to strike fear into my heart," Dean said.

Dean and Best finished up in the bathroom a few minutes later and headed back toward the beer garden. Dean pondered Best's reasoning.

It had been hard being here on his own, with only the guys to hang with. He had grown up in Queens with his Catholic father and his mother, who had been raised an Orthodox Jew, and his five brothers and sisters. Although his mother's family had basically ignored them until his grandfather had died, his father's family was a large, loud Italian bunch who made family holidays chaotically awesome. It had been hard to go from that, to the barracks and his team, to his lonely apartment.

He missed his big, boisterous family so much that he found himself Skyping them just to hear them bicker. He usually didn't have time to dwell on the shit storm that had screwed his career while he was working at Alpha Dog, but once he got home to his quiet apartment, it was harder to ignore. He tried to block out the past with TV or a trip down to Mick's Bar, but at some point, he had to sleep.

And he hated sleeping alone.

It would be nice to find someone for a no-strings-attached deal, but not many women could handle that for long, and he wasn't much for sleeping around.

Back in the beer garden, Dean spotted Violet and Tracy talking to a couple of people they seemed to know. One of the guys was edging closer to Violet, his hand brushing her shoulder as he picked up a lock of her hair. He was a short guy with dark spiky hair and skinny jeans.

Jesus, skinny jeans? It just wasn't natural.

Tracy spotted them and waved them over. As Best started to head that way, Dean said, "I'm going to grab another beer."

Best paused, looking from Violet to Dean with a shake of his head. "Sack up, man."

And with that sage advice, Best went to join the group, sliding in next to Tracy and throwing his arm around her shoulders with a grin.

Dean caught Violet watching him for half a second before she turned her attention back to the guy in front of her, suddenly hanging on his every word.

This is what you wanted, right? So get your beer and listen to some music. You came here for the concert.

Dean decided to do exactly that and, walking out of the beer garden, resisted the urge to look back at her one last time.

Chapter Three

VIOLET SWAYED TO the music as she sipped on her fourth wine in two hours, enjoying the buzz. Meghan Trainor was up next, and Violet was excited to cut loose and dance her heart out.

If only she was attracted to her dance partner.

It wasn't that she didn't like Robert Tran in general. He was a nice, if awkward, guy she'd gone to high school with, and although they'd been friends, she'd never been into him like that. Mainly because he was about eight inches shorter than her. She couldn't help it that it was her biggest turnoff. Being tall had always been a sore spot, especially when guys in middle school had called her giraffe.

To make matters worse, Robert was extremely opinionated and didn't mind pushing those opinions onto others. He was known for jumping from one soapbox to the next, which was probably why he'd been so good at debate. Violet thought he would have made an excellent politician, but he'd been talking about finishing up his med school program at UC Davis for the last thirty minutes, so maybe he'd gotten over arguing with people constantly.

Violet was a little intimidated by how put-together Robert seemed. She had one semester left to complete her bachelor's degree but still needed her master's degree and maybe even her doctorate. She wanted to help people suffering from severe depression, like her mother had been. Right now, she worked at Here to Listen, a national suicide hotline. It was astonishing how many callers had absolutely no support system. No counselor, no family or friends who understood. It was heartbreaking and gave her a better understanding of what her mother had gone through before she died.

Died. Even in her head and ten years later, it was still hard for her to say *suicide*. Her mother had committed suicide, leaving her three children alone with an unstable father.

But when she put it that way, it made her angry with her mother, and she didn't want that to consume all the good memories of her. So she always used the words *died* or *passed away.*

But even the words couldn't always banish the images of her mother in the bathtub, her pale face turned toward the door, her eyes closed...

And the water running over the side tinted red.

Violet blinked, pushing away thoughts of her mother, and refocused on Robert's lips.

Which were moving. Shit, how long had he been speaking? Trying to hide the fact that he'd caught her spacing out, she pointed to her ears.

"Sorry, it's loud. What did you say?"

"I said I'm glad we bumped into each other."

"Oh, me, too," she said. "It's good to catch up."

Suddenly he took her hand and brought her to him. When his arm wrapped around her waist and he gazed up at her with desire in his eyes, she swallowed.

Oh no.

"You know, I've liked you since freshman biology."

Why? Because your face is eye level with my boobs?

"You...You have?" Violet looked around for Tracy to save her, but her friend was a little busy with Tyler's tongue down her throat. Violet couldn't believe it. Tracy normally made men work harder than a couple of beers and some smooth lines.

No help from that quarter.

"I almost asked you out, too, but then your mom died and you always seemed so busy with family and everything..."

It was the standard explanation for why guys avoided getting involved with her. Her life was straight-up drama, had been for as long as she could remember, but it had only gotten worse after her mother died. Not many guys had wanted to date the girl who couldn't go out on a Saturday because her little brother had a sore throat and fever. It was like being a teenaged mom.

And everyone knew at least some of her situation, if not all of it. It was kind of hard to hide the fact that your mom had committed suicide when it was plastered on the local news stations.

Violet hadn't had a lot of friends to begin with, but most of them disappeared that first year. "*Her house is depressing,*" she'd heard one girl say, and another had told her she was scared of Violet's dad. It made sense; the girl had slept over one of the nights when her dad had ransacked her room for money and then screamed at her for over ten minutes before taking off. The only friend who had stuck it out was Tracy. Probably because Tracy understood how scary life could get.

But despite all the dark spots in Violet's life, the isolation and tough situations, it had been worth it to keep her family together.

And once again, she'd drifted off while Robert was talking. Damn it.

"Anyway, now that things are different, maybe we could get dinner sometime? My schedule will get crazy again once school starts, but my weekends are wide open now."

Violet didn't have a lot of experience blowing guys off, but she'd watched Tracy master the skill. Violet just wouldn't be as blunt. "Oh, Robert, that is super sweet, but I have a lot going on. My sister is going away to college in a few weeks, and between my job, my brother, and school, I don't have a lot of time for dating." Violet said a silent prayer that he'd drop the subject.

"Really? You don't have time for just one drink?"

"I wish I could, but I'm just too busy."

"We could keep it casual. Why don't I bring dinner by your place? Are you still living at your dad's?"

His persistence was another thing she remembered now. It was super annoying.

Glancing around, Violet caught sight of Dean towering above the nearby crowd. He was still except for the slight bob of his head to the beat of the music. She didn't actually think that Dean would rescue her, not after he had practically run away from her, but at this point, she was desperate. Staring hard at him, she willed him to turn her way.

Come on, dude! Make yourself useful.

"Believe me, if anyone would understand being busy, it's me. With my extensive schedule at school, I hardly ever leave my apartment." He gave her what she assumed was supposed to be a sultry look. "But I would definitely make time for you."

"That is such a nice thing to say, Robert, but I hardly even see Tracy anymore. I don't think I'll be free to date anyone until after this last semester, at least."

Violet glanced back toward Dean, redoubling her efforts to get his attention. Dean finally turned, and she widened her eyes.

"Well, if you can make time for Tracy, I'm sure you could squeeze me in."

Dean raised his eyebrow, and Violet flicked her eyes down to Robert and back.

"That's true, I could, but wouldn't you rather date a girl who is more available?"

"No, I like that you're busy. It means you won't get too clingy, unlike my last girlfriend, who wouldn't stop calling or texting, even when I told her I had to study."

Violet had a sneaking suspicion it was the other way around but didn't say that. Shooting pleading eyes at Dean, she tried once more. *Rescue me. Now.*

Dean, the bastard, grinned at her but made no move to help her.

Defeated, Violet tried waiting until Robert stopped talking about the supposed clingy girlfriend, but there seemed to be no end in sight.

"Hey, Robert, sorry, but I've got to go to the bathroom," she said, cutting off the rest of his bullshit.

Releasing her waist, he reached for her hand with a smile. "That's fine, I'll walk you over."

"You know, that's okay. I think my breakfast burrito isn't sitting well, so it may be awhile," she said.

Robert seemed at a loss for what to say, so she made a break for it.

Thank you, Morgan Tookers. Diarrhea does shut down everything.

Violet searched through her tote and grabbed a strip of gum from the back. Between the wine and the dancing, her breath was smelling kind of rank. She kept walking in the direction of the restroom, despite the fact that she didn't actually have to go. It was disappointing that this whole day was shaping up to be a bust.

Someone brushed against Violet's shoulder, and she turned, expecting to find that Robert had caught up to her. Only it was Dean, looking far too hot considering the evil soul that lurked beneath the surface. "I see you managed to escape."

The balls on this guy. He had encouraged her attention, ditched her, and then, when she really needed a hero, had left her to flounder.

She was done giving him the benefit of the doubt. He was a total jackass.

"No thanks to you. Couldn't you at least have pretended to be a nice guy for two seconds?"

He shrugged. *Shrugged!* "The guy was hobbit-sized. I figured you could take him."

"I didn't want to *take him*," she hissed. "I wanted you to come over and do that thing guys do to scare other men away so I didn't have to."

"Come on, how hard is it to tell a guy you aren't interested? It's better than leading the guy on."

Violet, fuming, stopped dead in her tracks and faced him with her arms crossed over her chest, sarcasm dripping from her tone. "I figured I'd just take a page from your book and suddenly have to go to the bathroom."

He didn't say much, at least not right away. Finally, he cleared his throat, clearly uncomfortable. "You're right. That was a dick move."

"Yeah it was." *Not that I ever thought you'd admit it.* "So, why are you following me? You've made it perfectly clear that I repulse you—"

"I never said you repulse me."

"You didn't have to say it; believe me, your attitude was all the evidence I needed." She choked on the last word and spun away before he saw the tears swimming in her eyes, nearly knocking a couple of teenagers over in the process.

"Watch it!" one of them snarled.

Violet ignored them and walked off the path, trying to get it together.

Unfortunately, she had no time before Dean took her arm and pulled her behind a corn dog vendor and away from the crowds.

"What are you doing?" she asked.

"I think we need to clear a few things up." He seemed so calm, almost amused.

Oh, hell no. He did not get to be an asshat and laugh at her when she blew up about it.

Pointing her finger at Dean's chest and breathing so hard she was sure fire was exploding from her nostrils, she advanced on him, furious when he didn't budge an inch. When she finally stopped, there were mere inches between them, her heaving chest brushing his as she raged quietly.

"Since the moment I met you, you've made me feel like I'm diseased. Wiping your hand on your leg, running off after I bought you a freaking beer without even returning the favor—"

"You want me to buy you a beer?" He still sounded like he was about to laugh at her expense, and it fueled her righteous indignation like wind on a wildfire.

"No, I don't want your stinking beer! I just want to know what it is you have against me. Is it that you don't like redheads? Am I too tall for you? Please, explain to me why you seem to be fluctuating between avoiding me and antagonizing me."

"I'm not sure."

"You're not *sure?* What the hell does that even mean?" Violet threw up her hands with a frustrated groan. "You know, I had plans today. I was going to sing and dance with my best friend, flirt with a hot guy. Maybe even hook up with him, who knows. Instead, I've been insulted by you, ditched by my best friend, and the only guy who has looked twice at me is a guy who was voted most likely to rule the world in high school." About ready to go bury her head in a corn dog and a whole bottle of whatever alcohol she could grab, she took a step away from him, her face burning with humiliation. "So, if you don't mind, I'm about to take the buzz I'm working on and upgrade it to a full-on bender."

Before she could escape, she was jerked back and pressed against the hard side of the food truck. Dean loomed over her, his face so close her eyes nearly crossed.

"You done throwing a tantrum?" he asked.

As his hard body moved into hers, tension hummed around them. "I was not—"

"Yeah, you're revved up into a full-on hissy fit, but I'm going to overlook that while I...clarify a few things."

The way his voice softened on those last four words made her body tighten, especially when she realized one of his legs was pressed between hers. His wide shoulders blocked her view of who might be watching them, and his hands were braced flat just above her shoulders. If she moved a fraction higher, he could graze her bare skin with his thumb, and just the thought of it made her nipples perk up against the sheer lace of her bra.

"First of all, yes, I was rude to you, but not because I wasn't attracted to you."

Violet held her breath at this, her eyes riveted to his lips.

"I was trying to save you."

Huh? Save her? She could hardly concentrate on what he was talking about, his proximity casting a spell of confusion over her. Maybe she'd been binge watching too much *Charmed*, but she was too caught up in the obsidian flecks in his brown eyes to fully process.

"From what?" Was that her voice? It was soft, dreamy, and not at all normal.

And good God, but were his lips inching closer? "From me."

"Are you dangerous?" Silly question. *If he was really dangerous, you wouldn't be putty in his hands.*

His right hand moved, and he began trailing one of his fingers along her temple and cheek, until the very tip smoothed over her bottom lip. "I would never mean to hurt you, but I'm not looking for anything serious."

That woke her up a little, and she frowned. "Neither am I."

His finger dropped, and he stared down at her grimly. "You say that now, but—"

"Okay, you know what, that's enough." The balls on him, getting her all revved up and then acting like she was just a soft piece of feminine fluff who didn't know her own mind. Putting her hands up against the wall of his chest, she pushed hard, but he wouldn't budge, so she settled for pointing her finger up between them, wagging it in his face. "Don't act like you know me or what I want. Don't just assume that I'm looking for a relationship because I have ovaries. I have too much going on in my life to handle anyone else's wants and needs, so the last thing I'm looking for is a boyfriend. And you might have learned that if you had bothered to spend more than ten minutes at a time talking to me tonight, instead of running away like a big wimpy asshat."

He leaned back but still didn't let her escape. "Big wimpy asshat, huh?"

Lifting her chin up, she didn't back down. "Yeah, that's right."

For several moments, he did nothing but stare at her, and the intensity in his eyes made her twitch. Finally, he nodded, as if coming to terms with his new title. "Fine, I made an assumption. I'm an asshat."

"Happy we agree on something," she said.

"But I didn't come here today looking to hook up. I planned to drink some beer, chill with my friend, and eventually head home to bed—alone."

Violet flushed. "Well, it's not like I was trolling for just anybody. If that were the case, I would be dragging Robert off to have my way with him in the parking lot."

"Are you saying I'm special?" he asked.

It was a loaded question, and her answer could be taken a hundred wrong ways. Why was it that the first guy she'd actually actively pursued had to be so complicated?

"Nope, you're absolutely right. Nothing special about you. There are still a few hours left for me to meet someone who doesn't make snap judgments and would love to make out with an attractive single woman who hasn't been kissed in six months, so if you'll—"

Dean's mouth closed over hers, stopping her tirade with the sheer heat of his soft, deep kiss. Violet melted on impact, her eyes rolling back as her lids closed. She opened her lips to the thrust of his tongue and felt a pool of joy bubbling up in her lower abdomen.

Holy shit. And you thought the sunshine was hot.

Violet could blame her weakness on the multiple glasses of wine, but it wasn't just that. It was about wanting something in the deep, visceral sense, regardless of the fact that she barely liked him. In fact, it was better this way.

If there was no attachment, then she couldn't get hurt.

For the last ten years, she'd played it safe. After her mother's suicide and the night her father, Jack, had left, she'd been sure she was numb to any more pain, but why risk it? It was partly why she put all of her energy into Casey and Daisy; she was prepared for them to leave, to not need her anymore, and she was okay with that. They would still be hers. It was them against the world.

Letting someone new into that dynamic could ruin everything and cause a disturbance that might cost her the only constants she'd ever had. Trust and loyalty took years to build, and even if she did eventually meet someone, she could never be sure. It was better to never know than to let someone in and have him destroy her.

But that didn't mean she couldn't participate in a little casual recreational fun every now and then.

Dean pulled away, breathing hard. As she opened her eyes, she found his own to be burning.

"I hope you'll take that as an apology."

"Sure." Reaching up behind his head, she pulled him to her once more. "How about you apologize again?"

Chapter Four

HOW THE HELL *did you get here?*

Dean wasn't sure. He'd had every intention of letting her go, but then he was kissing her again, tasting the sweet, minty interior of her mouth, and it had been one hell of a fight to stop the first time.

But as she pulled him closer, he groaned in surrender. He threaded his fingers through her thick hair and cradled her head, angling it to give his tongue better access. He loved the fact that she was tall, that he didn't need to break his neck to kiss her, and as he pressed his leg harder between hers, he felt her moan in his mouth.

He couldn't remember the last time he'd just kissed a woman, gotten caught up in the scent of her skin or the tight nubs of her nipples pressing against his chest through their clothes. The way she arched her back and thrust her hips against him as her hands slid into his back pockets. She actually squeezed his ass through the rough denim, and his cock twitched against her, aching to be touched, caressed by her silky hands.

Several high-pitched giggles close by pulled Dean up short, and he caught sight of a couple of teenagers watching them, one with a cell phone pointed their way.

Dean moved fast. He blocked Violet as he crossed the grass and yanked the phone away from the boy, who paled even as he protested.

"Hey, asshole, that's mine!"

Dean scrolled until he found the video gallery, ignoring the guy's attempt to be tough. Dean deleted the video and tossed the cell back to the kid.

"You're lucky you aren't getting it back in pieces. You better hope the next person you pull that on is as nice as me."

"Dude, you were doing it in public. You were asking for it," his friend said.

Dean didn't bother arguing. He should have known better; he worked with teen boys for God's sake, and in this day and age, everything was fodder for the Internet trolls. He hadn't been thinking straight, though. All he'd been thinking about for the last few hours was Violet.

Which was obviously a very, very bad sign.

Dean walked back to Violet, whose expression wavered somewhere between horrified and amused.

"I would have kicked the little shithead's ass," she said.

"I don't really want to be arrested tonight, if it's all the same to you."

"Yeah, I can understand why that would be a drag."

Her quiet laughter was hard to resist, and he found himself grinning down at her. "You think you're pretty funny, huh?"

"Considering how crazy my life is, it's better for me to laugh at everything than to cry," she said.

Although her tone was light, Dean caught the serious glimpse in her eyes. He wanted to ask her about the shadows in their depths, but once he did, they'd start sharing details about their lives. Get to know each other on a deeper level.

He needed to put some distance between them. "Why don't I walk you back to your friend? Maybe I can drag mine away so the two of you can dance and do whatever it is girls enjoy."

"That's a sweet offer."

"Well, I'm a sweet guy," he said.

She snorted, but he let it go as they headed back to the stage area. Their hands brushed several times, and he glanced over to see if she was doing it on purpose, hoping to get him to hold her hand, but then she stuffed them in the pockets of her shorts. Maybe she'd been telling the truth about wanting nothing more than a night of fun.

One night was something he could do.

They pushed through the crowd until they found Best and Tracy. Dean tapped Best on the shoulder, causing Best to pull away from Tracy's lips and flash him a disgruntled look. "What?"

"Can I talk to you for a second?" He was hoping Best would just go along with him, but that was too much to ask for.

"Worst wingman ever," Best muttered loud enough for him to hear.

Violet decided to help out by grabbing Tracy and squealing, "Meghan Trainor is next."

"Woo-hoo!" Tracy hollered.

Now that Best's toy was distracted, Dean led Best a few feet away from the girls. "What the hell, man? Why did you cock block me?"

Dean glanced over at Violet and Tracy, who seemed to be deep in conversation. "Because Violet wanted to dance with her friend and you've been monopolizing her."

"Since when do you care what Violet wants? I thought you were staying as far away as possible?"

That had been the plan, until you kissed her. Now, she's like an itch under your skin you want desperately to scratch.

That little bit of info was best kept to himself, though. "Well, since our rides seem to be pretty absorbed in each other, we figured that we better stick together in case you ditch us," Dean said.

"Uh-huh. I smell bullshit."

"Shut the fuck up and come on." Dean dragged him back over to Tracy and Violet. "You ladies want another drink?"

"Hell, yeah," Tracy said.

"She means thank you," Violet said.

"No problem. We'll be right back." Dean put his arm around Best's shoulders and used his thumb and forefinger to put the right amount of pressure on his clavicle, too subtle for anyone to notice. Best, to his credit, didn't flinch or put up a fight but walked along with Dean until they reached the corn dog vendor.

Shrugging him off, Best rubbed where Dean had hurt him. "I am trying to decide whether or not to kick your ass right now. Do you know how long it's been since I got laid?"

"Last weekend? Besides, what were you going to do, screw her on the grass? That's how you end up on YouTube, my friend."

"No, but we were headed for an early exit."

"I thought you wanted to see Jimmy Eat World?" Dean asked.

"Let's see...Have sex or watch a band?" Best actually held his hands up, pretending to weigh his options. "Yeah, I've got their album, I'm good."

Dean shook his head with a chuckle. "You are a sick, sick man."

They entered the beer garden and got in line. When the bartender waved them up, Dean said, "I'll take a glass of whatever wine you have."

"Red or white?"

Dean stared blankly. Now he looked like a damn idiot, but he had no idea; he hadn't really been focused on Violet's drink.

Her mouth, now that was another thing entirely.

"Which one tastes better?" he asked.

The bartender released a sigh louder than the crowd around him, and Dean bristled. "Are you seriously giving me attitude because I asked a question?"

"Whoa, easy buddy, I got this." Best stepped in, shooting the bartender his trademark easy smile. "He'll have Merlot, if you got it."

Dean wasn't sure what Merlot was, but as long as Violet liked it...

Best was right; since when did he care what Violet wanted? He had been convinced that being within ten feet of Violet would be an extremely bad call not one hour ago, and yet, here he was fetching drinks. And all because one amazingly hot kiss had changed his perspective?

Fine, it wasn't just the kiss. It was her and the way she affected him. It was her witty banter and her snarky attitude. It was the fact that she didn't know anything about him and wasn't afraid to put him in his place.

His attraction alone should have been a red flag, but she had said it herself; she didn't want anything more than a momentary distraction. No complications.

Exactly what he'd been looking for. She wanted him. Even if she hadn't said as much, her kiss had made that pretty plain. So, why not go for it? It was better than going home alone.

Best got Tracy a cup of wine and a beer for himself. Once they paid, they grabbed their drinks and headed for the exit, but the short, rotund security guy stopped Best.

"Sorry, but if you're buying one of those for someone, we have to check ID."

"You want to follow us back to where they are?" Best asked.

"Or they have to come here to collect their drinks."

Irritated, Best chugged his beer. When it was empty, he tossed the cup into the nearest trash and faced the guard once more.

"These are both for me."

"I see." The guard seemed amused. "Enjoy the concert, guys."

Dean exited first, while Best grumbled behind him about nosy assholes.

"He was just doing his job, man. Let it go," Dean said.

"Well, his job blows. And this coming from the guy who almost took off the bitchy bartender's head?"

"He was being a prick."

"How come you didn't get another one?" Best asked.

"Just not feeling it." Plus, Dean hoped he'd be driving Violet home later if his friend succeeded in hooking up with Tracy.

Dean picked up the pace, wanting to get back to Violet and see her reaction to the wine. As they came down the grass, Dean saw that her pint-sized admirer was back, pushing his way between Tracy and Violet as they danced. When she caught sight of Dean, Violet appeared relieved, almost happy to see him. His reaction to that glow of joy was unsettling. It was as if her warm gaze was pulling him to her by an invisible rope and he was powerless to resist.

When he finally broke through the crowd, he held out the cup of wine to her. "Since you're not really a fan of beer."

Her smile flashed so big and bright, it nearly blinded him. "That was very considerate of you."

"I'm a considerate guy."

She didn't comment as she took the wine; she just kept smiling.

The short dude glanced between them and held his hand out to Dean. "I'm Robert."

"Dean." The guy actually tried to squeeze Dean's hand harder than necessary, and Dean resisted the urge to crush the soft, dainty fingers in his.

"How do you know Violet?" Robert pulled his hand back and flexed it as if Dean had hurt him.

Little pussy.

Dean opened his mouth to answer, but Violet jumped in by taking his hand. "Dean and I have a friends-with-benefits thing going on."

Dean's mouth hung open for half a second, then snapped shut as Robert's expression shuttered and his lips thinned.

"I see. You didn't mention you were seeing anyone before," he said.

"Honestly, we don't really tell anyone. Like I said, we're casual. It works really well, since we're both so busy," Violet lied smoothly, impressing Dean further. Of all the things she could have said to run Robert off, he'd have never suspected she'd be bold enough for this.

Then again, she had pointed out that he had judged her too quickly and had no idea what she was capable of.

"Well, I don't want to intrude, so I'll catch up to my group. Nice to meet you."

"You, too," Dean said to Robert's back.

Tracy exploded into exaggerated giggles once Robert was gone. "Oh my God, I almost died! I can't believe you said that to him."

"Neither can I." Dean held up their entwined hands with a raised eyebrow. "Very convincing, but I don't think casual FWBs hold hands."

Violet pulled her hand from his and took a sip of wine before responding. "Thank you for playing along."

"Who says I'm playing?" He spoke quietly, hoping that Tracy and Best wouldn't hear.

"What do you mean?" Her brown eyes widened, and she nibbled on her lip, the sight of her worrying the soft pink flesh turning him on like crazy.

Dean glanced over at Tracy and Best, who were dancing closely and ignoring them, before leaning down. "Maybe I *am* interested in something casual...with you."

Chapter Five

VIOLET'S HEART THREATENED to pound right out of her chest. She'd been talking a big game, but could she really get involved with a guy she hardly knew…just for the sake of her hormones?

She definitely couldn't bring him back to her place. She had been fighting with Daisy for months about Daisy sneaking her loser boyfriend into the house when Violet was at work, and bringing someone home would just blow her reasoning all to hell. Despite the fact that Violet had raised Daisy, she'd never let Violet forget that she was just her sister, not her mom. Still, Violet had never let her boyfriends stay over, not that there had been many, and she definitely wasn't going to bend the rules for a friends-with-benefits situation.

"Did I cross the line?" Dean's breath warmed the shell of her ear, and her stomach clenched with lust. She really did love his voice, the deep tenor playing her like a guitar, pulling her strings taught in all the right places.

"No, I'm just considering," she said.

The music slowed, and all around them, people wrapped their arms around each other, swaying in time to the melody.

Dean slid behind her and circled his arms around her waist, splaying his hands across her abdomen. She shivered, desire pooling between her legs. His lips pressed just below her ear, trailing kisses down her neck to her shoulder. Violet closed her eyes and chewed her bottom lip.

"How about now?" he asked.

Violet released a breathless laugh. "You're bordering on likable. You should stop that."

"Absolutely." Dean stopped kissing her neck.

Disappointed, she made a face he couldn't see. "I said stop being likable, not the kissing," she said.

Dean's warm breath rushed against the back of her neck as he chuckled, but he didn't kiss her again. Instead, he swayed with her to the beat of the music, and Violet found herself relaxing into his body. Dancing with Dean was definitely a new experience, one she was enjoying way more than she should.

The song ended, but Dean didn't release her. As Meghan Trainor said good night to the crowd, Tracy was suddenly in her face, ignoring Dean behind her.

"Hey, so I love you, but I'm going to take Tyler back to my place. I'll call you in the morning."

Violet had known this was going to happen, but she didn't imagine it would occur so early. "Um, excuse me, but how am I going to get home?"

Tracy looked behind her, presumably at Dean. "You got this, right?"

Dean's chuckle ruffled the back of Violet's hair. "Yeah, I'll make sure she gets home safe."

"You better, because if she ends up in the Sacramento River, I will hunt you down like a dog and gut your ass."

Violet pulled away from Dean, uncomfortable that they seemed to be planning all of this without even considering how she might feel about it. "Can you hold my wine for a second?" Before he could answer, she placed her cup in his hand and dragged Tracy off a ways before hissing, "Okay, the very fact that it crossed your mind you may be leaving me with a deranged psychopath and you're willing to roll the dice on my safety anyway is making me reconsider the whole best friends thing."

"Oh, please, you'll be fine. Otherwise you wouldn't have let him suck on your neck like a vampire for the last four minutes," Tracy said.

Violet's whole face burned. "He was not!"

"Please, don't even try. I saw you with your eyes closed and your mouth open like 'Oh yeah. Oh, right there…'"

"I think I hate you."

"Okay, for reals. If you are really uncomfortable and want nothing to do with him, I'll take you home with us and you never have to see him again. It's up to you."

Violet pursed her lips, considering. It was now or never; did she want to take a chance on Dean or go home to her cold, lonely bed?

Just because he agreed to take you home does not mean you have to sleep with him. Unless you want to.

Finally, she rolled her eyes. "Go on. I'll stay here and enjoy the rest of the concert."

"Good, 'cause my offer was bullshit and I was going to ditch your ass anyway." Tracy threw her arms around Violet and squeezed her until her back cracked. "Love you!"

Violet bit the inside of her check to keep from smiling. "I don't believe you!"

Tracy didn't respond beyond blowing her a kiss. Tyler was talking to Dean, and Violet saw him hand Dean something before Tracy grabbed his arm and dragged him away.

Dean ambled toward her across the grass, avoiding dancing couples, and stopped in front of her with a grin.

"Guess you decided to trust me, huh?"

"Don't get cocky. I know self-defense, and if you try to put my head in a jar, I will not hesitate to make you a eunuch."

"God, what is it with women always going for the junk?"

"It's either that or your eyes," she said. Turning to face him, she crossed her arms over her chest. "So, what's the plan? Do you want to stay for the rest of the concert?"

"I'll leave that up to you. I wouldn't want to give the wrong answer and wind up blind and ball-less."

Violet laughed at the imagery. The guy really was funny when he wasn't being a full-on douche nozzle. Her mirth faded as their eyes met, and she wondered if he was waiting for her answer to his earlier proposal.

Unfolding her arms, she reached out and laid her hand on his bicep, squeezing the hard muscle without looking away. His mouth kicked up in the corner, a show of amusement, and his eyes blazed with what she could only guess was anticipation. Her stomach floated and dropped as if she was on a roller coaster as she realized that she wanted to leave. Right now. She wanted to get him alone, and it emboldened her.

Violet made sure she was loud enough to be heard over the music. "I promise if we leave now, I'll be gentle with you."

"All righty, then." Without further ado, he reached down and picked her up in his arms, cradling her high against his chest.

Violet squealed with laughter. "What are you doing?"

"We are getting the hell out of here."

"But my tote!" she cried.

With a heavy sigh, he turned back around and squatted down, juggling her as he grabbed the bag.

"You know, if you put me down, things would be a lot easier for you and less embarrassing for me." People kept looking their way, and she could have sworn she'd seen a few camera flashes. Still, she kind of liked being carried, although she could tell that he was getting tired and had to be burning up, if the beads of sweat on his temple were any indication.

"Yes, but since I am trying to make up for my earlier behavior, I figured I'd carry you to the car so you don't step in any mud puddles."

Fighting a smile, she said dryly, "My hero." Squirming against him as she tried to get comfortable, she finally gave up and poked his chest. "Are you made of rocks or something?"

"What?"

"You're all hard. Like The Thing." Not that there was anything wrong with being rock hard. She'd never admit it to Tracy, since all she ever did was mock her for being obsessed with men's bodies, but there was definitely something about a man with muscle.

In fact, Violet couldn't wait to see all of that definition for herself.

Dean released a rusty chuckle. "I'm not sure whether that was a compliment or not, but I'm going to take it as one."

Violet enjoyed her vantage point for a moment as she studied the square line of his jaw that was already showing some scruff. Her gaze moved along to the vein of his neck popping out against his skin, and she licked her lips, tempted to place her mouth there and find out exactly how salty his skin was.

Violet shook her head. All the wine must have gone to her head. Never in her life had she wanted to taste any man.

Squirming in his arms, she patted his shoulder. "Okay, muscle man, you have proved that you are strong like bull, but I think I can walk the rest of the way."

Without preamble, he dropped her to her feet and held out her tote bag. "Thank God, 'cause I have to admit, you are heavier than you look."

Violet grabbed the tote bag from Dean, shooting him a playful scowl. "That is not something you *ever* say to a woman, and especially not after you proposition her for sexy time!"

One of Dean's eyebrows hitched up as he grinned. "Sexy time, huh? Are we doing sexy time?"

When had this become a game? A few hours ago she'd written him off completely, and then he'd gone and kissed her socks off. Now they were bantering across a parking lot like they'd been flirting for years. It didn't really matter, she supposed. This was the most fun she'd had in a long time, and she didn't want it to end.

"Here we are." Dean stopped behind a black Ford truck.

Violet knew she wasn't sober enough to drive, and it suddenly occurred to her that he might not be either. "Are you okay to drive?"

Dean seemed surprised. "Yeah, I'm good."

Rummaging through her tote bag, she pulled out her portable Breathalyzer. She had bought two several months ago, one for Tracy, and a backup for her. She'd actually never used it, but sometimes Tracy was stubborn and didn't realize how loaded she was.

"Can you blow into this?" she asked.

"Is that a Breathalyzer?"

"Yes."

"You carry a personal Breathalyzer in your tote bag?" he asked.

"Yes."

"Is there something I should know about you?"

"I just like to be prepared." He gave her a skeptical look, so she figured honesty was the best policy. "And sometimes Tracy isn't the best judge of how sober she is."

Grimly, he shook his head. "My last beer was a couple hours ago, and I only had two."

"Still, please."

Dean took the Breathalyzer. "How long do I blow into it for?"

"Five seconds." Violet counted as he blew into the device.

He held up the little blue machine, and she was relieved to see the two zeros. "Thank you."

"Sure." He handed back the Breathalyzer. "That's actually a really smart thing to have on you, especially if you've been drinking.'

"I figured you'd think I was crazy or paranoid." She shoved it back into her tote and was taken off guard when he gently took her chin in his hand. As he tipped her face up to meet his, she sucked in her breath.

"Never feel bad about putting yourself first."

His words hit a little close to home. She hardly ever thought about what she wanted, except in the far-off future; she was too busy caring about everyone else's needs. Even before her father had left three years ago, she had put her siblings first, but once she had petitioned the court for guardianship, that was it. Her life was theirs until they left for college.

Except for tonight. Tonight was hers.

His thumb slipped up over her chin and rested against her bottom lip, tempting her to open her mouth and nip at the tip.

"I usually don't. This is the first time in too long that I've done anything just because I wanted to."

"Yeah?" He dipped his head, his lips brushing hers lightly, a teasing touch that hardly satisfied her yearning.

"You wouldn't be interested in coming back to my place to hang out, would you?"

Violet looked up at him from beneath her lashes. "That depends."

This time, his kiss was firmer, a burst of suction that left her knees wobbly. "On?"

She ran her fingertips along the back of his neck, nipping at his bottom lip. "If I come over, will you feed me?"

He chuckled, and their faces were so close she could count the tiny crinkles at the corner of his eyes. "We could pick up something on the way."

Just so you understand, you are about to say yes to going home with a man you just met whose kiss has the power to render you weak and kitteny.

And that was exactly why she was going to do it. Tomorrow, things could return to normal, but for right now, she was going to grab dinner with a sexy man.

From there, they would just have to see where the night took them.

"Then I'm game." She walked to the passenger side, but before she could reach for the handle, he was there, pulling it open for her. Violet climbed inside and grabbed the seat belt but realized he was still standing next to her open door.

"What? Are you double-checking to make sure I buckle myself right? Because I have done this before."

"Smart-ass." Dean slammed the door, and Violet watched him through the windshield as he jogged around to the driver's side. She flipped on the dome light and pulled down the visor, intending to reapply her lip gloss, but a photo covered the mirror. It was of Dean in camo with his arms around two smiling soldiers.

She slammed the visor back up as he hopped inside.

"It's funny, I didn't picture Tyler as a pick-up man."

"He's not; the truck is mine," Dean said. "I just hate driving in traffic, and he's used to it."

"Where are you from originally?" she asked.

"Queens, New York."

"Right, I heard New York is really quiet and tranquil, no traffic at all."

Dean leaned over and gave her hair a gentle tug, setting tingles loose across her scalp. "I rode the subway everywhere, so I never had to deal with traffic."

Violet thought he might kiss her again, but instead he released her, settling back into his seat.

If you continue to make out where anyone can see you, you will end up on YouTube. Cool your loins.

"So why does a city boy need a big ole truck?" she asked.

"Because I like to explore the world around me. Some of the best places are off the grid, and for that, you need four-wheel drive." Dean started the truck, turning up the AC, and Violet sighed as the cool air hit her heated skin.

"You're not planning on doing that now, right? No dark and secluded areas in the woods where it would be safe to hide a body?" Violet was only joking, but then she caught Dean's worried expression.

"I'm starting to think you're concerned I might really murder you."

"No, not really, I just have a sick sense of humor." Pausing briefly, she cocked her head. "Unless…Should I be worried?"

Before she realized what he was about to do, he gently brushed her hair off her forehead, the light touch sweetly searing her skin. "Don't worry, Violet. You're safe with me."

If he kept saying her name like that, Violet would believe anything.

FIFTEEN MINUTES LATER, Dean pulled through the Jimboy's Tacos drive-thru, handing Violet the bag of food. He normally avoided fried stuff, but the minute she'd suggested Mexican, his stomach had started growling.

"Mmmm, I love the smell of Jimboy's. I don't know if it's the grease or what, but nothing else compares." Violet held the bag under her nose and inhaled loudly, drawing a laugh from Dean.

"I'm more of a meat and potatoes kind of guy," Dean said.

"I can see that."

He glanced her way before he made a left out of the parking lot. "What, do we have a certain look or something?"

"No, I just tend to think of uber-masculine men as devouring rare steaks and heaps of mashed potatoes. On game day in high school, if Tracy and I weren't fast enough, the football players would clean out the cafeteria before we had a chance to get our food."

"Well, I don't know about rare steak, but I could probably scarf down my mother's entire brisket in one sitting," Dean said.

"Brisket?" she asked. "What's that?"

"Just a cut of beef. My mother was, is Jewish, so we had it most holidays."

"Oh." Dean waited for her to ask him something else about his family, but instead, she changed the subject entirely. "So, do you live alone or with Tyler?"

Dean should have been relieved that she didn't ask him more about his family, but instead, he found it odd. Most women asked a million questions, even personal ones, to pass the time until they hooked up.

Guess she really doesn't want to get involved.

"I live alone, and I'll apologize now for my furniture. I picked most of it up at thrift stores because I wasn't planning on staying this long."

"Where did you expect to be?"

Ah, there was a bit of curiosity in her. "Wherever they needed me. Most likely overseas."

"So, what is the holdup?"

Dean wasn't about to tell her he was waiting on his psychiatrist to clear him; she might start thinking he really was dangerous. "Just a lot of factors and red tape. It will happen, though."

"Huh." She didn't press him for more details, just sat quietly as he turned right on El Camino, and then left a few minutes later into his garage. He'd been lucky enough to rent the townhouse for a decent price, and the landlord hadn't even had a problem when he'd brought his dog, Dilbert, home. Some places had a thing against pit bull mixes, but Kenneth had been cool.

Dean parked and unbuckled his seat belt. "I just need to let my dog out back. He's super mellow, so you don't have to be afraid, he's just big."

"What kind of dog?"

"Pit bull mix." Best had guessed Dilbert was a pit because it was such a concentrated breed in the Sacramento area, but Dilbert could have been boxer and bulldog for all they knew. Whatever he was, he was a sweet, lazy-as-hell dork that Dean loved.

They walked inside, and Dilbert's heavy breathing deepened the closer Dean got to his kennel. "Hey, buddy, you need to pee?"

Dilbert kept looking beyond Dean to Violet, his tail wagging low and fast. Dean glanced back at Violet, his smile fading as he took in her wary expression.

"You got something against bully breeds?" he asked.

"You could say that."

He waited for her to say something else, but she just stood back behind his kitchen table. "Why?"

"I almost had my calf taken off by one before, so yeah, I'm a little nervous around them."

It was a tale Dean had heard often, but since working with Best and the other trainers at Alpha Dog, he had learned a lot about dogs. The biggest thing was that you couldn't judge an entire breed on a few bad examples.

"Well, I'm sorry to hear that, but Dilbert"—Dean paused to grab his dog's leash before opening the cage and clicking it on his collar—"is just a big doofus. He's pretty low energy and might sniff you to death, but other than that, he's a pussycat."

"He's a little big to be a cat, don't you think?" She eyed Dilbert, holding their food against her chest like a shield.

"I'm going to put him outside for a bit, anyway, but he'll win you over. Just wait." He walked past her with Dilbert, who tried to pull toward her for a split second before Dean corrected him. He opened the back door, and Dilbert lumbered outside before sitting patiently while Dean unclipped his leash. "Okay."

At the release command, Dilbert started sniffing across the lawn until he reached his favorite tree and lifted his leg. Dean snuck back inside to find Violet opening up his cupboards.

"Hasn't anyone ever told you it's rude to snoop?"

"I was looking for plates, not snooping," she said.

"Uh-huh."

"Okay, you're right. I was checking for body parts and pints of blood," she said dryly.

Geez, the girl had an obsession with morbidity. "Holy shit, what kind of movies do you watch?"

"I love true crime. For some reason, serial killers fascinate me."

"That is terrifying," he said. "But I'd never be stupid enough to keep trophies."

Her full lips twitched as if she was fighting a smile. "Trophies, huh? What kind of movies do *you* watch?"

"I don't watch a lot, but sometimes when I'm kicking back on my day off, I'll watch a *Criminal Minds* marathon."

"Ah, you got a thing for Shemar Moore?"

Dean tucked her hair behind her ear, shaking his head. "Nah, not my type. Yours?"

"Actually, I've always had a thing for Reed," she said.

Dean's eyebrows shot up in surprise. "The skinny kid?"

"What? He's like a lost puppy. You just want to snuggle him," she said, teasing.

"If he's a puppy, what does that make me?" he asked.

"A kitten."

Dean laughed again, the sound rough. It didn't happen very often, so he was out of practice. "You think I'm a kitten?"

"Mm-hm, is that a problem?"

"Usually kittens are small and fluffy."

"But you can cuddle kittens, too."

"Are you saying you want to cuddle me?" he asked, surprised.

The small, sexy smile that played across her lips was flirtatious and teasing, sending a beacon of lust straight to his cock.

"Let's eat first and see where things go," she said.

Sounds good to me.

Chapter Six

Being with Dean in a crowded park was one thing, but alone in his home, sitting adjacent to him at the kitchen table…he seemed bigger. Not that she was worried about *him*, not when his massive black and white hell hound was in the room.

Dean had finished his first taco and let Dilbert back in when he'd scratched at the door, assuring Violet that he'd give her a wide berth. Violet chewed the last bite of her burrito, watching Dilbert as he sat next to Dean's leg. The dog never took his eyes off his master's second taco, and if she hadn't been waiting for the dog to lunge for the food—and his hands by extension—she might have been amused. As it was, she was like a big bucket of nerves exposed to an electric prod: jumpy and jittery as hell. Not because she was scared, at least not of Dean, but because she was waiting for what happened next.

Being that this was her first casual encounter, she could only imagine how things were supposed to progress. Did she sneak off to use his mouthwash or chew some gum after dinner? What if he didn't and he had onion breath?

Oh, God, what if she went through with this and he was horrible in bed? What if he was so small that she had to lay there and fake it? The few lovers she'd had were okay, nothing mind-blowing, but she'd been satisfied.

If he screws the way he kisses, everything will be fine. Relax. Maybe you need another drink.

Violet wasn't going to ask for that, though. She didn't want him to think she was an alcoholic; he'd already looked at her funny about the Breathalyzer.

She just needed to catch a break. After all the bad shit she'd been dealt, she just wanted one night of forget-about-everything-else-except-this-guy's-body-on-hers sex. Was that too much to ask?

She wiped her hands on one of the napkins and swallowed. "Where is your bathroom? I want to wash my hands."

"First door on the left." He set his taco down and stood.

"What, are you going to follow me in there?"

"No, I just wanted to make sure there was a towel for you to dry your hands on."

"Oh. Thanks."

Violet followed Dean as he walked down the hallway and pulled a black hand towel from the linen cupboard.

"Here you go. Just hang it over the towel rack when you're done," he said.

"Okay." As she stepped into the bathroom, she closed and locked the door behind her. Leaning back against the cold wood, she closed her eyes.

Why is this so awkward?

Then again, it didn't seem like it was awkward for him at all. In fact, he appeared completely at ease, while she was sweating buckets.

Going to the mirrored medicine cabinet above the sink, she stared in horror at her wild hair and the black smudges under her eyes.

"Oh, God, I look like shit." She opened the cabinet to block out the reality of her appearance and curiously eyed the contents. Some aspirin, razors, a few prescriptions, and dental floss right next to a small bottle of mouthwash.

And a black box of condoms.

Violet's cheeks flamed, and she closed the mirror. Presented once again with her hideous appearance, she washed her hands and gently used the hand towel to clean up under her eyes. Running her hands through her windblown hair, she gave in and stole his brush off the counter. As she worked through the knots, she wondered why a man with such short hair even needed one but was grateful just the same.

Finally, presentable, Violet walked out of the bathroom but paused to look over a collage frame in the hallway.

A younger version of Dean stood in front of a tank with five other men in desert camo. He was smiling with his arms around their shoulders. Some of them made faces and flashed rock symbols while another sat on top of the tank flipping the camera off. A few of the faces seemed familiar, and she was pretty sure that they were the same men from the photo in Dean's truck.

Next to the group shot was an older photo of a man in a military uniform with a pretty dark-haired woman in a wedding dress and veil, her arms around his waist.

Violet heard Dean's approaching footsteps but ignored him as she studied the next picture, even as his arm brushed her shoulder.

"The one in the corner," he said, pointing up to a photo of him and another dark-haired young man buried up to their necks in the sand, "is me and my younger brother, Freddy. We'd all taken a family trip to Maine about five years ago, and everyone thought it would be hilarious to bury the two eldest in the sand."

"And who is this?" She pointed to the top picture of three pretty women in rose pink dresses holding bouquets. Two of the women were glaring at each other around the one in the middle.

"Those are my three sisters at our cousin's wedding. The youngest, Natalie." He pointed to the sister on the left. "In the middle is Audrey, and Dotty is the one who looks like she's about to punch Nat's lights out."

"And did she?" Violet asked.

"No, I stepped in just in time to pull Dotty onto the dance floor, where she burst into hysterical tears and soaked the front of my uniform."

"Why was she crying?"

"Because she was pregnant, and she was scared to tell my parents," he said.

Violet glanced back at the picture, studying Dotty. "How old was she?"

"Twenty."

Violet could understand the terror his sister must have felt. She experienced it nearly every day, worrying if she was doing right by her siblings. Wondering if they would have been better off in foster care.

"So, why does she look like she wants to kill your other sister?"

"Natalie had found the test and was blackmailing Dotty. Typical bratty little sister warfare." He grinned down at her like she'd understand, but she couldn't imagine breaking her sister's confidence for any reason.

"That's messed up." She didn't mean to sound so harsh, but tormenting someone you were supposed to love with sensitive information seemed cruel to Violet. She would never take personal information about her sister and use it against her.

Then again, it had just been Casey, Daisy, and her for so long, maybe they were abnormal. But if they were, they had a hundred excuses for being different. Their lives had never been easy, but after their mom died, their dad's drug habit had become uncontrollable. He couldn't hold down a job because he was always getting high, and whatever money he did bring in went straight up his nose. Sometimes he disappeared for days, and then suddenly, he was just there. And as horrible as it was, every time he left the house, part of Violet hoped he wouldn't come home.

As a teenager, she'd taken any job she could around the neighborhood and babysat for a few families who let her bring Daisy and Casey with her. She'd hidden the money she earned around their bedrooms until she could open her own checking account, but after her dad found one of her stashes—almost six hundred dollars—she'd installed dead bolts on all of their doors. Then it just became a race between her dad and her to see who could sell off family heirlooms the fastest.

When she'd first started college, she'd taken a self-defense course, and just before her twenty-first birthday, had completed her firearm safety course. On her birthday, she'd walked into the store and bought a gun and a safe to hold it. She'd spent hours at the range shooting, getting better and better all the time. Between the locks on their doors and the gun, Violet had finally started to feel safe.

The extra security wasn't just to keep her dad from ransacking their rooms. If any of his druggie friends stayed over, she needed her siblings to feel safe, too. Daisy and she shared a room, and the Jack and Jill bathroom led into Casey's. It had worked out well, especially on nights when her brother had been scared and crawled into bed with her anyway.

Three years ago, though, everything had changed. One night, her brother must have forgotten to lock his door, because she'd woken up to him crying. Daisy had been staying the night at a friend's house, and Dad hadn't been around when they'd gone to bed. She could still remember the panic that had gripped her when she'd heard the crashes and thumps coming from Casey's room. When she'd burst into the room to find her father throwing things around and screaming about money as he loomed over Casey, fear had been replaced by white-hot rage.

"I know you have some, you little shit."

One look at her brother's terrified face had sent Violet running to her room to get her gun from the safe. Her hands had been shaking so badly, she'd only managed to get one bullet in the chamber before Casey screamed again. When she got back to the room, her father was on top of Casey with his hands around his throat. She'd raised the gun and unclicked the safety.

With a voice far steadier than the rest of her, she'd said, *"Get off him before I blow your fucking head off."*

It was as if he hadn't heard her. Her breathing grew labored as tears pricked her eyes. This was her father. She was aiming a gun at her father's head.

Casey released a choked cry, and Violet shut off every doubt and worry, adjusting the end of the barrel for her warning shot. Before she could stress over what would happen after she fired her one bullet, she pulled the trigger, the bullet whizzing just over her father's head and imbedding in the wall, plaster exploding over Casey and her dad. She couldn't think about the fact that the wild-eyed man who turned toward her was still her dad, that despite this moment and all of the other bad ones before it, there had to have been some good ones, too.

All she could think about was Casey. Getting him away from Dad, no matter what.

Her dad scrambled off him, falling to the other side of the bed. When he stood up and wiped at a cut on his cheek, she held her ground.

"Next time it won't be a warning. You get out of this house and you don't come back, or I'll file assault charges."

Her dad had shaken off the pieces of drywall that coated his head and sputtered, "You're bluffing."

Violet could still feel the sweat sliding down her spine and the pinch of sorrow in her heart as her eyes had blurred. She'd told herself she'd cry later, but in that moment, she'd had to be strong. Firm.

She'd had to protect Casey.

"Try me."

Violet still couldn't believe it had worked. Maybe he'd been too high to notice the slight quiver at the end of *me*. All she knew was that in the three years since, he'd never tried to come home or contact them. Part of her wondered if he was dead, and sometimes she hated herself for missing him. She didn't miss the junkie who had made their lives miserable, but she did miss her dad, who he was in those rare moments when he wasn't consumed by the need for one more fix.

After he left, it took a while, but things finally started to come together. Violet filed for guardianship over her siblings and had to prove that with her father's addiction, she had been solely providing for them for years anyway. It had been a stressful time in their lives, but their judge had been sympathetic, and although a social worker was supposed to keep tabs on them, they hadn't seen one in years. But that was fine, because things continued to get better. Above all, they were happy and safe for the first time in too long.

Well, they *had* been happy, but with Casey's moodiness and acting out the past year, she wasn't sure anymore.

"Hey, you okay? You kind of went away for a minute there," Dean said.

Violet shook herself out of the past and back to the present. "Sorry, I was just thinking about my own sister. She can be a pain, I'll admit it, but we ultimately have each other's back." Mortified that he might have taken her observation the wrong way, she quickly tried to apologize. "I didn't mean to imply that you guys didn't have a good relationship, I'm sorry—"

Dean held up his hand, and she stopped rambling. "I didn't take it that way, and besides, it all worked out. Natalie got grounded for keeping the secret, and Dotty and her boyfriend had a simple wedding a month later before she blew up like an oil tanker."

"Oh, my God, you're horrible! I hope you didn't say that to her face," Violet cried.

"No, but I would have been within my rights. She called me Gonzo until high school because my nose was so big."

Violet studied him. "I don't think your nose is big. It's a nice nose."

"Thanks, but until my junior year I was pretty much a twig with a small head. I barely reached five feet five inches and was the kid who got his ass handed to him almost every day by guys who were bigger and meaner. Then, I grew six inches over the next year and started hitting the weight room every morning. By the time I enlisted, I wasn't the favorite victim anymore by a long shot."

"I definitely wouldn't try to shove you in a locker now." Violet grimaced at the lame joke, an attempt to fill in the conversation when all she really wanted to do was ask him more about his family. His life.

But that went against everything that he'd said all night. That this was casual, nothing serious. You didn't ask people you weren't interested in getting serious with about their childhood.

Yet several times tonight she'd bitten her tongue, tempted to do just that. First on the drive to his place and now. He was such an interesting enigma, but she didn't have the right to uncover all his secrets.

Especially since there was no way she'd be baring any of hers.

"Considering I haven't gone near a locker in almost twelve years, I think we're both safe."

Violet jumped when his arm went around her waist, and he squeezed her hip.

"Want some coffee?"

Coffee. Coffee was a good choice. It would make her more alert and less apt to say or do something stupid. Like get to know him.

And realize you might like him?

Yes, because that was the last thing she needed.

"Sure. Coffee would be great."

DEAN LED HER down the hallway with his hand still on her hip, enjoying the soft swell beneath his palm. He noticed that she had tried to tame her wild hair and the black smudges under her eyes were gone, and it made him smile. His sisters had once told him that if a woman primped around a man, it meant she was interested.

Wait, isn't interested a bad thing? What happened to not getting involved?

Dean's smile slipped. Since he'd been in Sacramento, he'd hooked up with a few women, but he'd never been concerned that it might get complicated. Mostly because, although there was always an initial attraction, they never did a lot of talking. Those occasions were under more obvious circumstances, too—like at a bar after several rounds.

But with Violet, they'd actually talked a little and flirted a lot. Despite his best intentions, he had a hard time putting her in the same box as other women. He hadn't asked her to come home with him just because she had been interested and available.

It was because of *her*. The undeniable chemistry between them that drew him closer and yet set off alarm bells. Sure, the sex might be fantastic, but what happened when they were done?

Stop worrying about what if, man, and concentrate on what's happening now. Day by day, that's all you can do.

But he liked the way she fit against him, his hand resting on the curve of her hip. He could tell she was nervous, too, but whether it was because she was second-guessing her decision to come home with him or because she was waiting for him to make his move, he couldn't tell.

"How do you take your coffee?" he asked.

"Creamer if you have it, milk and sugar if you don't."

"You got it." He released her reluctantly and headed toward the kitchen. "Have a seat on the couch while I make it."

"Your dog appears to be guarding the couch."

Dean glanced over to where Dilbert lay on the floor in front of the couch, his tail whacking the ground lazily as he met Dean's gaze. "He's not guarding, he's resting."

Violet shot him a doubting look, and he sighed. "Come on, Dil."

The dog grunted at him, his tail thumping harder.

"Come on, dude, I'll get you a bone."

Dilbert's ears twitched at the mention of a bone, but he still didn't budge.

Dean gave Violet an exasperated look. "Do you see? He's a sloth. Not even food will motivate him. Does that really look like a dog about to rip your throat out?"

Violet sat at the counter, her jaw clenched. "You don't need to make fun of me. Have you ever been attacked by a dog?"

"Yeah, I've been chased by a few of them," he said.

Violet lifted her leg onto the kitchen counter and turned it. He stepped closer to see the round, pale scars she was pointing at. "This is from a dog attack, so pardon me if I'm a little cautious."

Dean slid his hand over the smooth, soft skin of her leg, his rough thumb scraping along the way. As his gaze met hers, he tried to put himself in her shoes.

"How old were you?"

"Ten."

At ten years old, he'd been afraid of their basement, but it wasn't the same thing. The fear of being chased, of running for your life and thinking that these might be your last moments was something he could relate to as a grown man, but as a child…

Damn, he felt like an ass for making light of her fear. Just because Dilbert was a nice dog didn't mean they all were, that was true. He'd been a heel to not respect her genuine concern.

"I'm sorry," he said. "I shouldn't have brushed off your feelings about dogs. I'll go ahead and crate him for the night."

Grabbing a bone from the cupboard, Dean called Dilbert over to his large plastic crate. Inside was a plush bed and the stuffed duck that Dean had grabbed during their first trip to PetSmart. Dilbert came to his feet, stretching his back legs and then his front. Slowly, he took a few steps toward Dean, and when he finally walked into the crate, he lay down with a huff. Dean handed him the bone, and the large jaws opened, gently pulling the treat away. As he closed the door, he caught Violet watching them pensively.

"I thought he might try to take your hand off," she said.

"No, he's got a really soft mouth. Guess it comes with the lazy package."

"I'm sorry," she blurted. "You shouldn't have to crate your dog for me. Maybe we should just call it a night. I could call a cab or Tracy…"

Dean stood in front of the sink, washing his hands as he waited for her to stop rambling. When she finally trailed off, he turned to face her, keeping his expression blank, although he was more than disappointed at the thought of her walking out the door. "Do you want to leave?"

Her cheeks turned red as she looked down. "No, I just feel bad."

"He'll be fine for one night. I don't use the crate as a punishment, so he doesn't look at it that way. Relax."

Dean turned back to making coffee, and a few seconds ticked by before Violet spoke again. "Did you really mean that whole friends-with-benefits thing, or were you just messing around?"

Dean rested his hands on the counter, weighing exactly how to answer. She hadn't taken him seriously before, but he wanted her. Bad. Their initial jolt of attraction was what made him try to scare her off in the first place, but somehow she'd managed to override all of his common sense. Now, he had her in his house, asking him what he wanted...

And there was a good chance she was going to walk out that door anyway, no matter what she'd told him. Still, he owed her honesty.

Slowly he turned around to face her, leaning back against the counter. "Actually, I did mean it. It's all I'm looking for. I don't plan on being in town much longer, and I don't want to hurt you or anyone else when we say good-bye."

She didn't say anything, just watched him, and he could see the gears in her head turning.

"Would this be a one-time thing, or would we just hook up whenever the mood struck?"

He couldn't believe she was actually considering this. "It's up to you."

"You're right. How do I know you're even worth a second go-round?"

Dean's jaw hit the floor as indignation shot through him. "I can't believe you just said that."

"I thought you were all about honesty. And honestly, I'm not sure I'm ready to say yes to *any* kind of relationship until I see what you can do."

The coffeepot dinged behind him. "Well then, why don't we just see where the night takes us?"

"One last question," she said. "If we were to enter into a friends-with-benefits arrangement, would we have other friends as well, or just each other?"

This is getting too fucking complicated.

"Why don't we save that question for after your test drive?" He smirked when her cheeks caught fire. "You know, for someone who clearly knows what she wants, you tend to get embarrassed by frank discussions."

"I may not want something serious, but I've never really considered anything like this, either."

"Would it surprise you if I said this was a first for me, too?" He pulled two mugs down from the cupboard, already knowing what her answer would be.

"Actually, yes it would. I thought all guys wanted an FWB relationship."

Dean poured the coffee with a smile. "From what I've heard, it's a lot of work and it's not as easy as it sounds. Despite everyone's best intentions, it's hard to separate feelings during sex." He turned with her doctored coffee in one hand, still smirking. "Especially great sex."

"See, if you keep pumping yourself up like that, I'm going to go into this with high expectations. I'll expect God-like endurance and a penis the size of a Buick."

Dean almost made a joke about being called God during sex, but the last thing he wanted was to turn her off by being crass. "Here you go," he said, handing her the mug. "Wanna take this to the couch now?"

"Sure, thanks."

Dean sat down on the couch beside her and took a drink of the dark, bitter liquid. "Well, I can tell you right now, it's not as big as a car, but I think you'll be happy." He noticed her grimace as she tried her drink. "Too strong?"

"No, it's great," she said.

"Liar." He smiled to let her know he was teasing, and she laughed, a rich, husky sound that drew his gaze to the pale skin of her throat. The thought of kissing her as she laughed, feeling that vibration of joy against his mouth, left his dick straining against the front of his shorts, and he twisted around to face her so his hard-on wasn't as noticeable.

When her laughter subsided, a sheepish grin still stretched across her pink lips. "Fine, it tastes like mud with a hint of sugar."

"Ouch. Already criticizing my culinary skills?"

Violet set the cup on the coffee table and settled back into the couch, her hand resting a few inches from his leg. "Is coffee-making considered a skill?"

Dean shifted his body until the top of her hand touched the khaki of his cargo shorts. Fine, so it was a middle-school move, but it worked. Her hand turned over, and he felt the light glide of her fingers through the fabric.

"Since the rest of my cooking consists of protein shakes and TV dinners, I'm going to count it."

Her hand stilled on his thigh, and she looked at him doubtfully. "That's all you eat? You never cook?"

"Sometime the guys and I will barbeque some steaks or hamburgers, but otherwise, why go to all the trouble of cooking for just me?"

"Because you can't live on shakes and crap. Cooking is fun, even if it is just you."

The way she talked about it, her voice filled with excitement and passion, made him want to keep her talking. He liked her animated; it made her shine brighter.

"Do you cook?" he asked.

"Yeah, I can cook."

"Then maybe I'll just hire you to make me casseroles or something."

"Ha, or you could take a cooking class and learn to do it yourself," she said.

"Or you could just teach me." He was never this easygoing with a woman he hardly knew, but there was something about Violet that was warm and welcoming. Someone he could easily like and admire, on top of desire. It was why he'd suggested the friends-with-benefits arrangement. If it was going to be a frequent occurrence, there needed to be some level of trust to go along with the wanting, and being this comfortable with Violet was definitely a plus.

Just as long as their emotions stayed in check.

"Now?"

"Now what?" He'd been distracted by his deep thoughts and the adorable freckles on her nose.

Now her hand rested just above his knee, and she looked confused. "You want me to teach you to cook now?"

His arm stretched along the back of the couch and his fingers itched to dance along the smooth skin of her shoulder. "Nah, I don't even think I have anything besides frozen burritos."

Before he could make a move, though, Violet wrinkled the bridge of her nose and stood up. "Gross." Dean gaze followed the swing of her hips as she walked over to the kitchen. When she opened the fridge, she studied his shelves and tsked. "This is a travesty. All of your meals are liquid."

"But they're healthy. The green one is kale."

Violet made a disgusted face. "No one likes the taste of kale."

"They add lemon to mask the flavor."

Next she checked his freezer and pulled out one of his TV dinners with a laugh. "How is Marie Callender's chicken pot pie healthy?"

"Hey, it's got vegetables in it!"

She shut the freezer door with a thud and came back to the couch. This time, she sat down closer, and he adjusted so that the sides of their bodies met and pressed together.

Her hand cupped the side of his face, and he turned to look into her warm brown eyes.

"Just for future reference, if there is a next time, I like to eat real food. I'll even include a cooking lesson if you provide me with ingredients." Her hand dropped, but his cheek still burned from her touch. The only tasty thing he was craving was her mouth. "All contingent on how the first time goes, of course."

Dean hoped like hell he wasn't misreading the invitation in her eyes, but then he stopped thinking as he cupped the back of her neck with his hand.

"Speaking of firsts..." he murmured.

Chapter Seven

VIOLET'S HEART SLAMMED, sputtered, and vaulted as Dean's mouth dipped down, covering hers with lips as soft as cotton. She opened under him, and his tongue swept inside, deepening the kiss until her toes actually curled.

Her hands slid over his back, digging into the muscles before she looped her arms around his neck. Every nerve ending was going haywire as Dean's hands slipped down her back until he was cupping her ass, squeezing her cheeks as he stood up, lifting her with him. She yipped in surprise against his mouth and pulled away, gazing down at him as his hands supported her, pressing her to his body like he wanted them to fuse together.

"Wrap your legs around me."

She did so, squeezing him with her thighs. Dean nipped the column of her throat, the graze of his teeth like a shock.

"I want to taste every inch of you." His deep, rich voice was rough and utterly delicious as it vibrated against her neck.

"Oh..." A breathy moan escaped her before his mouth was back over hers. Violet returned his hungry kisses, opening one eye as he started moving. He carried her down the hallway to his bedroom, and she hardly had time to study her surroundings before he set her on the bed.

"Lights on or off?"

Violet stared at him towering above her, his hands gathering the bottom of his T-shirt. He brought it up and over his head, revealing washboard abs and a chest that would put The Rock to shame. Violet forgot what the question was, what she had for breakfast...Hell, that body would make any woman forget her own name.

"I don't know."

"On it is."

Dean dropped to his knees in front of her, spread her knees, and slid his hands under the legs of her shorts, pushing the fabric up. Bending his head, he placed his mouth on her inner thigh and sucked hard.

Violet had never imagined that sucking could be hot. Anytime her past boyfriends had ever tried, she'd been too worried about hickeys or other visible marks. But the quick, intense pressure of Dean's mouth on such a sensitive place made her back arch and her inner muscles clench. He released her flesh, kissing the spot softly before he sat back with a grin and reached for the button of her shorts.

It took Dean just a few seconds to slip her shorts down over her hips and thighs, tossing them aside with a flick of his wrist.

Waiting for his next move, Violet trembled with anticipation. When he crawled between her legs once more, she gripped the bedspread in her hands, staring up at the ceiling as his mouth traveled higher on her thighs. At every pull on her skin, she wanted to beg him to never stop the soft, feathery kisses sending lightning bolts of pleasure through her body.

As the heat of Dean's breath burned her through the cotton of her panties, she started to sit up and tell him he didn't have to. She had never enjoyed having a guy go down on her and usually just lay there, waiting for him to get bored. But when he hooked her underwear to the side and put his open mouth on her, she stopped breathing. Because his tongue was doing something amazing, sweeping up until it met her clit and pressing in with hard, fast flicks.

"Oh, wow..."

She hadn't even realized that she'd said the words out loud until he lifted his head, his lips glistening.

"You liked that?"

She nodded slowly, unsure how to answer. She'd had few lovers, and they'd never asked what she liked.

Violet watched him grab the sides of her panties and slide them down her legs. When they were off, he pressed her legs open wide, but she tried to close them, feeling too exposed.

"Don't." He ran the rough skin of his palms over her knees until they splayed over her inner thighs, pressing them back. "You're beautiful. I want to watch you come."

Violet hardly had time to process that before his mouth was back with a few of his fingers, and for the first time, Violet understood the difference between being with a boy and being with a man. As Dean hooked his finger, rubbing it over a place she hadn't even known existed, she cried out, and his words rushed over her.

"That's right, baby. Tell me what you like."

No man had ever touched her like this, and as his mouth closed over her clit, sucking it between his teeth and lightly pulling the hardened bud, she realized that this could become an addiction. This floating, tingling, *oh-my-God-I'm-going-to-crumble-into-a-million-pieces* feeling was too good to give up.

And as a thousand body-humming sensations rocked through her, she forgot about all her stress, all the pain of the past. She lost herself in Dean's touch, his mouth, the deep murmurs racing across her sensitive flesh. It was like a bubble had formed around them, blurring the rest of the world in a distant haze.

A safe place where nothing but pleasure existed.

Dean's other hand closed over her breast, and even through her shirt and her bra, it was amazing. Suddenly, the next flick of Dean's tongue and swipe of his finger had her crashing, crying out loudly, sure that her limbs were going to fall right off her body as they tightened and quivered violently.

Before she had even recovered, Violet heard a drawer open and close and the sound of a wrapper.

"Take off your top," Dean said roughly.

Violet lifted her head and watched him slide off his boxers, his long, thick cock springing free. She had never been so eager to watch a man strip down, but Dean was beautiful, like a statue sculpted by God as a reward for mere mortal women. As he ripped open the condom wrapper with his teeth, she remembered the sharp sting of them on her neck, and the memory raised gooseflesh over her skin.

"Violet, you're killing me, baby. If you don't get that shirt off, I can't guarantee its safety."

Understanding dawned on her, and she carefully pulled her shirt over her head. She didn't want it ripped in his eagerness. Although, the thought of a man so turned on he would rip her clothes off her body? Really hot.

Her hands were behind her, fussing with the clasp of her bra, when he picked her up and moved her to the head of the bed. One of his hands joined hers, and in seconds, he had her bra unsnapped and was sliding it down her arms.

"Should I be terrified that you can undo a bra with one hand? 'Cause that takes some serious skill," she said.

"My best friend and I used to practice in high school."

The image of a younger version of Dean sitting in his bedroom with another kid, trying to open a bra over and over made her giggle.

The giggle ended in a choking noise as Dean took her nipple in his mouth, sucking on her hard and fast. Violet cupped the back of Dean's head between her hands, holding him against her as she felt his hard cock, his hips rocking. Soon she was whimpering in frustration, wanting him inside her, yet wishing that this would never end.

Then Dean shifted over her and reached down between their bodies to adjust himself against her opening. As he pressed forward, she winced and her muscles stretched to take him in. She'd never been with anyone quite so big, and it had been so long since she'd done it anyway...

His body stilled over hers, and his lips brushed her lips, her cheek, before finally grazing the shell of her ear.

"Relax. We have all the time in the world."

IT WAS KILLING Dean not to move, but Violet was so tight around him, it had to hurt. And the last thing he wanted to do was hurt this sweet, beautiful woman.

Sweat broke out along Dean's forehead as he pressed a little more and then pulled back until only the tip remained. He clasped his mouth against her neck and sucked, hoping to distract her as he slipped further in again, a little more easily this time.

Dean felt her muscles relax around his dick, and her hands swept down his back and shoulders, leaving a trail of fire in their wake. Everything about Violet affected him, marking him. He wanted to please her. Wanted to take care of her.

"It's okay," she whispered. "It's better now."

Dean took her at her word and started to move, slowly at first with long, gentle strokes as his body protested, dying to drive into her like a battering ram. When her hips began to chase him, Dean lifted up on his arms, watching her face as he thrust inside her hard and fast, sheer lust ripping through him as her eyes rolled back and closed. Her pink, full lips opened, and a raspy moan escaped as he did it again.

And then he stopped thinking, stopped worrying as he lost himself in Violet. In the fiery mass of her hair spread out across his bed. In the sweet scent of her perfume and the heat of their bodies as they moved in sync, as if she was made for him.

When Violet's muscles spasmed around him and she dug her nails into his arms, he gritted his teeth, willing his body to hang on just a little longer.

"Oh, God, God, *God.*" The last word hit such a high pitch that it nearly shattered his hearing, and then she was trembling beneath him, her body tighter than a bowstring. He let go, yelling with his release as he came. Two more thrusts until he was spent, the tension draining from his body, and he lowered himself onto his elbows, resting his lips against her neck and trying not to crush her. Their rapid breathing caused her breasts to press against his chest over and over, leaving him still hard and aching inside her.

"I think you killed me," he said. Soft, breathless laughter made her clench down on his cock, and he groaned, reflexively jerking his hips. "Don't laugh, or you *will* kill me."

"Then stop making me." Her lips brushed his shoulder, and then she bit down, hard enough that he pulled back. "Didn't you…go?"

"Yeah, I went," he said.

"Then how come you're still…"

"Hard?"

"Yeah." She seemed concerned, and he laughed.

"Because you feel so damn good, I don't want to stop."

A devilish twinkle in her brown eyes accompanied the sweep of her hand from his shoulders down across his ass.

"So don't."

"You have no idea how bad I want to, but I have a feeling you might be sore in the morning if we go another round."

A sharp slap on his ass made him yelp. "Don't worry about me. I'm a big girl. I can decide whether I want another round or not."

Kissing her on the forehead, he climbed off her. "I'll be right back. Just going to get cleaned up."

Dean ignored her pout and reached under her to pull the covers of the bed down. "Here, climb in. I don't want you getting cold."

Violet did as he asked, and he brought the blankets back up over her.

"Thanks," she said.

She looks good in my bed.

The thought rushed through unbidden, and Dean shook his head as he turned his back on her. He didn't need to be thinking like that, especially since he was still reeling from the amazing sex they'd just shared.

Disposing of the condom in the trash can, he couldn't get Violet's expression out of his mind. Lips parted and glistening. Her eyes closed, her neck arched, her skin flushed a rosy hue. He'd never seen a more beautiful sight, and he wanted to see it again.

And again. Hell, if he wasn't careful, he was afraid he might become addicted to watching Violet come.

The point of this scenario is to not *get addicted.*

And he wouldn't, not really. Just because their situation needed to be uncomplicated didn't mean he couldn't enjoy it.

Dean grabbed another condom from the box in the cupboard and as an afterthought brushed his teeth.

By the time he walked back into the room, he thought that Violet might be asleep. She was curled up on her side facing him, her eyes closed and the blanket rising slow and steady. The blue of the comforter set off her red hair, which was spread out over his pillow in a fiery tangle. Her pale skin was scraped raw from his whiskers, and he hated to admit it, but the visual mark of him on her got his motor running again.

He flipped off the bedroom light, and the beam from the hallway lit up the room enough that he could still watch her as he climbed under the covers. He slid his arm under her head and started to pull her toward him when she moved. Curling her body against him with her head on his shoulder, her eyes popped open.

"Finally ready for another go-round?"

Dean's laugh turned into a choke as her hand slipped down and her long fingers wrapped around him, sliding up over the head of his length and back down slowly. She repeated the motion again, speeding up every time, and

Dean closed his eyes, giving himself over to her ministrations until his hips started chasing her motions.

Finally, he grabbed her hand and stalled her. Using his other hand, he ripped open the second condom with his teeth just before she took the package from him and rolled the condom down his cock at a torturous speed.

"You done playing with me?" he groaned.

"Almost." Her breathless whisper traveled up from under the blankets as she disappeared from view, and he felt the pressure of her mouth smoothing the latex down.

It was his breaking point.

He pulled her roughly up and over his body until they were nearly nose to nose. "You wanted another round?" Gripping his cock, he pushed into her until he was completely encased in her warmth and placed his hands over her thighs with a smile. "Then ride 'em, cowgirl."

The smile that spread over Violet's face was nothing short of breathtaking. She started to rock on him, and he used his hands to pull and push her back and forth as he listened to the hitches in her breath, waiting for them to dissolve into soft moans. And all the while, Dean watched her above him, her small, full breasts swaying with the flow of her body, her lashes fanned over the paleness of her cheeks. Every once in a while she would bite her lip, only to release it moments later, as if she couldn't contain her pleasure.

Dean liked that. He didn't want her contained. He wanted all of her, free and open with him.

As her motions started jerking and her rhythm faltered, Dean reached up and squeezed her breasts in his hands, running his thumbs over the nipples until she broke, her orgasm a thing of beauty. Every sound, every move she made was like a sensual dance, and as she slowed, her hands covering his pecs, she opened those beautiful eyes, and a soft, mischievous smile tilted the corner of her lips.

"I want to ride again."

Dean chuckled, caught up in this crazy girl who had taken him completely by surprise.

"Baby, you can have as many rides as you want." Gripping her hips, he lifted her up and slid her back down his length slowly. "But this one isn't over yet."

Chapter Eight

VIOLET WOKE UP slowly, aware that she was sprawled across Dean's hard body and that his arm had her pinned there as if he was afraid she'd escape. Smiling, she stroked her fingers over his skin. There was not a part of her body that wanted to leave the warmth of Dean's bed.

But her body didn't understand reality: This was just a night of passion that would be seared into her brain when she was old and gray. Dean wasn't her Prince Charming, and there was no happily-ever-after here. She couldn't afford a relationship, not with how crazy her life was now. Between taking care of Casey and Daisy, supporting them, and keeping Casey out of trouble, she already had her hands full.

So, how was she going to manage a casual relationship? Last night the concept had sounded great, especially since she'd wanted Dean intensely.

But there was no way she could take off in the middle of the night for a booty call, unless Casey just happened to be at a friend's house. And how could she possibly explain her situation to Dean without telling him everything about her past, her family?

No, she couldn't do it, no matter how explosively happy and satisfied it might make her. Amazing orgasms weren't worth screwing her family over.

As she tried to slide off him, she winced. Dean had been right; she was definitely sore.

"Where you going?"

His gruff question made her jump.

"God, you're a light sleeper."

Dean rolled over her, her head pillowed on his forearm. "Were you going to sneak off without a good-bye?"

"No, I was just going to use your bathroom."

He could probably tell she was lying. "Right. Well, you know where it is." To her surprise, he leaned over and gave her a hard, fast kiss. "If you are really nice to me, I'll take you out for breakfast."

"Actually, I should probably be getting home. Lots of stuff to do today." Besides, she wanted to be there before Casey and Daisy arrived.

"I can get you home with plenty of time for whatever you need to do," he said.

Violet got up from the bed, hiding her horrified expression. That was all she needed, to have some strange guy drop her off at her crappy, ghetto house.

Violet decided not to argue, at least not while she was buck naked. She gathered up her clothes as she made her way to the door and ignored his whistle. Her face burned, but it wasn't as if she hadn't let him see every inch of her last night.

And God, it had been good. Not just the sex, but letting go of all the crap for one night and just not caring. Just enjoying life and taking it by the balls.

Violet locked the bathroom and used Dean's mouthwash. She couldn't wait to use her toothbrush, disgusted by the film she could still feel across the surface of her teeth. She probably stunk, too. Searching through the cabinets under his sink, she came up empty on towels. Then she remembered the cabinet in the hallway.

Still feeling a little shy, she peeked her head out the door. "Hey, Dean, could you grab me a towel?"

Dean came out of the bedroom naked as a jaybird, and she glanced away, staring at her feet. Despite the fact that she'd had her hands and mouth all over his body just hours ago, staring at him was awkward.

"Here you go." Dean held the towel out but not close enough. To grab it, she'd have to step into the hallway.

"Can you bring it closer?"

"Nope." Waving the folded towel at her with one hand, his grin turned downright lecherous. "Come and get it."

Violet rolled her eyes and leaned out as far as she could…

Suddenly, Dean pushed the door open and grabbed her arm, pulling her out into the hallway.

Gripping her chin gently, he raised her gaze to his. "Want some company?"

Her traitorous knees weakened at the thought of running her soapy hands over all that gorgeous muscle, but damn it, she had to be strong.

Suddenly, Dean pressed her back into the wall, the towel trapped between their bodies as he kissed her, his hand searing her thigh, hip, and side as he trailed his fingers over her skin. Violet had just looped both of her arms around his neck when rock music blared from down the hall. Dean cupped her cheek in his hand, tracing her lips with his thumb. He kissed her again, sweeping his tongue across her lips before finally pulling away.

"Hold that thought."

What thought? Every time he touches you, thought and reason go right out the window.

He disappeared into the living room. "I don't know this number."

"I never answer numbers I don't know."

She wrapped the towel around her body as she padded down the hallway. She had left her tote in the living room last night and wanted to check her phone, in case one of the kids needed her. Pulling the tote up onto the arm of the couch, she rummaged through it until she found her phone. When she pressed the button to light up the screen, nothing happened.

Crap, her phone had died sometime during the night.

Dean's phone blared again.

"What's the number?"

He recited off the numbers of Tracy's cell, and she nodded. "Answer it. It's Tracy. She's probably been calling my phone, but it's dead."

"And now she's making sure you're not in a jar in my fridge."

"Most likely." Tracy would have been panicked when Violet didn't answer.

Dean answered, and after several seconds of silence, he held the phone out to her.

"Hey, Tracy," Violet said, taking the phone from him. "Sorry, my phone died. How'd you get this number, anyway?"

"I asked Tyler for it when you didn't pick up. Girl, you scared me to death! Why didn't you put it on that portable charger thing I got you?"

"I forgot it at home, but no worries, I'm fine." Glancing at Dean, she whispered, "Better than fine."

"Vi, honey, as much as I want to delve into all the details of your *better than fine*, we have a problem."

Dread took hold. "What's wrong?"

"There was a message from Casey on my phone last night. Apparently, he was trying to get ahold of you and figured you were with me. Babe, he got arrested."

Violet closed her eyes, fighting back the urge to cry. "For what?"

"He didn't say, but he's at the juvenile facility off of Bradshaw. I already called in sick, and Tyler gave me the address to your stud muffin's house, so I am on my way to pick you up. We'll head over to get Casey. With any luck, he hasn't done anything that will get him any time. Hopefully we can walk in and out with little trouble."

Violet wrapped her free arm around her middle, a comforting gesture as she turned her back on Dean. A thousand scenarios raced through her mind, each one worse than the last, and suddenly all she wanted to do was get to her brother.

"Thanks, Trace, I'll see you in a few."

"Ten four."

Violet clicked off the call and, taking a shaky breath, turned to hand Dean his phone. "Thanks."

"You okay?" he asked.

Violet blinked back tears, unable to speak past the lump in her throat. This was the third time Casey had been picked up by the police. They had let him off with a warning both times before and just driven him home, but last time, the officer had warned her that if it happened again, they were going to prosecute him. Once Casey had charges brought against him, she couldn't be sure Child Protective Services wouldn't come sniffing around. It wouldn't be the first time she'd handled CPS and kept her siblings with her, but what if her luck had run out?

Strong biceps wrapped around her, and she barely noticed the fact that she was basically falling apart in the arms of a naked stranger. She had wanted just one night of freedom.

And she was being punished for it.

Pulling away, she blinked several times, cursing the tears that escaped. "Sorry, I've got to get dressed. Tracy is on her way."

"Do you want to tell me what happened? Maybe I can help."

"No, thank you. It's just time for me to get back to reality." Violet started back toward the bathroom, but he dogged her footsteps.

"Violet, I know we don't know each other well, but if you're in some kind of trouble—"

"It's not that I don't appreciate the offer." She stopped in the doorway of the bathroom, blinking rapidly. If she didn't get inside, she was going to break down into a messy, weeping ball, and she didn't want him to see that. "There's just nothing you can do except let me get dressed."

Dean placed his hand on the door when she tried to close it, and she made the mistake of meeting his heavy gaze, so filled with concern.

"Can you please let go?" Her voice broke on the last word, and she hated that she still cried. Every time shit hit the fan, she was sure she had no more pain, grief, or tears left. But she did. She was weak, had always been weak.

Just like her mother.

Dean stepped back, maybe because he'd heard the desperation in her voice or because he got tired of trying. Whatever it was, she didn't care.

She just needed to escape.

"Thank you for everything." Closing the door with a soft click and locking it, she slid to the floor and sobbed into her arms.

DEAN STARED AT the closed door for several minutes, the sound of Violet's muffled sobs tearing into him like a razor blade. From the moment he'd laid eyes on her, nothing about this had been a typical hookup. And if he'd been any other guy, he'd have been dying to get her the hell out of his place.

Instead, he wanted to unlock the door and hold her again, to coax whatever was going wrong in her life out of her so he could fix it. It was what he did. As the oldest of six, he had always been the fixer. One of his brothers was being bullied? He busted the other kid's nose. His sister's boyfriend got a little too pushy? He handled it.

But how did he convince a girl he just met to trust him with her problems?

Someone knocked on the front door, and he reluctantly left his post to grab his boxers off the floor of the bedroom.

"Hang on," he called as he came back down the hall.

He pulled the door open, and Tracy didn't wait for him to invite her inside, just stepped right past him. She gave him a cursory once-over, her lips twitching slightly like she wanted to comment on his seminudity, but she refrained.

"Where is she?" she asked.

"She's in the bathroom. First door on the left."

She nodded and walked briskly down the hallway, knocking softly. "Vi, it's me. You about ready to go?"

"I'll be out in a minute." Her voice was raspy and wet.

"Damn it." Tracy glanced his way with a grimace. "Sorry for all the drama."

Dean motioned for her to follow him into the kitchen and was relieved when she did. "Do you want some coffee?"

"No, thanks. I'm on a caffeine detox. Haven't had so much as a sip in over a week."

"How's that going?" There was no way he could give up caffeine.

"It fucking blows," she said.

Dean started up the pot and turned back to face Tracy. "I know it's none of my business, but what happened?"

Tracy's face locked into a steely expression. "You're right, it's not your business."

Dean already knew that, but still, being pretty much told to fuck off in his own house rankled him. "Be that as it may, I've got a hysterical woman crying her eyes out in my bathroom, so if I can help, I'd like to."

Tracy seemed to be sizing him up, and he held her dark gaze, refusing to give an inch.

"Look, I don't know what happened between you two last night, but I'm not going to tell my friend's hookup intimate details about her life."

"Fine, that's fair." What else could he say when she was so very right? He didn't really want to know what was going on with Violet, did he? That would mean getting involved. Actually caring about her life and growing attached.

"Look, just so we have this all out in the open," Tracy continued, "Violet has a ton of shit on her plate. Whatever you two did, it's out of her system. She's not going to call, text, or write. You had a thing, it's over, and you can go your separate ways, right?"

Irrational anger coursed through him, despite the sneaking suspicion that it was exactly what Violet had planned. No lengthy, casual affair. Just a wham, bam, thank you, ma'am with her planning on taking off before he woke up.

And even though that was what he'd wanted, too, an insane part of him was actually butt-hurt that she wanted nothing more to do with him. Dean couldn't stop the sarcasm from lacing his tone. "Maybe she should decide that."

Dean hadn't heard Violet leave the bathroom, but as she walked into the living room, he started.

"Decide what?" she asked.

Tracy gave him a pointed *keep-your-mouth-shut* glare before turning a beaming flash of teeth at Violet. "Nothing, girl. You good to go?"

Violet's gaze flickered to Dean. "Yeah, I just... Do you mind giving us a minute? I'll be right out."

Tracy seemed perturbed at being dismissed but gave Dean a nod before walking out the door.

Dean studied Violet's red, splotchy face as she gave him a forced smile. "Well, this is a really awkward way to say good-bye, huh?"

"It's a first for me, yeah." Every fiber of his being wanted to reach out to her, to pull her into his arms and comfort her, but her body language was guarded, her arms crossed over her chest protectively, like she was putting up a barrier between them.

"I'm really sorry for falling apart like that. My life is just really complicated, which I may have mentioned, and it's why relationships just aren't in the cards for me." She ran her fingers through her hair, only making it wilder, and Dean wanted to smooth it back for her, cup the back of her head and bring her against him.

Still, he didn't move, simply let her ramble on.

"And thank you for last night, and well, everything. I had an amazing time."

Dean stayed silent, debating on whether to push her or not. It really wasn't his place to ask, he hardly knew her. Finally, unable to resist touching her, he reached out. Cupping her face, he smoothed his thumb over her cheek gently, holding her gaze with his, willing her to trust him.

Just because you've had your mouth on her body doesn't automatically give you clearance to her life story. Do you want her trying to divulge all your secrets?

But he wasn't the one hurting right now; Violet was. And even though it wasn't his right or concern, he didn't like to see her in pain.

"You sure I can't help?"

She covered his hand with hers and pulled it down with a squeeze before letting it go. "I appreciate the rescue last night, but I can take it from here."

Dean grabbed a sticky note and a pen off the counter and scribbled his number down. Handing it over to her, he said, "Call me."

"I will," she said.

But as she leaned up and gave him a light kiss, he knew she was lying.

Chapter Nine

FIVE MINUTES LATER, Violet stared out the window of Tracy's car as the signs along Highway 50 whizzed past, still holding the sticky note with Dean's number between her thumb and forefinger. She didn't know why she hadn't just crumpled it up and thrown it away the minute she'd walked out his door, but despite all of the shit hitting the fan this morning, she couldn't shake to image of Dean's dark eyes watching her with understanding. It had been so tempting to unburden her problems on him, a virtual stranger, but it wouldn't have been fair to saddle him with all of her drama.

"He gave you his number?" Tracy asked.

Violet stared down at the yellow sticky note with a sad smile. "He told me to call him."

"Like for another booty romp or..."

Violet sighed heavily, leaning her head back against the headrest. Frustration coursed through her at the ridiculous question. "Does it matter? I'm not going to do it. My life is way too messed up to drag some poor guy into it."

If there is no way you're ever going to call again, then why not just get rid of it?

Maybe because despite the reality that had crashed and burned all around her, she wasn't quite ready to let go of the beautiful night they'd had.

Oh, God, do you hear yourself? Get your mind out of the cornball fantasy clouds and back to the problems at hand.

"Besides, you gotta wonder what's wrong with him that he still wants to talk to me after I turned into a complete basket case."

"Maybe he dug it. Some guys get off on crazy," Tracy said, earning a dark look from Violet. "Just saying, the dude seemed into you. I pretty much pulled my crazy overprotective best friend gig, and he didn't even bat an eyelash. And you know how scary I can be."

Violet could just imagine Dean smirking down at Tracy while she threatened him, and the image almost made her laugh. "Yes, I'm sure you had all two hundred and fifty pounds of him quaking in his boots."

"I didn't notice any boots, but I gotta say, those boxers showed off a hell of a lot of sexy man cake. Mmmm... You have to tell me about his slice. Is he packing a full sheet?"

Violet choked at Tracy's crude euphemism.

"God, you are disgusting. I'm not telling you about his dick."

"Why not? You told me how Joe Vance never trimmed his fingernails and—"

Just the mention of Joe Vance and his Freddy Krueger nails inside her body made her cringe. "He was nothing like Joe."

"Ah, see, now we're getting somewhere," Tracy said.

Violet slipped Dean's number into her tote bag and tried once again to get Tracy to take a hint. "In case you forgot, I've got more important things to stress about than your need for a play-by-play of my sex life."

"So there was definitely sex going on?"

If Tracy wasn't driving a car at sixty-five miles per hour, she would have strangled her. "Trace, I swear—"

"Will you chillax? I am trying to get your mind off of all this shit with Casey." Tracy exited the freeway and made a hard right, turning Violet's stomach. She really needed to eat something.

Violet leaned her head back against the seat and closed her eyes. "I know."

But nothing would ever make her forget about Casey and Daisy. By the time she was eighteen, her siblings had become her world. Since then, she'd gotten a better-paying job, sometimes two, and taken classes when she could. But above all, Daisy and Casey still came first.

"I need to call Daisy and make sure she stays at Madison's until all of this is done," Violet said as she pulled out her phone, which had been hooked to Tracy's portable charger for a bit, and waited for it to boot up.

"What you need to do is move those kids out of that neighborhood. I don't understand why you don't get an apartment and just take them with you. Why the hell do you stay in that creepy house?" Tracy asked for the thousandth time.

"Because I can't afford rent, school, and the kids."

Besides, even though they couldn't afford all the updates the house needed, it was the only constant in their lives. Despite all the bad shit that had happened in that place, it was familiar.

So they stayed in the house. All she had to do was keep the lights on and food on the table—the rest she saved for their schooling and hers.

And in a month, Daisy would be going to college, and Violet would have only Casey to worry about. With the financial aid and scholarship Oregon State University had offered Daisy, she wouldn't owe a dime when she graduated. It was more than Violet could have hoped for. The most important thing was making sure Daisy and Casey would have a future.

Yeah, you've done one hell of a job, Ace. Your sister's dating a punk who is just like your dad, and your little brother is in juvie.

Violet dialed Daisy's cell and pressed her phone to her ear while it rang. Daisy's groggy voice came over the line. "Hello?"

"Hey, Dais. Do you think you could hang at Maddy's a little longer? I have to take care of a few things—"

"Whatever."

The call ended, and Violet sighed.

"Little sis is a real charmer, huh? Makes me glad it was just me growing up, sometimes," Tracy said.

Tracy turned into the juvenile center, and Violet got out before the car was in park with her wallet in hand. She knew that she probably looked like a mess, but she didn't want to leave Casey inside longer than she had to.

Upon entering, she walked through the security scanner and reached a large desk with a wall of glass attached. Behind it sat a rough-looking security guard who waved her forward.

"Hi, I got a phone call that my little brother was here—"

"ID," he said curtly.

Violet rummaged through her wallet and pulled out her license.

He took the ID from her hand and, after glancing up at her briefly, handed it back. "What's the name of the kid?"

"Casey Douglas," she said.

"Hang on." Tapping away at a keyboard, he pursed his lips and squinted his eyes. "Kid's being held until later this morning."

"What do you mean? I can't just post bail or something?"

"You brother is being charged with vandalism and possession of a controlled substance. He'll have a hearing today, but until then, he is going to stay with us."

Violet's head swam, and she gripped the side of the desk. "Can I see him at least? Please?"

"After he is processed—"

"Please, he's just a kid." God, she hated begging, but she had to make sure he was okay.

"Everything okay?" Tracy had come up beside her and wrapped her arm around her waist.

Violet saw the guard's gaze light up as he took in Tracy's dimples, and for the first time, the man smiled back. "I was just telling your friend that I'd be happy to let her see her brother for a minute. Why don't you ladies have a seat?"

"That is so nice of you," Tracy said.

As the two of them sat down, Violet whispered, "Thank you."

"I don't know how many times I have to tell you that a flirty smile will get you anything you want," Tracy hissed back.

"Maybe if I looked more like you—"

"Please, I would kill for your legs. I got two stumps."

Violet gave a choked laugh. "Have I told you I love you today?"

"All right, enough of that, or that man might hear you and get the wrong impression."

"Miss Douglas?" the guard called from the open doorway. "Come this way."

"I'll wait here," Tracy said.

Violet stood and followed the man into an empty room. "Have a seat. They're bringing him down now."

"Thank you so much."

Once the door was closed, Violet paced the room, trying to stop the shaking of her hands and the racing of her thoughts.

This is all your fault. If you hadn't gone out last night, this wouldn't have happened.

The door opened, and a guard walked in, followed by Casey's lowered strawberry blond head. The minute he glanced up and she saw the dark purple bruise swelling on the left side of his face, she cried out.

"You have five minutes," the guard said, shutting the door.

Violet didn't waste any time rushing to her brother and squeezing him tight in her arms. When he groaned, she released him swiftly. "What happened? Did one of the officers do this?" The thought of a grown man with a gun doing this to her five-foot-two, hundred-pounds-soaking-wet little brother burned through her.

"No, a bunch of guys jumped me," Casey said sullenly, avoiding her gaze.

"Who?" Violet would tear their lungs from their chests, beat them to a bloody pulp...

"I'm fine," he said.

"Casey, damn it, who did this?"

Casey looked at her with their mother's green-gold eyes, and she could see the pain and fear swimming in their depths. "Where were you last night?"

Violet's face burned. The last thing she wanted to tell her brother was that she'd let her phone die while she was screwing a guy she just met.

"I was at Tracy's; I just forgot to put my phone on the charger. I am really sorry, Casey."

"Whatever, I'm fine."

Violet could see that he wasn't fine, but she didn't argue. "At least let me see the rest of it."

After a moment's hesitation, Casey lifted his shirt. The right side of his body was so discolored there wasn't a patch of natural skin tone left.

Violet's eyes blurred as she stared at the evidence of the beating he'd taken, and she shook her head. "Did they take you to the hospital? You might have a broken rib or something."

"I'm fine, *Dr.* Douglas." He let his shirt fall, and she bit her tongue, trying not to lose her shit.

"The guard said you were being charged with vandalism and possession. What happened?"

"Assholes set me up. Luis and I were painting at the school—"

"Wait, do you mean tagging?"

"It's not tagging, Vi," Casey snapped.

Don't be combative. Just let him tell his story... Then, you can lecture.

"Fine, you were painting a mural without permission. How did you end up looking like someone took a bat to you?"

Casey's fists clenched, and his expression turned lethal. "Fucking Garret and his crew showed up, and they called Luis a rat because they think he told Principal White that Garret's been dealing at school. They jumped him, and when I stepped in, they started whaling on me. We heard the sirens, and they scattered, but Luis and I weren't fast enough."

Violet made a note to contact the school and find out who this Garret was. She had to make sure Casey would be safe at school. "And the possession?"

"Come on, Vi, it was just one joint."

Just the fact that he acted like it was no big deal after everything they had been through with their dad sent her blood pressure skyrocketing. "I'm sure that's the same thing Dad said before things got away from him."

"I am nothing like Dad," he said coldly.

Violet sighed and ran her hands over her hair. "I know, but you are in serious trouble, Case."

"Yeah, no shit, Sherlock. I kinda got that impression when they put cuffs on me and read me my rights."

"Which wouldn't have happened if you and Luis had stayed home—"

The guard stepped back in. "Time's up."

Violet gave Casey a gentle hug, ignoring the way he stiffened when she touched him. Lately he'd disliked anyone getting too close to him, even for a hug, and it twisted Violet up inside. He'd always been so affectionate, hugging her to the point that her ribs squeaked. Now he cringed if anyone tried to touch him.

"I'm going to get you out of here."

"I know," Casey said as he followed the guard out. He tossed her a cocky smile that didn't meet his eyes, and the door closed behind him.

Violet sat down at the table for a moment or two, trying to regain her composure. Finally, she made her way back out front, and Tracy met her with an almost gleeful expression.

"What's got you so happy?"

"Let's get outside first," Tracy said, leading the way out the door. Once they reached her car, she continued,

"So, I was talking to the guard, and he said that Casey's hearing will most likely be with Judge Gambit, since it's before lunch."

"And he'll go easy on him?"

"No, apparently he's a hard-ass, *but* Casey will most likely get sent to this new military boot camp for the duration of his sentence," Tracy said.

"How is that a good thing?" Violet asked.

"Because"—Tracy paused to climb into her car, and Violet did the same—"from what he said, it's way better than juvie."

"God, he's going to have legal fees, and I'm sure I'll have to pay a fine."

"You need a sugar daddy," Tracy said.

"Don't be gross." Violet couldn't stop the sneering face of Mr. Walker from flashing through her mind. He was a longtime friend of her dad's, but the guy gave her the creeps. She'd seen him around town a few times, and the way he watched her made her skin crawl.

"Well, you at least need a win. Because right now, with everything you do for those kids, you have a bigger heart than fucking Cinderella—and that bitch got a prince and a castle."

"I gave up on princes and castles a long time ago, Trace." Staring out the window, she pushed away the memory of Dean's dark eyes filled with white-hot desire. "Besides, I've been handling my business without a guy to rescue me. Why start now?"

Chapter Ten

One Week Later

VIOLET PULLED INTO the parking lot of Alpha Dog Training Program and parked in an open spot right in front of the large brick building. Peering at it through the windshield, she smiled.

"Hey, it doesn't look so bad. It doesn't have any bars on the windows."

She glanced over at Casey, hoping to see his normal glimmer of optimism, the one he always used to have, even during their hardest struggles. Instead, he was huddled against the door with his face turned away. Casey's public defender had encouraged him to plead guilty and apologize, which he had balked at until Violet had warned him that if he didn't cooperate, he wouldn't get to come home with them. He'd been sulking and silent since, lashing out at Daisy and her like they had been the ones who had gotten him in trouble. Violet had been trying hard to be patient with him, hoping that he would tell her what seemed to be bothering him, but he just kept shutting her out.

When they'd gone back for his sentencing on Friday, the judge had ordered him to report to Alpha Dog first thing Monday morning to begin his six-week sentence. Even though Violet had tried to convince him that it was a great opportunity and it could have been worse, his attitude hadn't improved.

Unbuckling her seat belt, she placed her hand on his arm, but he shrugged it off with a jerk.

So much for patience.

"Look, I know this sucks, but there is nothing either one of us can do to avoid it. You need to go in there, serve your time, and hopefully, the experience will teach you something."

"Like what?" Casey finally turned, his green eyes blazing at her. "Is it going to teach me how to be a man? How to say, 'Yes, sir?'"

"Maybe how to respect other people's property, for one thing!" she snapped.

"Screw you." Casey practically leapt from the car, slamming the door so hard the windows shook.

Violet took a deep breath and counted silently, trying to rein in her temper before exiting the vehicle. She was at her wit's end. She had tried everything she could think of to get Casey to talk to her, but he just said he was fine. She'd look into getting him a psychiatrist, but the only way insurance would cover it was if he was referred by a doctor.

When she'd brought up the idea, Casey became even angrier. The last thing she wanted was to push him so far that he took off—or worse.

Sometimes it made her question whether she'd done the right thing, keeping them together. Should she have let them go into the system? They might have ended up in good homes...

Violet shook her head. *Stop being an idiot. This is just a rough patch, and you love him. That's the most important thing to remember: You are stronger as a family, and you will get through this.*

At least, that is what Violet had told herself a thousand times over the years.

Another car pulled up alongside her, and a man in military camo got out of the driver's side. As he walked in front of her car to go inside, Violet watched him, imagining a different set of shoulders beneath the jacket.

Stop thinking about Dean.

It was hard, though. It seemed like anytime she had a moment to breathe, his face would flash through her mind and steal away all the air.

She'd made the decision not to call, not to continue the friends-with-benefits situation. It just wouldn't work with her life, and besides, if she was this distracted by him after one night, she couldn't imagine what multiple hookups would do. Getting involved with him would only derail her plans. She needed to focus on school, on getting Daisy off to college, and on Casey...

Why are you trying to convince yourself? It was one night. Eventually, you'll forget all about him.

Casey rapped on the car window, and Violet turned to find him pointing to the trunk impatiently. She popped the lever and stepped out just as Casey slammed the trunk shut, his backpack slung over his shoulder.

He hit the sidewalk before she did, but she was still taller than him and caught up without any trouble, grabbing his arm. "Casey, I don't want to fight with you. Please, just talk to me."

"There is nothing to say! We're going to be late." Casey jerked away and kept walking inside.

Violet wanted to grab him by the shoulders and shake him, but that probably wasn't the best plan outside of a building filled with guys who carried guns for a living. She walked behind him through the glass doors. Casey handed his backpack over to a security guard to be searched, and another waved a wand over him, scanning for weapons most likely. Violet waited patiently until it was her turn, letting her gaze wander over the spacious lobby and beyond to a narrow hallway...

Two men stood just before the opening, both in green camo pants and green T-shirts with hats covering their heads, and the one on the left was familiar to her...

When it hit her why, her stomach roiled violently, and bile burned its way up her throat.

Tyler. Tracy's Tyler.

"Shit!" Violet's hand flew to her mouth as Casey and the security guards glanced her way, all of them frowning.

Clearing her throat, she grimaced at the vile taste in her mouth and the awkward slipup. "Sorry, just remembered that I left my coffeepot on."

"You didn't have coffee this morning," Casey said.

Crap, she hadn't. "I know. I was making it but forgot."

They finished with Casey and waved her forward. While they went through her belongings with a fine-tooth comb, Violet's gaze kept shifting back to Tyler.

And then it hit her. Tyler and Dean worked at the same place. So if Tyler was there, that meant Dean ran this place.

Oh, God, what am I going to do?

She couldn't escape. Couldn't just leave before Casey was settled.

"Just wait right here while we get someone," the security guard with the wand said.

"Sure." Violet stood next to Casey, trying not to look at Tyler. The last thing she needed was for him to notice her and go find Dean.

It wasn't just that she hadn't called him after their one night together; it was that he had seen her at her weakest, and she hated it. She didn't let anyone see her like that, and yet he had been there when she'd broken down like an idiot. She'd been too embarrassed and reasoned that as sweet and understanding as he'd seemed, he was probably relieved that she hadn't called. After all, what normal guy would want to get into an FWB relationship with a woman who had locked herself in his bathroom and cried for a half an hour?

"What is up with you?" Casey asked.

"Nothing, why?"

He stared at her with suspicion, and Violet glanced down to where Tyler had been, but he was gone. The man he'd been talking to was walking toward them with a large smile on his handsome face.

"Hello, there. I'm Sergeant Oliver Martinez. Welcome to Alpha Dog."

Sergeant Martinez held his hand out to Violet first and then Casey, who didn't even bother taking it. His deep blue eyes narrowed at Casey's rudeness, but Sergeant Martinez dropped his hand without comment, as if it happened all the time.

"I'm Violet Douglas, and this is Casey."

"Yes, ma'am, we've been expecting you. Follow me, and I'll give you the tour and show Casey where he'll be bunking."

With any luck, she'd be able to escape the place without any awkward encounters.

Violet nodded and fell into step beside Casey...just as Dean stepped out of a room a few doors down.

Too late.

DEAN BLINKED AND rubbed his eyes as the words seemed to jumble together on the page. One thing he hated about being the director of a nonprofit was all the paperwork. He was going to have to get glasses if he kept at this for much longer.

As soon as that damn shrink gives you a pass, you are back in the field and out of here.

Dean got up from the desk and stretched. He had only been in the office for an hour and he was ready for a nap. He'd been having a rough time sleeping, and he couldn't blame it completely on his nightmares. It was hard to get a good night's rest when he couldn't erase the sweet scent of Violet from his bed.

Tracy had been right when she'd said Violet wouldn't call, but here he was, mooning over her like some lovesick kid anyway.

Why are you obsessing over a woman you spent one night with? You didn't want anything serious, right? She is doing you a favor, and you are fucking moping around like a pussy.

Dean didn't know why he couldn't shake her. The sex had definitely been amazing. Maybe he was afraid it would never be that good again?

Suddenly, Best burst into his office, grinning.

"Don't you ever knock?" Dean grabbed his coffee mug from the desk and started to walk past Best so he could refill it, but Best stopped him.

"I'm not sure you want to go out there, dude."

"Why not?" Dean snapped.

"'Cause Violet—you remember Violet, right? Your one-night stand?—well, she just showed up with a kid for the program. Figured I'd save you from the drama," Best said.

Violet's here? With a kid?

Dean pushed through Best and almost slammed into Sergeant Oliver Martinez in the hallway. "Whoa, slow down, man. Miss Douglas, Casey, this is our director, Sergeant Dean Sparks."

Dean didn't even acknowledge Martinez; his gaze was riveted to Violet's wide brown eyes staring back at him, excitement racing through his body to his heart, jump-starting a pounding that deafened him. Her already light skin paled to a frightening shade of white with a hint of green, as if his being there might just make her toss up her cookies, and disappointment churned deep in his stomach.

What had he expected? That she'd throw her arms around him with some excuse? That maybe she had lost his number and been wanting to call, but couldn't?

"What are you staring at?" a surly young man asked as he stepped in front of Violet.

Dean looked down at the kid. There was a definite resemblance between him and Violet, although the boy's eyes were green and his hair wasn't a brilliant red. He was also sporting the greenish-purple evidence of a fading bruise on his face.

Holy shit! If this boy was hers, she must have had him when she was barely a teenager. There was no way she was older than thirty.

No wonder she didn't want to get involved with you; she was protecting her kid.

Dean imagined what life had been like for Violet, and he wanted to beat the hell out of whoever her son's dad was.

"Sorry, your mom just looked like someone I'd met before." Dean held out his hand to the kid, who sneered.

"She's my sister, dumbass," the kid said.

Relief flooded through Dean, even as Violet gasped loudly. "Casey, apologize now."

Dean's eyes narrowed, but Casey's stony silence and fixed stare told Dean the kid was going to be a hard egg to crack.

"I'm sorry for my brother, Sergeant Sparks." Violet's voice trembled, and he wondered if it was her brother's behavior or being around him that was causing it.

"Don't worry about it." Dean caught her gaze again briefly before she shifted it away, looking at anyone but him.

Her brother getting busted must have been why she'd broken down at his place, but looking back, why? It should have been her parents' problem, not hers. Dean would have to study Casey's file. At least that would give him some insight into why the kid was so fucking pissed off.

"I was just showing them around before getting Casey settled in B," Martinez said.

"I can show them." Why was he pushing this? From the pinched grimace on Violet's face, he could tell she was probably praying he would go away. Why chase a woman who obviously didn't want to be caught?

This was a legitimate question, yet he couldn't give a reasonable answer. He just couldn't believe that something that had been so good for him could be so forgettable to her.

Martinez arched a brow but ultimately shrugged. "Sure, I just thought you'd be too busy."

Violet finally met his gaze and gave him a tiny shake of her head, a silent plea to stop.

"Nope, I'm free." Dean wasn't sure if he was punishing her for her rejection or just hoping to satisfy his curiosity about her, but he wouldn't back down now.

"Really, Sergeant Sparks, that's not necessary." She sounded guttural, as if she was speaking through gritted teeth, but that was too bad.

Dean's eyes bored into hers, silently telling her she had no choice. "I insist, Miss Douglas."

VIOLET SEARCHED THE area for any means of escape, but the hallway didn't allow for anywhere to hide.

When the judge had assigned Casey to Alpha Dog, Violet had researched the program. It had opened four months ago, taking in nonviolent juvenile offenders and putting them in barracks. Each teenager was assigned a dog rescued from a local shelter to train. Once their time was up, Alpha Dog helped place the kids with veterinarians, shelters, or ROP programs in animal behavior and health. There had been a bunch of testimonials from parents praising the program, and Violet had been so hopeful.

If only she had checked out the staff.

"Well, I'll leave you to it then." If Sergeant Martinez was aware of the tension between Dean and Violet, he didn't say a word.

Violet noticed Tyler grinning like a fool behind Dean, but Sergeant Martinez grabbed him in a headlock and led him away, laughing.

God, this was humiliating. Had Dean told all his friends about their night together? Now she wasn't just looking to escape, but silently willing herself to disappear. What if it got back to Casey?

"If you'll follow me, I'll give you the rest of the tour," Dean said.

Violet put her arm around Casey, who shrugged her off immediately. She tried to ignore the sting of his rejection, but his moods shifted so fast, sometimes it made her head spin.

She caught Dean's disapproving look as he stared down her brother and blurted, "Thank you, Sergeant Sparks. I'm sure you're very busy. It can't be easy keeping something like this running."

"No, but everyone pitches in and works as a team, Miss Douglas." His tone was so casual and calm, at odds with the blaze she'd seen in his eyes. Was he actually angry with her? He'd been the one to say he didn't get involved; why would he care if she didn't call?

Maybe he feels like you led him on, talking about all of that friends-with-benefits stuff? Or his manly pride is stung.

Violet bristled as the ridiculous notion washed over her. She did not want to deal with another sulking male; she already had Casey to deal with, she was not going to take it from Dean.

"Violet, please." It seemed ridiculous to keep up the formality when he'd seen her naked, but she had a hard time keeping the irritation out of her voice.

Dean nodded and started walking. As Violet trailed a step behind him with Casey, her gaze traveled over Dean's broad back and shoulders, and she wanted to kick herself.

"Through there are the kennels. Every program member is assigned a dog. It will be your responsibility to provide food and water, as well as train your animal. If at any time the animal is mistreated, you will leave the program and conclude your sentence at juvenile hall. We don't give second chances here. These dogs have been through enough."

"I'm sure the children have, too." Violet didn't like Dean's insinuation that only the dogs had suffered. Casey wasn't a bad kid; he had been through one traumatic experience after another and had always put on a brave face. If he was acting out now, he had his reasons.

Dean stopped, and she almost slammed into his back. He turned, and she found herself inches away from his broad chest, his dark eyes fixed on hers as he leaned in. "I know that. I can guarantee that while they are here, none of these kids will be mistreated, but unlike the dogs, they are not helpless. They can speak up and tell us if they are hurt, hungry, or need help. Animals cannot."

Dean's spicy scent encircled her, distracting her from what he was saying for a half a second. That erotic aroma had lingered on her clothes, and she hated to admit that it had taken her a day or two to wash her tank top. She'd wanted the comfort of him, something to chase away reality again without risking getting hurt.

How could you get hurt? It was just physical, nothing more.

Except that the physical draw of him had her swaying dangerously closer, and she could have sworn he'd dipped his head.

Suddenly, Violet was pushed back and Casey placed himself right in front of her.

"Back the fuck off my sister, asshole."

Dean looked away from her, focusing all of his irritation on Casey. "I was just explaining myself, Casey."

"No, you were getting up in her face and being a douche." Violet noticed Casey's hands clenched at his sides and was afraid he might take a swing at Dean.

Which would most likely get him kicked out of the program and add an assault charge on top of everything.

Violet wrapped her arms around her brother and swung him away from Dean, putting herself back between them. "Casey, stop it. Dean—Sergeant Sparks wasn't doing anything. He's just passionate about the program, that's all."

"He was getting in your face—"

"If that were the case, do you really think I'd have sat back and taken it?"

Casey's shoulders fell, although he continued to glare daggers at Dean.

Violet jumped when his breath rustled her hair. "Should we continue with the tour?"

She hadn't been aware he was standing so close, but now she could feel the heat of his body radiating against her back. Was he trying to get a rise out of Casey or her?

Violet stepped away and didn't face him again until she was next to Casey. "Lead the way, Sergeant Sparks."

Dean turned on his heels and started walking once more, pointing out areas and talking about schedules while Violet's mind wandered. She hadn't been completely lying to Casey; Dean had spoken about helping animals with a passion, like the way she talked about cooking. He was right that animals couldn't speak for themselves, however, a part of her thought he might have been trying to punish her for seeming unsympathetic to the dogs. She didn't particularly like dogs, but she didn't want them hurt or abused either. She wasn't a monster.

But she couldn't get into all that with Casey standing there, already shooting suspicious looks between her and Dean. She would just have to wait and explain herself to Dean after.

Dean walked past the kennel door and into a large cafeteria. "This is the mess hall. All the meals are served here. There's no food allowed in the barracks. And through here"—Dean took them into another room, where a bunch of kids were preparing food—"is the kitchen. Like I said, everyone helps."

The rest of the tour included the meal prep station for the dogs, the yard where they worked the dogs, and the gym. When they reached the room where Casey would be bunking, Dean pointed to a freshly made bed with a stack of clothes on top.

"That's your bunk. Get changed, and someone will be waiting for you outside this door. After your duties are done, there's class until lunch. Then Sergeant Best will assign you a dog. You'll learn some basic training and then go to class until dinner. After dinner, you'll report back to the kennels, and then lights out. Are we clear?"

"Yeah," Casey grumbled.

"And while you're here, it's 'yes, sir.' "

Violet caught her laughter before it escaped, coughing loudly.

Her brother knew exactly what she was doing and made a face. "Yes, sir."

"We'll work on it." Dean's gaze came back to her, her heart catching as their eyes held briefly. "I'll give you two a minute to say good-bye, and then I'll walk you out."

There was a promise to his words, and she shivered at the thought of being alone with Dean. Would he bombard her with questions? Would he rail at her in disappointment?

Or would he actually treat her just like any other worried parent?

When they were alone, Violet put her hand on Casey's shoulder and looked in his eyes. "Six weeks is nothing. And it doesn't sound too bad. You'll get to have a dog, finally. At least, for a little while."

Casey didn't say anything, just stared at the floor. Sighing, Violet kissed the top of his head, but he jerked away. "I love you, Case. I wish I knew what I did to make you so angry."

"You didn't do anything," Casey snapped. "Just go. I'll be fine."

Violet did as he asked, blinking back the tears. She closed the door behind her and avoided Dean's searching gaze. "Thank you for showing us around."

"I'll walk you out," Dean said.

"Really, I can find my way—"

"I can't let a civilian wander around the program alone. This here is Jorge," Dean nodded at an approaching young man with a wicked grin. "He's a good kid and will take care of Casey. Won't you?"

"Yes, sir." Jorge's gaze traveled over her from head to toe before he gave her a wink. "Ma'am."

"And after you've shown Casey to the kennel, I'll let Martinez know you're to run laps with that lazy dog of yours," Dean growled.

"Worth it, sir," Jorge said.

Violet opened her mouth to say something to the little perv, but Dean's hand rested on the small of her back, propelling her forward gently. The heat of his palm burned through her shirt and branded her skin. She'd been trying to push the memory of his hands from her mind, and now she would have to start over again.

The silence between them was so loud, it actually hurt her nerves. Why wouldn't he talk? He'd obviously been trying to get her alone.

Unable to stand it anymore, she blurted, "I appreciate you not telling Casey that we've met before."

Dean grunted. "That's an interesting way of putting it."

Okay, he's definitely perturbed. "And I'm sorry I didn't call, but as you can see, I kind of have my hands full."

Dean's hand fell as they reached the lobby, and he shrugged. "It's fine, really. We had fun. It doesn't have to be anything more than that."

"Oh, well"—What the hell did she say to that?—"thank you for being so understanding."

"My pleasure," he said.

Considering how eager he'd been to give them the tour and get her alone, this conversation was a bit anticlimactic.

Silence stretched between them once more, and Violet twisted her hands in front of her nervously. "Dean—"

"Violet, is that you?"

Violet saw Tyler sauntering up to them and grimaced. "Hey, Tyler."

"Such a surprise to see you. How are things?" Tyler asked.

Violet glanced at Dean, who appeared to be clenching his jaw tighter than a steel trap. Obviously, Tyler was trying to make an awkward situation worse, and irritation pricked her temper. "About as well as can be expected, I guess."

"Isn't that the truth?" Tyler actually put his arm around her and gave her shoulders a quick squeeze. "Hey, but that concert was fun, right? When you see Tracy, tell her I said hi."

Violet shrugged off Tyler's arm with gritted teeth. "I'll do that."

Tyler slapped Dean on the back with a grin. "Well, I'm sure you two kids have a lot to talk about."

"Get the fuck out of here," Dean said with a snarl.

Violet's gaze shifted back and forth between the two as Tyler took off down the hall laughing. "I hope he doesn't mention the concert to anyone. The last thing I want is any of this getting back to Casey."

"I'll make sure he keeps his mouth shut. We're supposed to be professionals, although you probably couldn't tell. I apologize for Sergeant Best."

"It's okay, you can't always control the things your friends do." Violet almost reached out to touch his arm but dropped it at the last minute. Between the security guards and Tyler waiting in the wings, she didn't want to cause any more talk. "I really do feel bad about how things happened after…"

Dean cut her off with a shake of his head. "Violet, listen, we both got what we wanted. We said we'd try it once, and we did. No apologies, recriminations, or regrets. But in light of Casey and the fact that we'll be seeing each other a lot during his stay, let's just forget it ever happened."

How was she supposed to forget about them when she'd be seeing him every day for over a month? How was she going to forget those lips on hers, trailing down her body and making her scream? "Can you do that? Just forget that anything ever happened?"

It wasn't a fair question, considering she'd been trying to do that very thing before today, but it had seemed like there was something more he'd wanted to say to her. Had she read into all of his looks? The tour? Had he really just been acting normal, and she'd seen something more because she'd wanted to?

He looked her dead in the eye, his expression blank. "Honestly, I'd forgotten about it until you showed up here today."

Violet didn't believe him, not really, but his words cut deeper than any knife. Despite her resolve not to call him, she'd had a hard time concentrating on anything but him while he'd pretty much told her she was completely forgettable. Damn if that wasn't a kick to her pride, and he probably knew it. She'd really tried to hold onto a shred of dignity, but what was the point? She'd already made a giant ass of herself.

"Right, well, on that totally humiliating note, I am going to go and..." *Run my car off the overpass?*

Without finishing the sentence, she spun around and raced for the exit like a coward.

Chapter Eleven

LATER THAT AFTERNOON, Dean took Dilbert's leash in his left hand and flexed his sore right hand, satisfaction coursing through him as he remembered the dark shiner Best was now sporting. He'd deserved the hit after embarrassing Violet, and Dean wasn't sorry he'd done it. Too bad he couldn't put all the blame for her discomfort at Best's feet. He hadn't exactly been kind to her, either.

But what had she expected him to do? Rejection had never sat well with him, and despite all the crazy baggage she obviously carried, he'd been into her. Had been interested in seeing more of her.

And she had given him the big fat brush-off.

It hurt, but he had no right to take it personally. He should have just let it go and treated her like any other parent.

Except she wasn't a parent, which brought up more questions.

Dilbert started to lean lazily against Dean's leg, and he scowled down at him. Dilbert panted back adoringly. "Mutt, get off my leg."

Dilbert closed his mouth, catching his top lip in his teeth as he cocked his head.

When they'd first been assigned to Alpha Dog, Dean had gone with Best to the shelter, and Best had asked if they had any dogs set to be euthanized. They'd shown them back to a room filled with kennels and cages. Best had taken his time, putting each dog through a series of tests and exercises to grade their temperaments.

When they'd gotten to Dilbert, they had already chosen four dogs to take back to Alpha Dog for training. One of the volunteers had come in then and broken down crying. She'd shown them photos on her phone of Dilbert in funny hats and glasses—an attempt to get him adopted. It had been too hard for Dean to watch, and he'd said he'd train Dilbert himself. Best had still tested his temperament, and he'd passed with shining colors.

There was only one issue with Dilbert—he was a sloth. He slept as much as Dean would let him and was slow as molasses. Still, Dean had grown attached to the big lump, so he kept him, using him for demonstrations. Dilbert had gone through the entire search and rescue program, which was Dean's department, but he was definitely better suited to be an instructor's pet than a full-on working dog. Dean still held out hope that he would find Dilbert a home before leaving, but if he didn't, he could always send Dilbert to live with his brother Freddy or his mom and dad. Being a house dog would be just up Dilbert's alley.

Dean and Dilbert followed along behind Best, who was taking Casey down the row of available dogs, telling him what was expected of him. Dean had already decided to take the kid into his training group, telling himself it had nothing to do with pumping the kid for information but knowing it was a lie. He wanted to know why Casey had such a massive attitude, especially where his sister was concerned.

"So, without further ado," Best said, stopping in front of a kennel, "this is Apollo."

Dean looked in at the four-month-old black Lab and hound mix named Apollo. Apollo and his brother, Zeus, had been dumped in front of the program when they were just a few weeks old, skinny and dehydrated. Best had taken them to his veterinarian for a wellness check and discovered that although they were malnourished, they were otherwise healthy.

"His ears are too big for his head," Casey said. "His name should be Dumbo."

"You can call him whatever you want, just make sure it's consistent," Best said, opening the gate. As he led the puppy out, Dean didn't miss the way the boy's face softened.

Best handed him the leash and a pouch full of treats. "Take good care of him. He's a tough little guy."

I get the feeling his new master is pretty tough, too.

"All right, Casey, let's join the other guys outside and get started," Dean said. He noticed the shift in the kid's body when he addressed him, but he ignored it. It was Casey's first day, and he would try patience first. Violet wasn't wrong; most of the kids in the program had been through some form of trauma or another. Sometimes patience won out over a show of force.

The puppy strained to get closer to Dilbert, whose tail-thumping was about as excited as he got. Dean nodded at Best and headed for the back door that opened into the yard. As Casey and Apollo followed alongside him and Dilbert, Dean broke the silence.

"So, you live with your sister?"

"Yeah."

"How is that?"

"Fine."

The irony of his next question made Dean smile. "You're kind of taciturn, aren't you?"

Unlike Dean the first time he had heard it, Casey knew what the word meant, and from the dark, twisted look on his young face, it obviously ruffled his feathers.

"If you think you're going to pump me for information on my sister, you're delusional."

Dean really hadn't been trying for information on Violet in this instance, and when they were just a few feet from Dean's unit, he stopped and faced Casey. "Look, Casey, I'm interested in what's going on with you and every kid who walks through that door. My goal is to make sure you don't end up back in here or worse. I'm not gonna lie, your sister is beautiful, but she's not in my unit. You are."

Dean put his hand on the kid's shoulder and would have said more, but Casey jerked away violently and yelled, "Don't touch me! Don't you ever fucking touch me!"

Dean put his hands up in the air, and Liam, a young man who had been with him for a couple of months, jogged over with his dog, Ranger, in tow. Ranger was a black and white medium sized dog with a ton of energy who had come a long way in the last few months with Liam's gentle hand guiding him.

"Everything all right, sir?" Liam asked.

"Yeah, Liam. This is Casey. Let's get him set up in line."

Liam was a tall, thin kid with dirty blond hair and crooked teeth. He had been caught shoplifting and earned a three-month sentence at Alpha Dog. Dean had read his file—a junkie mother followed by four foster homes. When he'd run away from the last one, he'd stolen a sack of groceries and an iPod, the latter of which he hoped to sell, but had been caught at the door.

Dean had pulled him into his group and found out that Liam was a natural leader and had been taking care of other runaways he'd met. The other kids in the unit turned to Liam when there was a dispute. Dean thought the kid deserved better than the hand life had dealt him. Liam was just past sixteen, and Dean had been searching for some way to help him get out of the system.

"Come on, dude," Liam said.

Casey eyed Dean warily as he followed Liam into formation. All of the kids were to keep three feet between them and hold onto their leashes at all times.

"Attention!" Everyone except Casey stood straight, and Dean waited until Casey finally copied Liam's stance. "We have a new unit member, Casey Douglas. Please answer any questions he may have and help him feel welcome. He is in Barrack B. Who is in B?"

Liam, Jeff, and Carlos raised their hands.

"Good, you can keep an eye on him and make sure he's settling in. Now, let's get started."

Dean brought Dilbert along and made him sit. "Your dog should always be sitting, whether in front of you or alongside you. Dilbert, about-face."

Dilbert shifted to a sitting position next to Dean. It wasn't nearly as fast as some of the other trainers' dogs, but Dean gave him a treat anyway.

As Dean continued the lesson, he tried not to think about how much he enjoyed this part. Teaching the kids, seeing their faces when their dogs followed a command perfectly...They needed this program, and Dean wanted it to succeed and spread. That was the military's goal: to open up facilities like this across the country. It created new job opportunities for military personnel and established good rapport with the community.

But it wasn't where Dean belonged. He wanted to be back where the action was, needed to prove that he wasn't done. That what had happened wasn't his fault.

Pushing that day from his mind, he barked, "Next up, down-stay! Let's go."

"Hey, Sparks!" Martinez called from behind him.

Dean turned around, irritated, but walked over to where Sergeant Oliver Martinez stood by the fence, his blue eyes watching Dean with concern.

"What?" Dean growled.

"Your psychiatrist called. You missed your appointment this morning."

"My appointment is tomorrow. It's always Tuesday morning." Every week, the same conversation over and over.

Martinez gave him a fierce frown. "No, remember I told you she'd called and had to change it to today because she was going out of town, and you said yeah, fine?"

"Fuck." He couldn't have her thinking he was skipping out on his appointments. Not when he was so close to getting back what he'd lost.

"Lucky for you, I am a smooth-talking voodoo daddy and told her you had an emergency pop up with one of the kids. Asked her if you could come in an hour."

Dean laughed with relief. "Thanks, man. I'm glad you answered the phone. Best would have left me out to dry."

"Yeah, you owe me two because I'm about to take over your class for you while you get the hell out of here and handle your business. And start updating your appointments in your phone like you live in this century."

Dean didn't point out that up until Oliver had met his girlfriend, Evelyn Reynolds, he'd been just as clueless as Dean when it came to technology. He didn't have the time to bring it up if he wanted to make it to Rita Wentworth's office.

He raced through the facility with Dilbert puffing beside him. When they stopped off at his office for his keys and wallet, Dean put Dilbert in his crate. The dog sucked down half his water bowl before collapsing onto his fluffy dog bed.

"We're going to have to work on your stamina, Dilbert, my man."

Dilbert let out a loud, doggy sigh as Dean closed his office door. He started running again until he made it outside to his truck. Checking his dashboard clock as he turned the key, he figured he would make it to Rita's office with ten minutes to spare, as long as the roads were clear of construction.

Dean's thoughts started drifting to what he was going to say to Rita today. He'd given her every detail he could remember about the day of the bomb, from the smell of smoke and burning flesh to the ear-splitting sound of his brothers' screams. Still, she just kept telling him, *"Okay, we'll pick this up again next week."*

Dean just wanted her to tell him what in the hell she wanted. What would it take for her to just sign off and give him his life back?

Maybe the truth. Maybe if you told her about the nightmares, she could give you something to help you sleep.

But if he told her about the dreams, about the anxiety and the sleepless nights, she'd have everything she needed to keep him out of the action. She'd probably try to shove a bunch of medications down his throat, and he didn't want to be all drugged up like a zombie. He wanted to be the guy people could count on.

He just wanted to feel needed—not lucky. People had told him over and over *how lucky* he was to be alive, *how lucky* he was to get a post stateside and not have to go back.

Dean pulled into Rita Wentworth's office lot and parked before walking inside to the quiet, whitewashed sitting area. A landscape of a cottage surrounded by wildflowers was the only splash of color in the room. Even the couch he sat down on was cream colored, which probably explained the NO EATING OR DRINKING sign on the opposite wall.

Rita stepped out into the hallway, her hand on the back of a woman who was wiping at her cheeks furiously with a tissue.

"I'll see you next week, Susan. Call if you need to talk sooner than that."

"Thank you, Rita," Susan sniffled.

Once Susan disappeared out the door, Dean stood as Rita faced him, her blue eyes seeming to pierce his soul. He assumed she was in her early fifties by the lines on her face and threads of gray in her jet-black hair, but he had never been a good judge of women's ages.

"Dean, how are you doing?"

"I'm fine, Rita. Just fine."

"Good." With a fluttering wave of her hand, she asked, "Should we get started then?"

VIOLET WAS JUST wrapping up her day at the hotline and wished she had called in today. Her day had gone from bad to worse, first with Dean and then with school. She'd gotten to her summer class only to find that it had been canceled. No e-mail or text from the teacher, just a note on the door that said *Class canceled. Sick.*

"So sorry you wasted precious gas to drive to campus this morning, but I am probably off getting my nob waxed," Violet had said aloud in a fake British accent, mocking the professor. He was a pompous, sexist ass, but his class was a requirement she needed.

So, she'd gone in early for her shift at Here to Listen, figuring it would keep her mind off of things, but that hadn't helped either. She had spent most of it distracted, worrying about Casey and how he was doing on his first day. She had almost called several times but stopped herself. The last thing she wanted was to pester them so much that they kicked Casey out.

Or are you just worried you might get Dean on the phone and have another awkward conversation?

"Sometimes, I just feel like no one can see me. Like they don't even notice that I'm drowning," the caller said softly on the other end of the line, bringing Violet out of her head. She was glad that the caller couldn't see her cheeks burning guiltily. It wasn't fair to these people for her to tune them out. It was just one more person letting them down.

Trying to make up for her insensitivity, she said, "I can imagine that is very hard to deal with. Really, anytime you need to talk, please call us. And it is really important to let your family know how you're feeling, too. Sometimes, people just get busy and don't mean to push others away. If you just sit them down and voice your concerns, I am sure that they will be there for you."

"I will try talking to my husband tonight."

Violet wasn't sure if she really would, but she could only listen and advise. She couldn't make people do what they weren't ready for.

"I think that is a great first step."

"Thank you for listening. It helped," the caller said.

Guilt shot through her. "You're welcome, and take care, okay? All right, bye."

Violet disconnected the call and groaned. Slowly she climbed to her feet and went to grab her time card.

"Are you working Friday, Violet?" Sean Lambert asked.

Sean was a funny guy who had started at Here to Listen as part of a community service gig and been hired after his hours were up. Now he was a liberal arts major working on his doctorate to become a college professor in English lit.

"Yeah, I think so. All depends on how much my sister has packed. She leaves at the end of the month for Oregon State."

"Well, maybe if you don't have to help your sister, we could go for coffee or dinner...a movie...?"

Violet stared at Sean. They had been bumping into each other for months, and she'd never gotten that vibe from him. Never experienced the desire for more than just a casual hi and bye. And even if she could afford to date someone right now, it wouldn't be Sean. Not after learning exactly what explosive passion felt like. She couldn't go back to settling for a pleasant time with someone who was just there to stave off the loneliness.

"I'm sorry, Sean. I'm actually seeing someone," she lied.

"Oh, well, can't blame a guy for trying." He gave her a hesitant, awkward smile before escaping back to his cubicle.

Violet left the building with a heavy sigh, cursing Dean Sparks for basically ruining her. Before, she would have been completely satisfied to settle for a date with Sean, just to get out of the freaking house for a few hours. Now, it was as if every other man's flaws and shortcomings had been magnified. Sean was nice and funny, but he talked a lot and about boring things, like weird facts and historical references that were too random to be interesting.

Instead, she'd rather sit at home and fantasize about a man who wanted a relationship less than she did and was now completely taboo. There was no way she could hook up with Dean while Casey was at Alpha Dog or even after. If her brother wasn't pissed off now, he would be if Dean started coming around. It was completely off the table.

An hour later, Violet stumbled up the steps to the house with her hands full of groceries, still thinking about Dean. She had been trying to protect the both of them, but she should have just called to let him know that an FWB thing was out of the question.

Do you really think he cares? He probably has girls lined up to be his booty buddy.

That thought was terribly unpleasant, to say the least.

Violet, already irritated by her train of thought, hollered for her sister. "Dais! Can you help me put away the groceries?"

No answer besides rock music thumping through the ceiling. "Figures."

It was a little after four in the afternoon, and Violet glanced around the kitchen at the dirty dishes still in the sink with disgust. All summer long Daisy had slept the mornings away, hardly lifting a finger to help with the cleaning. At night, she was either working at Safeway or out with her friends, but Violet was done letting her get away with being lazy. Violet hadn't wanted to be an annoying nag for the remainder of time Daisy was home, but apparently, that was the only thing her sister responded to.

Dropping the groceries in the kitchen, Violet pushed the play button on the answering machine. She kept the house phone for emergencies and people she didn't want to have her cell phone number.

"Hello, Miss Douglas, this is Mrs. Paulsen with Child Protective Services. I stopped by today to do a home visit and speak to you about Casey, but it looks like you were out. Please call me as soon as you get in so that we can connect before Casey's release. My number is 916-555-9087. Thank you."

Perfect. This was just what they needed; after years of having CPS ignore them, they were right back under their microscope.

Violet started putting the cold and frozen stuff away first, grumbling at the way her day had gone, when a loud bang upstairs startled her, and she jumped a foot in the air.

"Daisy, you okay?"

No answer, and the music had stopped.

Worry shot through her like a bullet, and she headed for the stairs. Climbing them swiftly, she reached Daisy's room and turned the knob, but it was locked. "Daisy?"

"What?" Daisy answered, her voice muffled.

"What are you doing?" she asked.

"Working out," Daisy said, giggling.

Violet heard a deep chuckle join hers and closed her eyes, counting to ten. Her sister was seventeen, almost eighteen, and she was already aware of how Violet felt about her boyfriend, Quinton Harris. The guy was a druggie loser, but Daisy had spent the last six months trying to convince Violet that she was wrong about him. That he was a good guy. Violet thought her sister was blind, but too much arguing just seemed to drive her sister closer to him.

Still, she did enjoy making the worm squirm. A twenty-two-year-old guy should know better than to mess around with a seventeen-year-old.

"Well, tell your *exercise partner* he's got two minutes to get his ass out of this house or I'm calling the cops, and if you want me to rent that U-Haul for your stuff, you better finish doing the dishes like you promised."

Muffled cursing and scrambling came through the door, warming Violet's heart.

"Douche bag," Violet said, loud enough for him to hear.

"Bitch."

Violet heard Daisy snap at him to not call her sister a bitch, and she grinned.

And then she heard the distinct sound of a slap, and her sister cried out.

Violet ran to Casey's door, planning on using the adjoining bathroom to get in, but it was locked, too.

Violet yelled at the top of her lungs, "If you hit my sister again, motherfucker, you're dead."

"I didn't hit her, did I, baby? Why don't you just mind your business?"

"I'm fine, Vi. He didn't hit me."

"One minute." Violet took the stairs two at a time and ran to her parents' old room, now hers. Punching in the combination to her safe, she pulled out the extra door key for the bedrooms and her gun. It wasn't loaded, but it sure would make that little prick piss his pants.

When she reached the top of the stairs, she yelled, "I'm coming in, Dais."

"Shit," Quinton said.

Violet turned the key in the lock and threw the door open. Quinton was already halfway through the two-story window in a T-shirt and boxers, his pants in his hand.

Violet pulled out her cell phone and pretended to dial. As she held the phone up to her ear, she raised the gun. "Hello, some guy broke into my house and attacked my sister…"

"Violet, no!" Daisy yelled as Quinton disappeared, probably to scale down the side of the house. Violet went to the window and watched him fall the last few feet to the ground and hollered, "Yeah, you better run, punk!"

Violet shut the window and slipped her phone into her pocket. Setting the gun down on the bench seat under Daisy's window, she sat on her sister's bed. Violet held a hand out and traced the obvious red imprint across her sister's left cheek. Her sister wiped at her wet, green-gold eyes, wincing when Violet touched the slap mark.

"I should have loaded the gun and pulled the trigger."

"Shut up," Daisy whimpered. "It was an accident."

Violet dropped her hand as it clenched in frustration. Daisy wasn't stupid, so why was she saying something so ignorant?

Probably the same reason Mom always made excuses for Dad. Love.

Which only proved to Violet that she had been smart to keep men at a distance. If love made you blind and complacent, she would pass.

"Someone tripping over your big feet is an accident; someone hitting you because they don't like what you said is assault."

"Why can't you just stay out of it, Vi? I'm almost eighteen and leaving for Oregon in a few weeks. How are you going to control who I see when I'm a state away?"

Violet rubbed her hands over her face and groaned. "If I wanted to control you, I would have locked you up in a convent the minute you brought that piece of garbage home. In fact, I think I've been pretty understanding about your feelings for Quinton, but no more." Violet pulled out her phone and took a picture of her sister before she could turn away. She held it up for her to see. "No one who loves you would do this to you. And if I catch him anywhere near this house again, I *will* call the cops."

"Fuck you! You are not my mother!" Daisy cried.

Violet swallowed down the lump of pain in her throat and stood up. "I know I'm not Mom, but I love you, Daisy. Love is about making sacrifices and putting other people's needs before your own. You aren't thinking straight when it comes to that mother—"

"I didn't ask you to give up your life for me!"

"You didn't have to, that's the point. No matter what you say or what you do, I'm always going to love you. Can you say the same about Quinton?"

Daisy lay down with a sob, and Violet sat once more, gathering her in her arms. Violet waited for her sister to push her away, but she didn't. Daisy clung to her, shaking with the force of her tears as Violet stroked her chestnut hair and rocked her. Speaking from memory, she recited the words of her mother's favorite book, *Love You Forever* by Robert Munsch.

"I'll love you forever, I'll like you for always..." As her sister started to quiet, Violet closed her eyes.

As she spoke, she remembered the softness of her mother's voice when she read the story, and her chest felt like someone was standing on it. She had loved and adored her mother, even when she'd have one of her dark days. When her mother would lock herself in her room, Violet would take care of Daisy and Casey. And after her suicide, Violet had continued to do that, but looking at where they were now, Violet knew she'd screwed up. Her brother was in constant trouble, and her sister was in love with a dirtbag.

After raising her brother and sister, it was hard for Violet to imagine having kids of her own. Not that she didn't love kids and think about having them eventually, but what if she screwed them up, too? What if she chose a loser like her mother and sister had?

Or worse yet, what if as time went on, she turned out like her mother?

There were already so many similarities. Violet cried at everything and internalized every hurt she'd ever received, stacking them up inside like Jenga pieces. She was afraid that someday the pieces would become too high and tumble down. That eventually, all the hurts and unhappy memories would just be too much for her.

Like her mother—who at thirty-five had taken her own life, leaving her children alone with her drug-addict husband and no other family to speak of. It was why Violet never forgot that she had other people depending on her, why she kept busy.

Because she couldn't be alone with her thoughts, memories, and fears. She didn't think she could handle going through the stress and pain of having her own children, especially if there was a chance that she might not be strong enough to endure all the ups and downs. She had four more years, and then Casey would be going off to college and living his own life.

Then the only person she'd need to worry about was herself.

But sometimes, she thought about what her life would be like if her mother hadn't killed herself. If she had finally left Violet's dad and started over. If Violet had been free to have a normal childhood, to fall in love…

Only fantasy didn't do anyone any good. Fantasy was just another word for disappointment.

Chapter Twelve

Two weeks later

DEAN HAD MANAGED to avoid Violet every time she'd visited Casey, but it didn't mean he wasn't aware of her. Glancing at the clock, he knew there were just sixteen more hours until her arrival. The woman was like clockwork, coming the same time every day, sometimes with another young woman he assumed was her sister, but mostly alone.

Dean had gone through Casey's file, and it was no wonder the kid was pissed off. His mom, Elaine, had committed suicide when he was still a toddler, and his father, Jack, had taken off on them three years ago. The only constant he seemed to have were his sisters.

It had been surprising to learn that Violet was his legal guardian, but with everything he knew about her, it made sense. She was essentially a single mom, keeping everyone at bay while trying to raise two kids when she was basically still a kid herself.

After reading the file, Dean had decided it was better to keep his distance from her. As much as he was drawn to her, she hadn't been lying when she'd said she had a lot going on.

Except now, he was worried about Casey. The kid seemed to be adjusting to the program well. He followed directions and had settled in fine with his bunkmates, but if any of the instructors tried to draw him out of his shell, he closed himself off. He definitely had something against men, though considering what Dean had read about his dad, who could blame him? However, Dean suspected that Casey was dealing with something more. His mood swings and violent reactions to being touched were more than just teenaged angst.

Whatever had happened to the kid, Dean knew that it was bad. Casey probably needed to see a professional, but considering Dean's aversion to shrinks, he wasn't exactly the best advocate.

Which meant he would have to contact Violet and come up with a plan to help Casey. He could keep things professional. Treat her just like any other parent.

Except when you talk to any other parent, you can't actually picture them naked.

A knock on his office door pulled him from his thoughts, and he barked, "Come in."

Liam opened the door and stepped inside. "Sorry to bother you, sir."

"No problem, Liam, I was just doing paperwork. I appreciate any excuse to avoid it, so have a seat." Dean waved to the chair in front of his desk and sat back. "What's on your mind?"

"It's about Casey," Liam said, looking uncomfortable.

"What about him?"

Liam hesitated, and Dean sat forward. "Liam, if he's done something, I need to know—"

"He hasn't done anything wrong, sir, but...He has night terrors. Violent ones. In one of the foster homes I lived in, the kid I shared a room with had them, too. I think someone hurt him, Sergeant Sparks, or is still hurting him. I just...You've helped me a lot, and Casey's a good kid, so I was hoping maybe...Maybe you could help him, too?"

After four months of working with teenagers, Dean had learned that it was hard for most of them to ask for help.

"Just to be clear, you think someone is hitting him?" Abuse would make sense, but who? Violet? Dean couldn't picture it, not with the way she protected the kid.

Maybe one of her boyfriends?

He hated to admit that the thought of Violet tangled up with another man made him want to smash something.

"Or worse, sir. Some of the things he said...I get the feeling it might be worse than that."

Dean's blood ran cold at the horrors that flashed through his mind. *Something worse.*

Casey was small, easy to overpower...

"Thanks, Liam." His voice sounded like a guttural growl, and he cleared his throat. "You're a good friend."

Liam stood, his expression worried. "Can you not tell Casey I told you anything? I don't want to break his trust."

Such a good kid. Hopefully when he gets out of here, he'll be able to catch a break. "I won't say anything. Besides, it's not as if he actually said anything to you, so he doesn't need to know that you told me about the nightmares."

"Thank you, sir."

As Liam left his office, Dean pulled Casey's file for Violet's number. It would be easier to talk to her over the phone, where he couldn't see her face. Especially since he already knew that if she cried, he wouldn't be able to resist comforting her.

He got her voicemail and went for a completely professional message. He didn't want her to get the wrong idea and think this was a personal call. "Hello, this is Sergeant Dean Sparks. I need to speak to you about Casey."

Dean left his office number and hung up. He should give her a chance to call back, but if Casey was suffering, it was important to get him help sooner than later.

Glancing at the clock on the wall, he saw it was after six. He could swing by the Douglas home and sit down with Violet. Casey was going to be in his care for another four weeks. He couldn't be afraid to deal with Violet.

He was a grown man, after all. He could control himself.

NO MATTER HOW many times he told himself he didn't want to see her, it didn't stop his heart from pounding as he pulled into the Douglas's driveway fifteen minutes later. The two-story house was dark brown and looked like it needed a new roof at the very least. The yard was overgrown, and as he neared the front porch, he noticed a few of the boards appeared a little iffy on their load-bearing abilities. It actually looked like something the neighborhood kids would call haunted, but he knocked on the door anyway.

A young woman answered the door in a tank top and shorts, flashing him a flirtatious smile.

"Whew, happy birthday to me. Whatever you're selling, put me down for two."

Dean remembered his younger sisters' friends practicing their wiles on him and knew how to deflect feminine interest. "I'm Sergeant Dean Sparks. I work at Alpha Dog Training Program. I need to speak to Violet Douglas about Casey."

"How about you show me some ID, hot stuff. How do I know you're not one of those sexy home invaders putting on an elaborate ruse to get inside and cut us into little bits?"

First Violet with her serial killer obsession and now her sister.

Dean pulled out his ID and handed it over. She looked it over, her forehead wrinkling in concentration for far too long. Pretty sure she was fucking with him, he held his hand out. "Do you want to call the program, or can I have that back?"

"It looks legit, but then again, I watch *Supernatural.* You could have made this at Kinko's, for all I know."

"Look, if you want to get your sister, I'll wait out here—"

"I'm just fucking with you! Violet's in the kitchen. Come on in." She stepped back to let him pass and held her hand out to him. "I'm Daisy, by the way."

Dean glanced around the living room and took in the aged wallpaper, the brown shag carpet. Threadbare furniture and an old box television were arranged around the small space, and the walls were filled with pictures in a wide array of frames. It was as if they'd picked up whatever they could find and slipped the pictures in.

Dean crossed the room and studied the pictures, one by one.

"That's my mother holding Casey the day he was born. And that's Violet and me in our Easter dresses when I was six and she was thirteen."

Dean stared at the picture she indicated. Violet had her arm around her little sister's shoulders, and the two beamed at the camera in puffy dresses covered in flowers and ribbons.

"Violet told me that Mom got the dresses at Goodwill for a couple of bucks. They were two sizes too big for us, but she cut them down and sewed all those flowers and ribbons on to dress them up. Violet always said our mom could make a burlap sack beautiful."

"Dais, who was at the…door."

Dean turned around at the sound of Violet's voice and stared at her. Her red hair was piled on top of her head, and she had on an apron over a T-shirt and shorts. White flour covered her hands, and it looked like she was holding a ball of dough between them.

She was so beautiful, he almost forgot to breathe.

"What are you doing here?" she asked.

"Actually, I needed to speak to you about Casey. I have some concerns."

"What kind of concerns?" she asked.

Dean glanced toward Daisy. "Can we speak in private?"

"Um, sure." Nodding in the direction of the kitchen, she left the room with Daisy on her heels. He could hear them whispering, but it was too quiet to understand.

When Violet came back into the room, Dean turned back to the photographs and noticed that only one of them contained a smiling man with deep creases around his eyes. "You don't have many pictures of your father."

"He was never home," she said impatiently. "I'm sure you've read Casey's file and know why."

"Yeah, I did. I can't imagine having to raise my brothers and sisters—"

"I didn't *have* to do anything."

Dean faced Violet, her crossed arms and blazing eyes, and realized he'd said exactly the wrong thing. Again.

"I fought to keep them with me and was lucky I got the right judge. I love them and would do anything for them."

"I didn't mean it that way, Violet. I was trying to give you a compliment. What you're doing is admirable. Not everyone would step up."

"Obviously, or we wouldn't have so many kids in foster care." With a heavy sigh, she uncrossed her arms and spoke calmly. "Look, do you actually have something to tell me about my brother?"

Her attitude rubbed his patience raw. Why was she being so rude to him when he was just trying to help her brother?

"I have reason to believe that your brother is being abused," he said bluntly.

Violet sucked in her breath sharply. "Why do you think that? Did he say something?"

"Did you know Casey suffered from night terrors?" he asked, ignoring her questions.

"He has nightmares sometimes, yeah, but we haven't exactly had it easy."

"I understand that, but one of his bunkmates came to me because Casey said some disturbing things during these nightmares, and it has me concerned."

"A kid told you all this?" Violet said.

"A young man I trust. It's enough to make me think Casey should talk to someone."

Violet sank into one of the worn chairs, her face leached of color. "Oh, God." She covered her mouth, and Dean saw her eyes well up. "I did this. This is my fault."

Before he realized what he was doing, he was on his knees in front of her. "Violet, this isn't your fault. I am not even sure I'm right—"

"He's changed. Just this last year, he hasn't been the same. He was always so happy, even after..." She seemed to catch herself and wiped at her eyes. "I'll look into finding someone."

"In the meantime, we have counselors at the program. I'd like to set him up with Dr. Linda Stabler. She's really good, at least from what I'm told."

Violet nodded her head, and Dean took her hands in his. "I have to ask. Do you know who could have been abusing your brother?"

"No. No, I have no idea," she said.

Dean hated asking, afraid that she would take it the wrong way, but he couldn't help himself. "What about a boyfriend?"

Violet's head jerked up. "I don't bring men around Casey and Daisy."

"What about your sister?" Dean didn't want to analyze the relief her admission brought him. He didn't think Violet could've handled it if she found out someone she brought around had hurt her brother.

Violet tensed up, and Dean could tell she was considering the possibility that someone her sister knew could have hurt her brother.

Violet pulled her hands from his and wiped at her cheek. "I appreciate you coming by, Sergeant Sparks, but I can take it from here."

VIOLET'S MIND RACED as she thought back over all the times that she'd been at work and it had been just Casey and Daisy at home. Had Daisy ever left Casey at home with Quinton?

Quinton was an abusive bastard, but the thought that he might take advantage of a kid half his size turned her stomach.

Still, she wasn't going to question her sister with Dean in the house. For a brief moment, she'd wanted to sink into the comfort he offered, to lay her head on his chest and let him wrap his arms around her. To let his strength hold her up for a little while. But he was still a stranger, and she already had enough people up in her business.

"Violet, I'd like to help you," he said earnestly.

"I don't need any help. We're doing fine."

"From the looks of this house, it seems like you could use some," he said.

Violet stood up angrily and placed her hands on her hips. "We have a roof over our heads, food in the cupboards, and the lights are still on. We're *fine*."

"I'm not saying you aren't fine, Violet. What are you, twenty-five?"

"I'm twenty-four," she said.

"And you've been taking care of your siblings for how long?"

"Long enough to know this works. Look, Daisy is heading off to college in a few weeks, and I have a semester left before I have my degree. After that, I'll be able to get a better-paying job and get Casey out of here." Violet held her tears at bay, refusing to break down again. "We don't need you getting involved. I'll talk to Daisy and Casey, and we will handle this together."

Dean stood still as a statue, saying nothing. The only part of his body that showed any life were his eyes. Emotions swirled through the dark depths—possibly frustration and definitely pity.

Twisting her hands in front of her, she fought the urge to scream at him. God, she didn't want his pity. She just wanted him out of her house so she could sort through her shit without an audience.

"I'll set Casey up with counseling appointments this week," he said finally.

He's just trying to help Casey. You don't have to be such a bitch to him.

It wasn't about him—or her, for that matter. She needed to get to the bottom of this on her own, and he would only complicate things for them.

For you, you mean.

"Thank you for coming by, really. I appreciate you looking out for my brother."

Dean nodded before walking out of the house and closing the door behind him.

Unable to stop it, she raced into the kitchen and hurled the contents of her stomach into the sink. As she clenched the counter and heaved, a comforting hand rubbed her back.

"You heard?" Violet asked.

"I've never left Quinton alone with Casey. I'd never leave Casey alone period, I swear," Daisy said.

Violet began to sob, believing her. Part of her was relieved that Daisy wouldn't have to bear any guilt for this, but the rest of her just wanted to know everything.

"It's okay," Daisy whispered.

"No it's…not." Violet tried to calm her breathing, but she was sucking in air like she was drowning.

"We'll talk to Casey, and once he tells us who did it, we'll call the cops."

"If Casey hasn't talked about what happened before, what makes you think he'll tell us about it now?" Violet asked.

"I don't know. My overwhelming optimism?"

Violet couldn't stand that Casey had kept something like this inside. He must have been so scared. Why hadn't he come to her?

"I can't believe I didn't see this coming."

"You knew something was going on, just not what. You can't blame yourself for this."

Violet held her head over the sink, waiting for the nausea to pass. There was no point in arguing with her sister; no matter which way you sliced it, part of what had happened to Casey was her fault. At some point, she'd put her brother in a vulnerable position.

And he had paid the ultimate price for her mistake.

"Sergeant Sparks seems like a good guy. You were kind of harsh."

"I slept with him." Violet wasn't sure why she'd told her. Maybe because she was so tired of secrets, but her sister's calming circles on her back stopped.

"For real? You had sex with that guy?"

Violet nodded and turned on the faucet, rinsing her mouth and the sink out.

"Shit, and here I thought you were a sexless prude."

Violet spun around to face her sister. "Why would you think that?"

"Because you never bring guys home—"

"Of course not. This is our home, and the fewer people we have coming or going, the better," she said. "Besides, how do I hold the high moral ground and tell you not to screw that douche bag in your bedroom if I'm doing the same thing?"

"You do like your moral high ground." Daisy smiled only briefly before her expression turned serious. "I wanted you to know that I've decided to break up with Quinton."

Violet paused, surprised for a second before stifling the urge to jump around and do a dance to the common-sense gods. Of course she refrained, but she couldn't keep the bright tone from her question. "Why?"

"Because I'm going to be in Oregon, and he'll be here. And I love him, I do, but…" The tremble in Daisy's voice shook Violet to her core; she wanted to hug her sister but waited patiently for her to finish. "He's just not who I see when I think about the future, you know? I want someone who's…well, nicer for one thing."

Violet weighed whether or not to ask, finally giving in. "That slap wasn't the first time, was it?"

Daisy avoided Violet's gaze but not before she saw the sheen of tears in her sister's eyes. "No, but it wasn't just that. I want someone who thinks I'm beautiful and smart and funny and nice—"

"You *are* beautiful, smart, funny, and nice! That is exactly what you *deserve* from the man who professes to love you."

"But I want someone who thinks those things about me, even when they might not be true."

Pulling her sister into her arms, Violet squeezed her tight. "Dais, it doesn't matter what anyone thinks about you. All that matters is how you feel about the person you are. And just in case you were wondering, your big sister thinks you're amazing."

"Thanks." Daisy laughed as she pulled away, wiping at her eyes. "Look what you did, you made me mess up my makeup."

"Sorry, I was trying to be supportive." Tucking a chestnut strand behind her sister's ear, Violet asked, "When are you going to do it?

"I called him this morning, but he didn't pick up. Figured I'd meet him sometime this week, do it face to face."

"Do it in a public place, please." Violet didn't trust Quinton. He was too volatile.

"Geez, Vi…"

"Humor me," Violet said.

"Fine, I'll make sure and tell him when we're surrounded by plenty of witnesses."

"Thank you."

Suddenly, Daisy hugged Violet back, hard. "You're a good sister."

In the last ten years, Daisy had never said those words to her. It was always understood that she loved Violet, but damn, it sounded good to hear it aloud.

"Thanks. So are you."

"No, not really. Not like you. I don't think I could have done what you did for us," Daisy said. "Sergeant Sparks was right. You're pretty special."

"I'm not. I just couldn't lose you guys." The words sounded selfish to her ears, and she shook her head, wiping at her watery eyes. "I don't know, maybe you would have been better off in a foster home, instead of living in this hovel with me."

"Stop it. You did the best you could, and no matter what happens, I hope you know that. Who knows where we would have been if you'd made a different choice, but I'm standing *here* on my eighteenth birthday. I'm leaving for college, and that's partially because of you. You are the best big sister in the entire world."

Violet hugged Daisy back, overwhelmed by her words. Then, suspicion rolled in. Daisy was laying it on awfully thick…almost like she wanted something.

And then she chuckled wetly. "You saw the car out the window?"

"You mean the black Honda with the red bow and *Happy Birthday, Daisy* written on the windshield?"

Violet's light amusement exploded into loud laughter. They had shopped for cars last week, and Daisy had fallen hard for the car, but she'd only saved three thousand and the guy was selling it for eight. After telling Daisy no, Violet had called the man back and asked if she could have it looked over by a mechanic she trusted. Later, she'd met the guy for coffee and asked if he'd take six thousand for it. At first, he'd balked, but eventually he'd let her have it for six thousand five hundred.

"Yes, I mean *that* car. Don't you want to know how I got it?"

"No, I knew you'd get it," Daisy said.

"How'd you know that?" Violet asked.

"Because you can do anything, no matter what obstacles are in the way."

Violet released a giggle and squeezed Daisy until she cried, "Oxygen becoming an issue!"

"I don't care that you are buttering me up, I needed to hear that."

Violet's little chicken timer went off, indicating the cake had cooled enough, and she let Daisy go to pull the cake out of the fridge. When they were kids their mother had baked their cakes, and Violet had since carried on the tradition, getting pretty good at decorating along the way.

"Can I go see it?" Daisy asked.

"Sure, the keys are in my purse on a Hannah Montana key chain," Violet said.

"Ugh, that's going in the trash," Daisy said.

Violet pulled her frosting kit from the cupboard, her mind wandering back to the problem at hand. Why wouldn't Casey have told her about the abuse? It didn't make any sense to keep this from her, especially since she'd be the first one to support him. Did he blame her because she'd been working and going to school? Did he think she didn't have time for him anymore? Or was he embarrassed?

And how was she going to bring it up to him? What if whoever had hurt Casey was hurting someone else? If she waited until he was home, would he open up more than if she brought it up while he was at Alpha Dog?

No, this couldn't wait. She would try to be as cautious as possible, but she had to let Casey know that she was here. That no matter what, she had his back and that he didn't have to be afraid anymore.

One thing was for sure; until she talked to him, nothing, not even Daisy's excited squeals, could distract her from her dark thoughts.

Chapter Thirteen

VIOLET SAT IN one of the Alpha Dog visiting rooms the next day, twisting her hands in her lap painfully as she waited for Casey. She'd hardly slept last night, trying to imagine how she was going to ask him if Dean's suspicions were correct. The scene had gone a hundred different ways in her head, but the worst was when he walked out of the room without saying anything.

The door opened, and Casey came in, looking sullen.

"Hey, I brought you some of Daisy's birthday cake," she said.

"Thanks." He sat down and reached for the cake, pulling the plastic wrap off the top.

"So, how are you? How's your morning so far?" she asked.

"It sucks, thanks for asking. That dick Dean has been up my ass since I got here."

"Is he picking on you?" He better not be punishing her little brother because he was upset with her.

"No, he's just annoying. All fake caring and wanting to help bullshit."

Relief rushed through her. "Maybe it's not fake. Maybe he really does care about what's going on with you."

"Yeah, right, he just wants me to like him so you'll go out with him."

Violet's face burned. "He does not want to go out with me, Case. I think his concern is genuine." Gathering her nerve, she added, "You know, he came to see me about you."

Casey picked up the plastic fork and took a big bite, talking around the cake in his mouth. "Yeah? Did he tell you how swell I'm doing?"

"Actually, he told me that he suspected you've been hurt by someone."

Casey froze midchew and then swallowed slowly. "What do you mean?"

"I mean that he came to the house last night. He asked if I knew who might be hurting you, and I told him I had no idea." Reaching across, she grabbed his hand and squeezed. "Is it true? Did someone…hurt you?"

"What, like rape me? Come on."

But despite his derisive tone, Violet noticed the slight tremor in his voice as he stabbed his cake.

"Casey, it's important that you know it's not your fault—"

"Thanks, Dr. Phil."

"—but you need to tell me who it is."

"Why? Even if something had happened, why the hell would I tell you?" he asked.

"Because I'm your sister and I love you."

"But what good could you do? Track him down and shoot him? Would that make it all go away? Did chasing Dad away help us? Really?"

The sting of his words was sharper than any slap. She wanted to yell and rail at him that she'd done it to keep him safe, but she held her temper in a vice grip. "I think not being around a meth head or worrying about him doing something to us when he's out of his mind is a very good thing."

"But we're still constantly paranoid, always worried that CPS is going to come in and take us away. I mean, is this how you imagined your life, Violet? Taking care of us and working your ass off until you're thirty and then waking up to realize you have nothing?"

He's just trying to hurt you. He's on the defensive and trying to turn the focus off of him.

But his words were like a thousand tiny needles pressing into her skin at once. She was afraid that her dream was just that and that eventually she'd end up wasting all this time and money on an education that didn't help her get a better-paying job. She'd heard horror stories about people getting out of college and getting a job that started just above minimum wage, with mountains of student loan debt. She wouldn't have the debt, but at the restaurant she averaged about seventeen dollars an hour on a slow night with tips. There was no way they'd ever get out of Del Paso Heights on that.

"We're talking about you, not me. And the reason you should tell me is so we can go to the police and tell them what happened."

"Nothing happened, okay? He tried, I got away, just…Just drop it, okay?"

Violet swallowed back her happiness that Casey hadn't been molested. "But what about the next kid, Case? What if he's not so lucky?"

"Shut up," Casey whispered, his voice cracking. "Shut up, shut up, shut up! Why does this have to be put on me, huh?" Casey stood up screaming, and Violet backed away from the table as he grabbed at his hair. "Why don't you just leave it be instead of always being such a nosy bi—"

"Hey!" Dean's bark from the doorway startled them both, but his dark gaze was focused on Casey. "What's going on in here?"

Casey glared mutinously.

"Answer me now, Casey!"

Still, her brother said nothing.

"Sergeant Best!" Dean hollered.

"Yes, Sergeant Sparks." Best stepped into the room behind Dean.

"Take Casey out into the yard and have him run a mile. Then I want every pile of poop in that yard scooped up."

"You heard him, kid. March," Best said.

"Is that really necessary?" Violet asked.

"Your brother is in my facility, and he needs to learn that he is lucky to be here," Dean said. "While here, he will show every instructor, kitchen worker, guest, or janitor respect. No exceptions."

Casey pushed past Best without saying good-bye to Violet.

This had definitely not been one of the scenarios she'd played out in her mind.

"Are you all right?" Dean asked gruffly.

Directing her anger at the only person left, she snapped, "What, were you listening at the door?"

"My office is right across the hall, and I heard shouting. I know he's going through a lot, but he has no right to speak to you that way, and you shouldn't let him get away with it," he said.

Why did people think that they could dispense unsolicited advice and she would just accept it graciously? What made him think that he knew what was best for them more than her?

"Oh, so now you're giving me advice on my brother's manners? That must be so awesome for you, getting to stand there and be self-righteous and all-knowing when you actually have no fucking clue what we've been through. You don't know anything about my brother, my sister, or me, for that matter, so why don't you mind your own business?"

Violet's whole body trembled with adrenaline, frustration and rage radiating across her skin. Going after Dean made her feel powerful, free.

"You were the one advertising your business loud enough for everyone to hear, so don't get mad at me just because you don't give a shit enough to demand respect."

All of her self-loathing and doubt came flooding back, extinguishing the brief victory. She wanted to rail at him that her family respected her and that once again, he was talking out of his ass!

But unfortunately, whenever she got flustered, she had trouble being particularly clever or articulate.

"Fuck you."

"That's really nice. I try to help you, and you tell me to go fuck myself."

Fine, so it hadn't been classy, but it had given her a beat to think. "I never asked for your help. That's what you just don't seem to get. I don't need it, and yet, here you are, giving me all the help I never wanted." Covering the half-eaten cake with plastic wrap again, she left it on the table and grabbed her purse. "You can give that to my brother or throw it away, I don't care."

She started to walk past him, but he slammed the door before she could walk through it. Violet spun around to face him just as he advanced, pressing her back into the door.

"Why are you like this?" he asked.

"Like…Like what?" He was so broad, so tall, that as he leaned over her she actually felt short.

"Why are you so fucking determined to make me stop caring?"

Violet blinked up at him, a lump of regret building in her throat. "Because I don't have anything left for you."

Dean's hands came up to frame her face, smoldering heat blazing from his gaze. "Oh, sweetheart, you are so very wrong."

Violet hardly had time to gasp before his mouth seared hers, his tongue dragging across her lips and then pushing inside. The press of his body against hers liquefied her entrails, her muscles, her bones. Every part of her was affected by the taste and scent of him as he sweetly punished her with his kiss.

Wrapping her arms around his waist, she pushed back, meeting the thrusts of his tongue with unleashed passion. She had never understood the romance novels that had a hero and heroine fighting one minute and making out the next, but right now, she totally got it. The blood pumping through her veins, the frustration leaking out of her as they touched and stroked and melded together.

Someone turned the knob and pushed on the door, but with both of them leaning against it, it wouldn't open. Dean pulled away first, and she gasped for air, staring up at him as they both tried to catch their breath.

"Hey, is everything okay in there?" someone asked from the other side.

"Yeah, it's fine. We'll be out in a minute," Dean called.

"Ooooh-kaaaay," the guy on the other side drawled.

Horror burned Violet's cheeks. Someone might have heard them and guessed what they were doing. Oh, God, what the hell was wrong with her? Casey would never forgive her if he heard from someone else.

She finally got her bearings and dropped her arms from Dean's neck, placing her palms on his chest to push him off. "I have to go."

Dean didn't release her right away. "Are we going to talk about this?"

"No. No, we're not." Ducking under his arm, she put some distance between them, taking a few deep breaths before she faced him again, his back now to the door. This poor guy seemed to always be there whenever she was at her worst, and he'd definitely felt the whip of her emotions. It wasn't fair, any of it.

"I am sorry for what I said. I was being defensive, and you didn't deserve it." It was true, but more than that, they couldn't keep doing this. Especially not here.

What does that mean? That it's okay to kiss him like you can't get enough as long as no one knows?

No, that wasn't what she was thinking. It just seemed like every time they ended up in the same room together, they were always drawing closer, touching. As if they couldn't help themselves, which sounded completely insane, even in her head. Human beings could control their urges.

Except for when the subject of her uncontrollable attraction was giving her that half smile with the teasing edge. The one that made her warm all over.

"I don't know, that wounded me deeply. I might need more than an apology," he said.

Violet shook her head, fighting the urge to smile back. "You never give up, do you?"

"No, I do. Lucky for you, though, it takes a lot to make me write someone off."

The sincerity in his expression tugged at her emotions, making her feel almost shy. Definitely awkward, so she joked, "I wouldn't say lucky…"

"Ouch again. You definitely owe me." He opened the door but stepped back into the doorway, blocking her escape.

"And what is it that you want?" Her heart skipped into a gallop as his eyes raked her from her toes back up to meet her gaze.

"I'm not sure yet. I'll think about it."

The insinuation wasn't lost on her, and her snark returned as she walked through the doorframe, inches away from him. "I don't want you to hurt your brain."

He dropped his head, his mouth so close she almost thought he was about to kiss her again. She silently screamed at herself, but her body wouldn't move, as if dying to know if he'd dare. The hallway looked empty, but that didn't mean it would stay that way.

Dean didn't kiss her, though. Instead, his warm breath fanned over her lips as he whispered, "I promise that whatever I come up with won't put you out in the slightest."

If it involves being near you, it will more than put me out. It will put me in danger of getting too close.

AN HOUR LATER, Dean sat at his desk keeping a tight rein on his temper. Across from him stood Casey, with his arms crossed and a stubborn expression plastered across his face.

"I'm not going to some stupid counselor, and you can't make me."

Dean leaned back in his chair, studying the boy. He was lucky Dean hadn't grabbed him by the scruff of the neck after the way he'd talked to Violet. It had taken every ounce of discipline to remember the kid was hurting and lashing out. That he needed normalcy and understanding, not more violence.

Still, Casey knew how to push every button Dean had.

"Actually, as you are still under my care for the next few weeks, I can. It is my decision whether or not you need a professional to talk to, and I believe it is in your best interest."

"You don't know dick about me or what's best for me!"

"Actually, I know quite a lot about you," Dean said, standing. "Your mom died ten years ago when you were four, your father left, and you have been raised by your older sister ever since."

Casey glared at him mutely, and Dean softened his tone. "I know something bad happened to you, and I am not going to push you to tell me about it, but you need to tell someone. Otherwise, you'll never move past it."

Dean could see the internal struggle in Casey's face. He hadn't quite mastered the ability to mask his emotions, and Dean could tell he'd struck a nerve.

"Whatever," he said, his voice choked up.

As Casey started to slam out of his office, Dean said, "I didn't excuse you."

Casey turned around with a clenched jaw and a defiant gleam back in his eye. "May I be excused, sir?"

"Yes, you can report to the mess hall."

Casey walked out without bothering to close the door. Dean took a deep breath and reminded himself that these kids had been through things most adults couldn't handle. They'd had their trust broken more times than they could count, and he had to earn their respect.

But it took all of his resolve not to go after Casey and make him scrub the bathroom floor with a toothbrush for being such a turd.

Of course, Dean would have to be blind not to compare Casey to Violet and her own defense mechanisms. After she'd thrown him out last night, he'd driven around for a while before going home, seething. It wasn't right that she carried this burden alone.

If only they realized Dean really did want to help Casey, and not just because he was Violet's little brother, although he couldn't deny that was part of it. Every time he closed his eyes, he saw her wide, tear-filled eyes. The worry and pain written all over her face had made him want to ignore her wishes and stay.

But Casey, too, had been getting to him, especially in those brief moments when he brightened. Like when Apollo accomplished another command and Casey slipped to his knees to give him a hug and a biscuit or two.

Moments like that showed Dean who Casey was beneath all the anger and distrust, and Dean wanted to erase all the bad for him. To look after the three of them, Daisy, Casey, and, of course, Violet, and keep them safe.

But if he pursued Violet, it would mean taking on all her problems as his own. And despite the fact that she'd been surviving for ten years taking care of two kids when she was basically a kid herself, she was struggling, that much he could see. Did he want to take that on, knowing he wouldn't be staying?

News flash, hotshot, what makes you think she wants you to? She's made it pretty clear she isn't interested in you.

Except her kisses said otherwise.

At the time, she'd made him so frustrated and furious that it had been a choice between kissing her and shaking her, and he'd chosen the former. And man, what a kiss. He'd been so caught up in her that when Best had knocked, he'd almost told him to fuck off. It had only been the brief flicker of panic in Violet's eyes that had told him not to push for more.

He wanted more from her, though. It wasn't fair or right, but he would never stop craving her if he kept denying what was between them.

God, what a selfish bastard he was. His life had been good, filled with stable, loving parents and a supportive extended family, while she had needed to grow up way too fast just to compensate. She'd told him she didn't have anything left for him, but at this point, he'd take anything from her. Even if it was just her friendship.

Not that she'd ever believe him, though, especially when he mauled her in visiting rooms.

What Dean needed was an olive branch. Something to show her that he could be trusted. That he could be her friend.

Suddenly, an idea struck him, and Dean picked up the phone, dialing.

"This is Sergeant Kline."

"I was thinking about taking a group out a week from Saturday for a community service project. You in?"

"Sure, what's the project?"

"Home improvement. Let's recruit ten of the kids who have been here awhile and want to earn some extra privileges. I figure we'll leave about oh six hundred and be back by lunch."

"Sounds good, I'll enlist the volunteers and let the parents know. What about their dogs?"

Dean grinned. "Best is working Saturday. I'm surc he won't mind ten extra dogs."

Chapter Fourteen

Ten Days Later

On Friday afternoon, Violet carried two mugs of coffee into the living room—one for her and one for Mrs. Paulson from Child Protective Services. When Violet had called her back to set up the appointment, she'd wanted to push it off until after Daisy was at Oregon State U and Casey was home, but Mrs. Paulson had insisted on sooner. Violet had given up her afternoon shift to work six until two in the morning, which meant better tips, but she hated getting home so late and leaving Daisy alone.

Technically, she's an adult now, and once she's a full state away, she's going to be on her own anyway.

Which was actually rather terrifying, but there was nothing she could do about it.

Just like there was nothing she could do but deal with Mrs. Paulson head-on. She seemed nice enough;

probably midforties with short brown hair and a brown pantsuit. Her eyes seemed a little tired behind her wire-framed glasses, and she smiled as Violet handed her the mug of coffee.

"Thank you. I really shouldn't have another cup, but I have hours to go and not a lot of gas left in my tank." Mrs. Paulson laughed at her own joke, and Violet smiled politely.

"I can imagine."

Mrs. Paulson took a sip from her mug and hummed in approval. "Perfect." She set down her mug and pulled out a relatively thick file. Violet saw Casey's name on it just before Mrs. Paulson opened it wide and licked her finger to thumb the pages apart. When she finally reached a blank one, she pulled out a pen and looked up at Violet expectantly. "Should we get started, then? As you can imagine, we have some concerns regarding Casey's troubles over the last year. I've gathered reports that he's been picked up by the police several times but received only warnings. Has something changed in the home?"

"No, nothing." Violet had learned early on that the less she said in these situations the better, especially with her tendency to ramble.

"Has Casey confided in you about any bullying at school?"

No, he hadn't confided in her, not really, but Violet had gone by his school after his arrest and talked to them about the boys who had attacked Casey. After a bit of a fit on her part, they had called the boys and their parents in for a meeting. Violet had agreed not to press charges with the police, who had taken photographs of all Casey's injuries on intake, as long as the boys received some kind of punishment at school. They had all agreed, including the principal.

"There were some boys that he was having trouble with, but I arranged to meet with their parents at school, with their principal moderating. And Casey is seeing a counselor at Alpha Dog." Violet didn't want to bring up the alleged abuse, especially when Casey hadn't been ready to talk to her about it.

"I see." Mrs. Paulson took another sip of her coffee and waited a beat before the real interview began. The woman asked her everything from what her hours at work were to how long Casey was alone in the house and how many guests they had during the week. Violet didn't bring up the fact that at nearly fourteen, Casey could technically be his own babysitter, but instead just answered the barrage of questions shot at her, one after another.

And then, Mrs. Paulson asked, "Do you ever speak with your father?"

Violet stiffened, a wave of emotions crashing over her. "No. Not since he left three years ago."

"I see here that you own a handgun. How is it stored?"

Still shaken from the mention of her dad, Violet's voice wavered. "Unloaded in a safe in my room."

Mrs. Paulson stared at her, suspicion lurking in her blue eyes. "Do you mind leading me to it, so I can double-check?"

"No, of course not." Violet stood up and headed back into her bedroom. Opening the closet, she punched in the combination.

"Does anyone else, primarily Casey, have access to the code?" Mrs. Paulson asked behind her.

"No." Violet stood up and stepped back while Mrs. Paulson squatted down in her place. As she inspected the gun, Violet waited patiently. She'd been up-front with CPS three years ago about the gun, and because she had gone through all the proper channels, taken safety courses, and kept it locked up tight, they hadn't objected.

Mrs. Paulson closed the safe and stood, her lips pinched thinly. "Although the gun is stored correctly, I just want to warn you that having a gun in the house with a child, especially a teenager, is dangerous."

It wasn't the first time someone had said something similar to her. "I understand all the risks and take every precaution." Violet wasn't about to tell her that she took Casey shooting and had shown him the proper way to handle the gun, even though she believed that it was the right move for them. Ever since she'd pulled the gun on her dad, she'd been worried that Casey was secretly scared of her or at least afraid of the weapon. She'd thought that if she showed him how to use it properly and helped him get comfortable with it, his nightmares might stop.

Unfortunately, there was nothing she could do to change the fact that his father had attacked him.

Mrs. Paulson walked out of the room with Violet close behind. As she made notes in Casey's file, Violet sat down, trying hard not to worry at her nails as she waited.

Finally, Mrs. Paulson closed the folder and held her hands together. "Well, that's all I need for now. I'm going to stop into Alpha Dog to speak with Casey, but at this time, I don't have any concerns. Very few young women would take on the care of their siblings. You are to be commended."

Violet hated being praised for doing what she thought was right but kept her mouth shut. "Thank you."

Mrs. Paulson finished off the rest of her coffee and stood. Violet showed her out, and the minute the door closed, the tight coil in Violet's chest loosened. She had been dreading the meeting all week, worried that Mrs. Paulson would find something that would make her uneasy and worth challenging Violet's guardianship. Violet was beating herself up already worrying about how Casey was doing with the counselor; she'd been by every day this week, and he still wouldn't see her. It hurt, badly, but she had to remind herself that whatever had happened to him, Casey was suffering, too.

A SHARP RAPPING sound erupted, startling Dean awake. As his head came flying off his desk, he realized he'd fallen asleep at work again. It was the third time this week, and he was running his hands over his face, trying to wake up when Martinez walked in.

Dean could tell by his friend's face that he knew what Dean had been doing.

"Dude, I don't mean to overstep—"

"So don't," Dean growled. Climbing to his feet, he walked over to his mini fridge and grabbed an energy drink.

"But I'm going to anyway. I know you don't want to talk about what went on over there, but you should at least get that shrink of yours to prescribe you something to help you sleep. Otherwise, you're going to get worn down, and you know what can happen if you let this go too far."

"I don't need drugs." Dean chugged until the can was empty and crushed it with one hand. "I'm fine."

"You aren't fine, man. You forget, I've known you since you first got back and we were in group together. As long as you keep denying that you need help, you'll continue to hit a brick wall. If you want to get back to active duty, you're going to have to open up."

Dean leaned on his desk with his head down, closing his eyes against the pounding headache that was exploding through his brain.

Martinez, Best, Kline, and he had all been in group therapy together. They also had all been lucky to end up at Alpha Dog, especially after they had bonded over their lack of sharing in group. They had always supported each other and believed that their issues were no one's business but theirs.

Only Dean had made the mistake of telling Martinez about his nightmares, and now it was coming back to bite him in the ass.

"I'm just having a bad week, is all," Dean said.

"Does it have anything to do with Casey Douglas's sister?" Martinez asked.

If Dean was going for honesty, he would have said yes, but he didn't want the guys talking more than they already were. Whoever said men didn't gossip was full of shit.

"No, just having a rough time. And I don't know what Best told you, but nothing was ever really going on with her."

"Really? Then why are you and Kline taking some kids over to her house for community service?"

Martinez watched him expectantly, but Dean was ready for his question. "We're doing it as an olive branch for Casey. The kid has had it rough, and I figured this would be a nice way to get into his good graces." Dean wasn't going to mention that the branch was being extended to Violet, too.

"If you don't want to tell me about her, that's fine, but I am serious about you getting some help. What if you're driving down the road and fall asleep? Or you stay awake for so long that sleep deprivation makes you hallucinate? You might lose more than your chance to get back into action if you aren't careful."

"I'll go to bed early tonight. Really, you have nothing to worry about."

Martinez gave him a doubtful look, then shrugged. "Fine. The main reason I came in here was to let you know that we've got a new intake coming in this afternoon, and Best has gone off to temperament test a few dogs one of the shelters called about. And Megan is waiting in the lobby for her interview."

Megan Bryce was Martinez's girlfriend's best friend and had come through for Alpha Dog a few months ago when one of the trainers couldn't be at their big charity auction. They'd been putting feelers out for more trainers, and Martinez had suggested giving Megan a shot.

Although she wasn't active military, she'd served six years before her knee injury and had the experience and knowledge to help them out.

"You can send her in." Dean's phone rang, and as Martinez walked out the door, Dean picked up. "Alpha Dog Training Program, Sergeant Sparks."

"Sparks, this is General Reynolds. How are things going over there?"

The general was in charge of everything and everyone on the base, and Dean knew from having watched Martinez get the shaft from him a few months ago not to be anything but polite. "Everything is going well, sir."

"That's great."

For the next several minutes, the general rattled off his weekly list of questions, and Dean answered them dutifully, from how many kids they had taken in to when they would be holding a demonstration for the dog's abilities.

And then, the general surprised him with a boatload of praise.

"You know how important this program is, especially to the community. I know that you want to get back into the field, but I wanted to extend my gratitude for the job you've undertaken. I have heard nothing but praise about you and your staff. Let's hope it continues to grow and do well."

"Thank you, sir. And yes, I do want to get back to doing my job—"

"Until your psychiatrist gives you the green light, I'm afraid this is your job." The general's tone wasn't harsh, only firm, and Dean's jaw clenched in frustration. He was so sick of being powerless.

"Well, I'll let you get back to work. Keep me updated, Sergeant Sparks." The general hung up, and Dean groaned loudly, wishing for something to hit.

Even if it's not what you would have chosen, he's right. This is your life, and you have a job to do.

Chapter Fifteen

VIOLET CURLED DEEPER into her comforter on Saturday, willing the obnoxious sound of a lawn mower to go away, but the persistent roar continued. It was too bad, too, because she had been having the most amazing dream. She'd been lying in a bed of marshmallows as Dean Sparks poured melted chocolate over her, licking it off along the way. And despite her conscious decision to keep away from him, enjoying his attention in her subconscious was permissible.

The lawn mower was joined by something that sounded like a weed whacker, and the overwhelming urge to destroy whoever was ruining her day off fired up her blood.

"Mother of God," she growled. Peeking out from underneath the blanket at her clock, she groaned aloud. "It is six thirty in the fucking morning."

The engine's buzz grew louder, and she could have sworn it was coming from outside her window. Climbing clumsily to her feet, she wobbled toward the window and lifted the curtain.

And stared dumbly out at the group of men surrounding her house.

"What the fuck?" she yelled, but none of them could hear her above the noise. Dropping the curtains, she grabbed her zombie slippers from the end of her bed. Slipping them on as she hopped out of her bedroom and into the living room, she almost collided with Daisy, who looked ready to rip someone's head off.

"What the fuck is going on?" Daisy asked.

"That's exactly what I said."

Violet unlocked the front door and threw it open so hard it would have punched a hole through the wall without the doorstop. On the porch, she bumped into a young guy carrying a bucket of paint and a brush.

"Sorry, ma'am," he said.

"Who are you, and what do you think you're doing?" Violet asked.

"Um, we're doing community service, ma'am. Sergeant Sparks brought us to clean up your yard and house," he said.

Why that sneaky, conniving son of a bitch.

Hadn't she told him she was fine and she could take care of her family? She definitely didn't need his charity.

Violet's eyes narrowed to slits as she sought out Dean, who was standing with his back to her. She'd recognize those broad shoulders anywhere. A tool belt rested over his jean-clad hips, and as he turned, she noticed that he looked good in a faded New York Yankees ball cap.

Damn him. Why couldn't he have just stayed in her dreams instead of stepping all over her reality?

"Hey, isn't that your fuck buddy?" Daisy asked.

"Don't call him that," Violet barked just as the kid with the lawn mower killed the engine. All male eyes turned their way. Dean's dark gaze slid over her from top to bottom, and her nipples hardened against the cotton of her tank top.

Crossing her arms over her chest, she ignored the quivering of her knees as he approached with another man right behind him.

"Did we wake you?" Dean asked.

"No, the sweet sound of bluebirds chirping on our windowsill did," Daisy said.

The man behind Dean laughed then looked sheepish. "Sorry about that, but we wanted to get an early start before it got too hot."

"What are you doing?" Violet asked.

Ignoring her question, Dean introduced the man at his side. "This is Sergeant Blake Kline. This is Violet Douglas and her sister, Daisy."

Blake held out his hand to her, his smile a flash of white on his tan face. "Nice to meet you."

Violet took his hand politely. It wasn't his fault that she wanted to kill his friend with her bare hands. Blake held his hand out to Daisy, who walked back into the house with a huff.

Violet gave Blake an apologetic smile as the guy dropped his hand. "She's not a morning person."

"I got that," Blake said. "I'm going to unload the lumber."

Blake walked away before she even got out her, "What lumber?" But that was fine, as the man she wanted hadn't moved off her steps.

Wanted to talk to, *you mean.*

"Of course," she muttered to herself.

"What?" Dean asked.

"Nothing. Are you going to tell me what the hell you're doing?"

"Well, I've got a couple of guys cleaning up the yard and several more painting the house. Blake and I are going to work on the rotten boards on the porch, and—"

"Maybe I need to be clearer. Why…the hell…are…you…here?"

He gave her that knock-her-on-her-ass grin. "Because once a week, we do some form of outreach service in the community. Sometimes we take the kids and their dogs to local senior centers or we pick up trash in the park. Today, we're going around to random houses in need of repairs."

"Random?" Violet seethed with humiliation. *Random my ass.* "And how did my house become random?"

The jerk had the nerve to look exasperated, as if *she* was insulting *him.* "You ever been told not to look a gift horse in the mouth?"

"Except I don't need your horse or your charity." As she glanced around the yard, a hopeful thought struck her through every other emotion boiling up inside her. "Is Casey here?"

"No. Work detail goes by seniority; it's a way for kids with longer sentences to earn privileges." His tone held a touch of apology as he added, "If it were up to me, I would have brought him, but it would have looked like favoritism. And I know you're worried about people talking."

His reasoning made sense, even if she was disappointed. Although, if he was really worried about people talking, then he wouldn't have picked her house for this field trip.

Especially since she'd been perfectly clear about not needing his help.

"As much as I appreciate your thoughtfulness, I really must decline your work detail. My house is fine just the way it is."

"Really? Because this porch is on the verge of becoming a death trap. How are you going to pay for someone's medical bills, let alone a lawsuit if someone falls through the planks?"

His bluntness raised Violet's hackles, and she ground her teeth together painfully. "You're an ass."

"I've been called worse, usually when I'm right." As if he didn't give a damn either way, he shrugged. "I guess if you really don't want us here, you could always call the cops. You might manage to get us shut down, and then all the kids we help would go back to juvie, including your brother, and all the dogs would be euthanized, but if you feel that strongly about it..."

Violet battled the urge to scream at him. For ten years she'd been handling everything for her family and doing her best. And now Dean swooped in with his hero complex and proved that she wasn't good enough.

That all her fears about failing her siblings were spot on.

God, if she didn't escape back inside she was going to break down and bawl again. Which was exactly why she should avoid the man, even in her dreams; every time they had a run-in, she ended up an emotional wreck.

"Do whatever you want. It's not like I can stop you."

She turned on her heels and headed back inside, slamming the door behind her so hard it shook the whole house.

Climbing back into her bed, she pulled the covers over her head and sucked in several shaking breaths.

Stop behaving like a child hiding out in her room. Piece your pride back together and tell them to get the fuck off your property or pitch in and help. You cannot stay in here all day.

Violet didn't agree. Staying in her room sounded like an excellent idea.

DEAN STARED AT the closed door, the eyes of his charges and Blake burning holes in his back. If they hadn't heard the exchange, Violet's dramatic exit would have been clue enough that they weren't wanted there.

Damn it, why did she have to be so stubborn? His olive branch definitely hadn't worked out the way he'd hoped. He'd expected a little resistance at first, but ultimately, he'd figured she'd see it was all in good faith.

Why the hell had she flown off the handle?

Just let it go, man. Just go about fixing the place and let her cool down.

But no one had ever accused Dean of being smart.

"I'll be right back," Dean called to Kline as he opened the front door and walked inside. He headed through the living room and knocked on the closed door by the stairs, taking a chance that it was Violet's room and not Daisy's.

"Go away." Violet's voice was muffled, and he ignored her.

Walking into her room, he saw her shape under the comforter and stood over the bed. "I'm not trying to get one up on you or anything. This is my way of apologizing for the other day—"

Violet threw the blanket off her head as she sat up. Long, tangled red strands stood on end, and Dean had to bite the inside of his cheek to keep from smiling.

And then he met her red-rimmed, furious gaze, and his amusement melted away.

"Apologize? If you want to apologize, then you pick up a phone, dial my number, and if I answer, say, 'I am sorry.' You don't bring a bunch of guys to my home because it's such a run-down hellhole that someone has to fix it."

Dean sat on the edge of her bed, his hand raised slightly in case she took a swing. "I never said your house was a hellhole."

"You used my house for a community service project. You don't have to say it."

Dean realized too late why Violet was so angry with him, and he felt like the world's biggest tool. "Everyone needs someone in their corner, Violet. That's all I was trying to do with all of this. I get that you don't like asking for help, and maybe you don't think you need it, but this wasn't anything more than a gesture of friendship."

"Friends? That is really all this is to you?"

Smoothing down her static-charged hair with one hand, he hesitated. His answer was more complicated than yes or no. Did he want her trust? Yes. Did he want to be friends with her? Absolutely.

Was that all he wanted? No, but he couldn't have everything he wanted. Not unless he chose to derail all of the plans he'd made for his career and future. If he gave up on going back to being a soldier, then he would always be the guy who choked. Who failed his unit when they needed him the most.

And he wasn't ready to do that yet, not for anyone.

"Yes, I came here as a friend. To do something nice for you. I wasn't trying to make you feel like shit about your house; I get that you have had to deal with a lot." Dean stared into her face as his fingers played with a soft lock of her hair. "Let us do this for you."

The tension in Violet's body seemed to drain from her, yet she caught his hand and pulled it from her hair. Her expression was earnest and intense. "I can't."

Dean sighed in defeat. There was only so much he could do, and he wasn't going to force this on her, despite his initial intentions. "I'll let the guys know."

"No." She tugged his hand as he started to rise. "I just meant that I can't let you do it *for* me. If you are going to work on my house, then I want to help."

Dean's thumb trailed over the soft skin of her palm, but he didn't argue. "I'd never say no to an extra set of hands."

"I wouldn't have let you even if you'd tried."

VIOLET'S SKIN HUMMED where Dean had touched her, and she was loath to pull away from the sensation. Just moments before she had been ready to deck him for sticking his nose in her business, but his sincerity had put a chink in her armor. If he wanted to be her friend, then helping was okay. Tracy helped her all the time and vice versa.

And truth be told, she didn't have a lot of friends to call on. And he'd already seen her at her worst, so what would be the harm in letting him be there for her?

Because the way he makes you feel is very unfriend-like.

As evidenced by the somersault her stomach did when he squeezed her hand and stood up.

"Well, I'll get back out there and let you change."

Violet climbed out of bed and stood with him, struggling to find something to say. "I am sorry that I nearly took your head off, but next time you decide to do something nice for a friend, you might want to wait until eight a.m. Maybe nine."

"I'll remember that, for next time." Pointing at her feet, he added, "By the way, what are those supposed to be?"

Violet glanced down at the slippers he was staring at. The plush gray faces had red felt sores and a dangling eyeball. "They're zombies."

"You have a thing for zombies?"

"No, they scare me, always have."

"Then why do you have them?" he asked.

"Because I have a fourteen-year-old brother with a wicked sense of humor," she said, smiling. Casey had gotten into zombies when he was ten, but she never let him watch any movies because she was afraid he'd get nightmares. She'd finally given in when he was almost twelve but insisted on sitting with him in case it was too scary. Turned out she was the big sissy, and it had been a constant joke in their house.

The slippers were her favorite birthday gift ever, especially because it tickled Casey so much for her to wear them. Apparently he had collected recycling and taken a few odd jobs to pay for them so they would be a surprise.

Dean chuckled. "I'd have done the same thing to my sister. It's a sign of affection, believe me."

"I know," she said.

"Well, off to go crack the whip. I want to get the kids back in time for afternoon visitation. Plus, all their dogs are being handled by Best, who wasn't happy about it."

Violet wasn't sympathetic, not after Best had been so tactless at Alpha Dog. "Somehow, I don't think I'll feel bad about that."

"Me neither. Believe me, I've covered for him enough, he can take this one."

As Dean left her room, Violet wasn't sure she hadn't lost her mind. Dean's close proximity seemed to send her into turbulent mood swings; one minute she was beyond livid, the next she was a simpering pile of goo.

It wasn't right. It wasn't healthy.

So why didn't you just kick him out?

That was an excellent question.

DEAN HADN'T EXPECTED Violet to actually come outside fifteen minutes later dressed in jeans and a ratty T-shirt, a tool box in one hand and a pot of coffee in the other. Daisy came out behind her with a bunch of mismatched mugs and set them on the porch railing.

"I'll be back," Daisy said.

"Hurry up. You aren't getting out of this," Violet called, earning a face from Daisy.

Dean tipped the brim of his hat back and took off his work gloves. "What's all this?"

"I figured everyone could use some coffee, and Daisy's gone to get donuts."

Dean had a feeling she just didn't want to feel obligated to him for anything, and he could respect that. Climbing up to study the mugs, he picked up a Darth Vader mug and held it out. "You got any milk and sugar?"

"Yeah, on the counter in the kitchen. I'll get it."

Dean followed behind her with his mug, figuring there was no sense in her carrying the milk and sugar outside for him. Kline took his coffee black, and as for most of the kids, he wasn't sure they needed the caffeine.

He hadn't gotten to check out her kitchen yet and was surprised to find most of the appliances had been updated, unlike the living room. There was even a standing mixer on the counter, similar to the one his mother had begged his dad for five Christmases ago. Since he'd been the one to pick it up for his dad, he knew it wasn't cheap.

"What do you use that for?" he asked.

She glanced at the mixer as she set the coffeepot back on its station. "My mother's old one broke a few years ago. Daisy got a job at this fancy kitchen store in Roseville and used her discount to buy it for me." Violet gave him a rueful smile as she continued, "I was so mad at her for wasting her money, but she'd told me this bullshit story about how the owner had given her an additional thirty percent off, so it wasn't as much as I thought. I knew she was lying because I'd met her boss, and there wasn't a generous bone in her body. I was so glad when she took the job at Safeway. They love her, and the manager even helped her get a transfer to a store close to Oregon State."

"That's awesome," he said.

"It is. She gets benefits, too, so that works out well."

As he doctored his coffee, he thought about his youngest sisters, who were twenty and twenty-two, and couldn't believe the difference in maturity. He imagined them in Violet's shoes and didn't think they could hold it together the way she did. With all the odds stacked against her, Violet was something else.

"I should go ask everyone else if they want some coffee," she said suddenly.

"And I should get back to the porch before someone falls through and gets stuck."

"Har har, my porch isn't that bad," she said.

"It's no longer considered a porch, it's a termite's dinner," he said.

"Whatever." She rolled her eyes at him as she walked past with the pot, and his gaze traveled down to the sway of her hips. It was so subtle he knew it wasn't a conscious motion, but it hypnotized him, sending him into a state of arousal inappropriate for the crowd outside.

"Are you coming?" she asked from the open doorway.

"Yeah, one second." Closing his eyes, he tried to conjure images of dead dogs and fish guts, but her ass was officially burned into his retinas.

And it only got worse as the morning wore on. Every time she bent over to pick something up or knelt down to hammer in a nail, it was like a lightning bolt to his crotch. Everything about the woman turned him on, even her eating a chocolate donut. He watched that little pink tongue lick the chocolate off her lips and had actually taken a step toward her. Pictured pressing her back against her ugly house and taking her mouth, sliding his tongue in to taste her.

Jesus, he was horned up. *Where's a bathtub full of ice when a guy needs it?*

He had to put some distance between them or he was going to explode. He'd thought that trying to be friends would be easy, but the more time he spent around her, the more he remembered what she had going on under her clothes and the heat of her tight little—

"Hey, Blake, can you help me for a second?" Violet asked. "I can't seem to pull this nail out."

Dean caught Kline's gaze as his friend started to stand up, but one firm shake of his head stopped him. A slow grin spread across Kline's face, but Dean ignored it.

"I got it." Dean went to kneel next to her, distracted by the sweet scent of her. As his hand covered hers, she jumped, and he wondered if she'd experienced the same jolt he did when they touched.

She pulled her hand out from under his and let him have the hammer. He focused on wiggling it, loosening the nail from the board until it finally slipped out. He held it out to her, and their fingers brushed as she took it, the air crackling with tension as she let out a soft breath. He noticed the flush of her neck and cheeks, the rosy hue making her plump lips appear darker.

Someone kicked his ass from behind, and he almost fell on his face. Catching himself on his forearms, he glared over his shoulder at Daisy.

"Stop hitting on my sister and get back to work."

One glance at Violet's scarlet face told him that she had been just as caught up as he was, but as he stood up, he noticed a couple of the kids had realized there was something going on.

"You want to spend the afternoon doing up-downs?" he asked.

They scattered like rabbits, and he grunted at Daisy as he passed.

"Where are you going?" Kline asked. Dean could hear the laughter in his voice.

"Going to take over weed-whacking for Jorge."

"Need to work out some frustration?" Daisy called after him.

Dean sent her a scowl at the same time Violet told her to shut up.

Chapter Sixteen

A FEW HOURS later, Violet was loading a bunch of water bottles into plastic bags to send with Dean and the rest of the guys and trying to ignore the bite of shame and humiliation. Dean probably thought she had money stashed away that she used on fancy mixers and stupid slippers instead of the upkeep of her home, but she had been telling the truth. For the longest time, she'd tried to keep the yard under control, but then she just didn't have time for it all.

Besides, it technically wasn't even hers. It was her father's house—and if he ever came back, at some point he would realize that he could get a lot of meth from its sale.

But as she walked outside and stood back to admire their work, she couldn't believe the difference. The dark, gloomy brown had been repainted a pretty blue-gray. The trim had been painted white, giving it a fresh, clean look.

Dean came up alongside her, the brush of his arm against hers raising gooseflesh over her skin. She wished she could forget about this reaction to him, but it had been a battle all day. Every time he came near her, it was like a magnetic pull drew her closer. He smelled of spicy cologne, cedar, and sweat—a heady combination that made her want to invite him in for a shower.

A long, hot shower where she ran soap over every inch of his body with her hands, watching droplets of water leave rivulets down his chest and abs.

God, what was happening to her? One freshly painted house and she was ready to rub her body against him like a cat in heat.

"I'll come back tomorrow and paint the porch, but I think it looks good." Dean's voice was laced with amusement as he added, "Of course, it's easier to see when you have your eyes open."

Oh, God. She hadn't realized she'd closed her eyes, and as they flew open, his deep rumble of laughter washed over her, drawing a blush into her cheeks.

"Sorry, I was resting my eyes. I think I might need a nap."

"I promise tomorrow I'll wait until nine," he said.

Blake was loading up the boys into the van and gave them a little wave as he closed the door. "I'll see you back at the program. Violet, it was very nice to meet you."

"You, too." Violet started to call for Daisy but noticed the Honda was gone. She must have snuck away when Violet was in the house.

Dean waved to Blake as he drove away. When his dark gaze focused on hers once more, she became aware that they were alone on the street, a hundred feet from her bedroom.

"Well, I better get back," he said.

"Dean..." She placed her hand on his arm to stop him from walking away. "Thank you for what you did. I appreciate it, I really do."

"But?"

But I'm starting to think I might like you.

Actually, it was more than a notion. She had spent most of the day catching herself watching him. The muscles in his arms straining against his T-shirt as he carried wood. Tiny beads of sweat giving his tan skin a sheen that was nearly as hypnotizing as his smile—when someone coaxed one from him.

It wasn't just her attraction to him, though. It was the way he had taken the time with the kids to show them how to use a tool or when he'd called Tyler to check on his dog. That he'd carried in all the coffee mugs and started washing them without being asked, and even when she'd told him to leave them, he'd just finished up and set them in the drying rack. That he held the door for her and Daisy, and at one point, when she'd hammered her thumb, he'd cradled her hand in his so gently, examining the bruised digit. For a split second, she'd thought he would try to kiss it and make it better, and when he hadn't, she'd been disappointed.

Which was proof enough that she was in big trouble.

"But you've done enough. You don't need to come back tomorrow; I can finish the porch."

"I like to finish something once I start," he said curtly.

"And I appreciate that, but I'm sure you have better things to do than to waste your day off coming over here and working. Really, I—"

Before she knew what he was doing, his hand shot out and caught the back of her neck gently, bringing her closer. "I am trying to be your friend."

Violet was stunned and a little defensive at his dark tone. "So you've said, but I'm sorry that I have trust issues. Most men don't paint your house unless they want something."

His gaze glittered at her in the afternoon sunlight like stars flashing in the night sky, and it was so arresting, she couldn't move.

"I'm trying here, Violet, but you're making it as hard as possible to be a good guy."

"Why, because I don't just take you at your word?" She could hardly hear her own throaty question over the pounding of her heart.

"No, because you push my buttons so hard I want to haul you over my shoulder, take you inside, and strip away every defense in your arsenal with my hands and mouth."

Violet held her breath, her body tight as a bowstring as she waited for him to make a move.

Instead, he released her and walked around the back of the truck. "Instead, I'm going to get in my truck and go back to work."

Violet bit back the urge to tell him no, to ask him to stay. But it wasn't a good idea.

Except her heart just wouldn't let him leave. She knocked on his passenger-side window, and when he rolled it down, she said, "If you insist on coming over to paint, then I'm cooking you breakfast tomorrow."

Dean's dark eyebrows shot up, surprise written all over his face. But the twinkle in his eyes and the slow, sweet grin beat down all her doubts with a hammer. "What are we having?"

"You like sausage? Biscuits and gravy? Bacon and eggs?"

"Yes, yes, and who doesn't?"

"Okay. See you tomorrow, then."

"I can't wait."

DEAN WAS SITTING on his couch later that evening, scrolling through his DVR. He'd popped a couple of Tyle nol when he got home, hoping the sheer exhaustion from working his ass off today would lull him into a dreamless sleep, but as he'd closed his eyes, they had come anyway, like a bad horror movie playing in his head. He'd gone back out to the living room to find something to hold the memories at bay.

Nothing looked good, and his mind started drifting, searching for any kind of happy thought, like his mother used to tell him to do as a child when he'd get a shot.

It wasn't that surprising that his current happy thought had a pair of chocolate brown eyes and fiery red hair.

There was a knock at the door, which drove Violet's face away as Dean jumped. Glancing down at Dilbert, who was lying with his head in Dean's lap, he asked, "You expecting somebody?"

Dilbert's ears twitched, but otherwise he didn't move. Dean slid out from under his chin, and the dog groaned, then rolled onto his back, letting out a loud snore.

"It's okay, you lay there while I get it. If it's an ax murderer, I'll let you know."

Dilbert opened one eye for half a second and then closed it.

Dean opened the door to find Sergeant Oliver Martinez and his dog, Beast, on his doorstep.

"Hey, man, what's going on?" Dean asked.

"Nothing, just coming by to see what you were up to. I tried calling, but you didn't answer." Martinez stepped into the house with Beast, not even waiting for an invitation. "Figured I'd take a chance."

"Something wrong?" Dean asked.

"Nah, Eve is out with her friends, and I just didn't want to sit at home alone."

"Aw, were you lonely?" Dean teased.

"Eh heh, shut up."

Dean chuckled as he went to the fridge. "Want a beer?"

"Sure, thanks." Martinez sat down on the couch, disturbing Dilbert, who woke up, saw Beast, and started barking excitedly. The two dogs were good friends and both wiggled as they turned in circles, sniffing each other's butts.

Dean handed Martinez the beer as he sat down. "You know, the only time Dilbert moves at a pace faster than snail is when you bring that behemoth over."

"Yeah, he's a leader, like his master. He starts to howl when he hears a fire engine and gets all the other dogs in the neighborhood going. I've been getting the stink eye when I leave my house."

The dogs chased each other around the couch and down the hall. Dean finally hollered at them to chill when the picture frames on the walls started to rattle.

"Your moose is going to bring the roof down on us," Dean said.

Beast had earned his name, being a huge mutt with a flat face and powerful body. Best thought he probably had some mastiff in him, which would account for the drool and flatulence Martinez was always complaining about. Despite all of Beast's quirks, Martinez had fought for the dog when it was discovered he suffered from severe separation anxiety and would no longer be eligible for military dog training. Like Dilbert, Beast was used to demonstrate obedience for the kids, but other than that, he was just a spoiled pet.

"Naw, we'll be fine. So, what's new with you? Any progress on getting that psychiatrist of yours to give you the green light?" Martinez asked.

Dean shook his head. He'd gone for his weekly session, and like every time before, she was insistent they talk. She wanted to know how he was sleeping, if he was suffering from any anxiety or depression. If there was anyone special in his life. His answer was no to all; the last thing he wanted to do was give her anything she could use to keep him permanently riding a desk.

Although, giving her nothing wasn't helping either. In nine months, any time he'd asked when she was going to clear him to return, she'd say, *"That all depends on you."*

Which was bullshit, because if it were up to him, he'd have been gone already.

"No, she's just dicking me around. About ready to request a new evaluation."

"That sucks, man, I'm sorry," Martinez said.

If anyone would understand where Dean was coming from, it was Martinez. Several months ago, Martinez was at Mick's and stepped in when some drunk asshole was getting a little too aggressive with a couple of girls at the bar. When he subdued the guy and had him arrested, he'd had no idea he was messing with General Reynolds's son. As a result, the general had taken him off active military police rotation and stuck him at Alpha Dog to help plan a fund-raiser. Martinez had been pissed off and bitter about being reassigned, until he'd fallen for the general's daughter, Eve, and realized he loved working with the kids and dogs more than he liked dealing with the assholes in his squad.

"You've been there, too," Dean said.

"Yeah, but my situation was a little different. I was benched because of the general's personal issue with me, not because they were worried that I might be suffering from PTSD."

Those four letters ran down his spine like an ice cube on chilled skin. He didn't have PTSD. It was normal to have nightmares and be haunted by something tragic, but that didn't mean he had a problem. He didn't drop to the ground when he heard a car backfire or drink until he blacked out. He was dealing. Why did no one understand that?

"I don't have it. I'm fine, but thanks for the support."

"I'm just speaking the truth, bro. They are covering their asses, and it's a bunch of red-tape bullshit, but you've just got to play along until you're cleared. There's no way around it, sorry to say."

"Yeah, I know." Dean couldn't be mad at his friend; that was just the way Martinez was. Speaking the truth, no matter how brutal it may be.

"Besides, I thought you liked being the director and working with the kids at Alpha Dog. Why would you want to go back there?"

Because you want to prove that you won't choke again in a crisis.

"I'm just not ready to be out, you know," he said.

"I didn't think I was either, but I gotta say, I don't miss the stress," Martinez said.

"I also don't have a beautiful woman to come home to every night." Violet's face flashed through Dean's mind, but that was so complicated. She was hot and cold with him, swearing she wanted nothing to do with him, then looking at him like it was only the two of them in the room.

"What about Casey Douglas's sister? You two seemed pretty together when you barred the door to the visiting room," Martinez asked.

Even though it was Martinez and not Best, Dean was still defensive of Violet. Her one worry was being discovered, and he wasn't going to let it happen. "We did not bar the door."

"Maybe *she* didn't, but I've seen you when you want something. Besides, Best told me about you two hooking up before her brother even got there," Martinez said.

"Best has a big mouth," Dean said.

"That doesn't change the fact that something is going on with you two. You took a group of kids out to her house to clean it up and wrote it off as community service. So, if you aren't hooking up, what are you doing with her?"

Dean leaned forward and ran his hands over his face with a groan. "I have no idea, man. I don't want anything serious, you know that, but with Violet...I mean, the girl has got drama up to her eyeballs and trust issues that would make most psychiatrists want to put her in a lab and study her. But I just can't get her out of my head."

"You know, once Eve and I let go of all the reasons why we shouldn't be together, everything just seemed to make sense for us," Martinez said.

"She says she doesn't have room for me in her life," he said.

"So prove her wrong."

To what end? Even if he could convince her that they could have something more, there were no guarantees he wouldn't be gone next week, and then what was he supposed to do? Just leave her high and dry like everyone else in her life?

"I don't even know what I want from her, so why make it complicated?" Dean asked.

"Because if you really think you could love this girl—"

"Whoa, I never said love. Besides, she's been through a lot, and when I get new orders, I don't want to hurt her."

"So be her friend. But if you just let her keep thinking that there is no place for you, then that's exactly what's going to happen. Fortune favors the brave, *mi amigo*."

"I might also send her screaming to the cops for a restraining order if I push too hard," Dean said.

"Well, I didn't tell you to stalk her, man. I just mean that you should show her that whatever qualms she might have mean nothing because you're a good guy. You're exactly what she needs."

Dean laughed. "That easy, huh? 'Cause it seems like no matter what I say, I'm going to end up being that guy she'll tell her friends about. The cautionary tale about one-night stands."

"Well, if you end up being that guy, at least it means she'll remember you."

Chapter Seventeen

THIS IS A *disaster.*

Violet surveyed the chaos that was her kitchen the next morning. She'd been up since seven, unable to decide what to make, so she'd ended up with a bit of everything: chocolate chip pancakes, biscuits and sausage gravy, bacon, and sliced watermelon and strawberries. Plus her mother's special breakfast pizza, which was still baking.

"Holy hell, what is the occasion? I already had my birthday breakfast," Daisy said as she walked into the room.

Violet glanced at the clock in horror. Dean would be there any minute, and she was still waiting on the breakfast pizza to finish.

"I got a little carried away making breakfast for Dean."

"Ah, Dean. Your boom-boom friend."

"Don't call him that, and it's not like that anyway. It's a thank-you for yesterday and for coming over to paint the porch."

"Then shouldn't the rest of the Shawshank crew be with him?" Daisy's innocent expression didn't fool her for one minute. "You know, there is an easier way to tell him thank you, and it doesn't cost a fortune in food. You just take him to your room, get on your knees—"

"Jesus, I don't want to hear this from you, because now all I can picture is my little sister doing *that*."

"I could have read it in a book."

Someone knocked at the door.

"Shit, how do I look?" Violet asked.

"Hmmm, it's better if you don't know," Daisy said helpfully.

"You are such a brat." Violet wiped her hands on her apron and headed for the door.

"I'm only trying to help you," Daisy called after her.

Violet opened the door and found Dean standing on her porch with a brightly colored bouquet in one hand and a bottle of orange juice in the other.

"Sorry, if it had been dinner, I would have brought wine, but I figured this was more appropriate," he said.

The gesture was so sweet, it caught her by surprise for a minute, and all she could do was stare at the bottle. She'd never had a man over for any meal, but somehow, she couldn't imagine any of the men she'd dated doing the like.

And flowers. He'd brought her flowers.

Violet cleared her throat, trying to get rid of the lump in it. She'd never had a guy bring her flowers before. The urge to throw herself at him and give him a bone-crushing hug was overwhelming.

"Do you not like orange juice? I could run and get something else?"

Great, she'd taken too long to answer, and he thought she didn't like it.

"It's fantastic, thank you. You just caught me by surprise. We don't get very many dinner guests, and..." *Stop rambling.* "I love orange juice."

Violet stepped back to let him inside, and he held out the flowers to her. "It smells really good in here."

"Thanks, I just—" The oven dinged. "Excuse me a second."

As she raced past Daisy, her sister said, "Aw, he brought you flowers."

"Will you go make yourself useful and set the table?" Violet set the flowers on the counter and pulled on her oven mitts. She had her head in the oven when she heard Dean's voice behind her.

"Were you expecting an army to come with me?"

Pulling out the cast-iron skillet, she set it on a hot pad and watched his gaze skitter from one full plate to the next. "I know, I went a little overboard. I guess you should never cook when you're hungry," she said.

"It is awesome. Honestly, I appreciate all the trouble you went to. I haven't had anyone cook for me since my mom at Christmas." He snatched a piece of bacon and came up alongside her, munching on it. "What's that?"

"Breakfast pizza. It's a potato crust with eggs, peppers, cheese, onions, mushrooms, and spinach."

"Hmm." He had moved behind her and was currently bending over her shoulder, his hands resting on the counter, boxing her in. "That sounds amazing. Where did you come up with that?"

"My mom used to make it." She hardly recognized the husky tone in her voice, but his proximity was driving her to distraction.

"I can't wait," he began, tracing his fingers along the side of her neck—"to eat it"—his lips pressed a light kiss right under her ear—"all up."

He nipped her skin, and she moaned softly, forgetting for a moment that they were supposed to be just friends.

"Okay, you two are super quiet in there," Daisy said. "So I'm giving you to the count of ten to get your clothes back on before I come in to get glasses. One..."

"Your sister reminds me of mine," Dean said, stepping away from her.

Self-consciously, Violet pulled on her ponytail, as if Daisy might be able to see where he'd kissed her and she needed to cover it up. "An evil devil's spawn put on this earth to torment you?"

"Exactly."

Violet grabbed the plate of bacon, avoiding Dean's reaching hands as he tried to steal another slice. "I bet your mother banned you from the kitchen while she was cooking."

"How did you know?"

"Ten!" Daisy opened the swinging door just as Violet was ready to come through. She stalled long enough to whisper to Daisy, "Remember that I know where Mom kept all the baby pictures."

"So? I was adorable. Bring it, sister."

"Not during your bowl-cut phase, you weren't," Violet said.

"You're all talk!"

"We'll see."

DEAN SAT BACK in his chair half an hour later, rubbing his stomach with a groan. "I think I might explode."

"You and me both," Daisy said with a laugh. "Violet's pancakes are the best. I could eat them forever. I keep telling her to quit school and open a restaurant, but she won't listen."

"It's a bad time to start a business, and besides, even if I was interested, I don't have the experience. I'd end up bankrupt in a year," Violet said.

"Such bullshit. The only time I've had cooking like yours is when we went to that little place in Placerville. What was it called?"

"Sweetie Pies," Violet said.

"Mmmm, that was good." Daisy turned to Dean. "Don't you think my sister could have her own successful eatery?"

"I would definitely be there for every meal," Dean said.

"See! You sell yourself short, Vi," Daisy said, taking another bite of her pancakes.

Dean grinned at Violet from around the vase of flowers she'd set in the middle of the table. He liked that she hadn't stopped smiling since he'd taken his first bite of her breakfast pizza and hummed with appreciation. Right now, she was easy to read; she liked taking care of people and being appreciated. He got the feeling she didn't get praised very often.

"Well, thank you both. Dean, you're going to have to take some of this home with you. We'll never finish all this before it goes bad."

"I'd be happy to take some of it off your hands."

"Those pancakes are mine," Daisy said.

"I'll arm wrestle you for half," Dean countered.

"Not fair! You have arms the size of tree trunks."

Dean couldn't remember the last time he'd sat around a kitchen table with anyone other than his own family and laughed so much. The Douglas girls were definitely good for him.

Who says you're good for them, though? They don't need another man in their lives who is just going to abandon them.

But last night after Martinez had left, Dean had sat on the couch and thought about his options. While Casey was at Alpha Dog, Dean would still bump into Violet, whether he tried to avoid her or not. And if he was being honest, he had stopped wanting to avoid her, even if it was for both of their sakes. He liked being around Violet, and if he got deployed again, did that really mean they had to end this thing before it even got started?

Especially since Violet was far from immune to him. He hadn't meant to kiss her on the neck in the kitchen, but being that close, with the warm scents of vanilla and chocolate and Violet in the air, he couldn't resist.

Didn't want to resist. Not anymore.

If only he could get Casey to come around to giving him a chance. It wasn't as if he hadn't tried, but the harder he pushed, the more pull the kid gave. Dean couldn't ask about his sessions with the counselor, but he had the feeling Casey still wasn't talking.

Violet stood up and started to gather dishes, but Dean beat her to it. "You cooked. We'll clean up."

"We? What's this we shi—" Daisy took one look at his hard gaze and shut her mouth. "On it, boss."

When Daisy disappeared with a stack of dishes into the kitchen, Violet whispered, "You're going to have to teach me that look sometime."

"It's the same one my dad used to give us when we were kids. One glance in our direction, and we scattered."

"Ours yelled a lot, but usually because he didn't want to be bothered with us," she said.

Placing a hand on her back, he gave her a comforting rub. "I'm sorry."

"Hey, we survived. You hear horror stories about kids getting ahold of their parents' stash and overdosing or starving because their parents forgot to feed them. Believe me, it could have been worse."

Daisy came into the room to gather more dishes, shooting Dean a disgruntled look. "Thought you were going to help me?"

"Bossy as your sister." Dean shot Violet a wink. "Why don't you go relax?"

"Actually, I'm going to go take a shower since you two have this handled. I think I actually have pancake batter in my hair."

Great. Now he was going to picture her standing under running water threading her hands through her long hair.

"So, do you like my sister, or are you just trying to get back in her pants?" Daisy asked once Violet had gone.

"She told you?"

"Yep. So which is it? And by the way, there is only one right answer," Daisy said.

Dean grabbed several platters, balancing them on his arms. "I like your sister. I'm just trying to be her friend."

"Does that usually work for you?" Daisy grabbed a box of gallon Ziploc bags from the cupboard, her expression doubtful. "'Cause if a guy liked me enough to sit back and be my friend, I'd think he was a puss."

Anger rushed through Dean. "I'm not a puss."

"Hey, no offense, pal, but it's true."

"Saying you meant no offense doesn't change the fact that I'm very offended," he said.

"Oh, cry me a river! You want my sister? Then man-up and ask her out."

Being told to man-up by a teenaged girl was humiliating, to say the least. "Thanks for the pep talk, but I can handle my own shit."

"Just because you two are walking on eggshells around each other doesn't mean the rest of us have to. All I'm saying is my sister needs to get a life of her own. After this week, I'm gone at college, and it's just going to be her and Casey. And I guarantee you Casey is not going to want to stay in and watch *The Breakfast Club* on a Saturday night." Sealing the baggie of pancakes with a snap, she continued, "So hop to it, Sergeant."

Dean wasn't sure about getting into his relationship—or whatever it was—with Violet with her adolescent sister.

Especially when he wasn't sure exactly what he was hoping for yet. "I'm not sure how much longer I'll be here before I get deployed again. That's been my goal at least, and I still don't know what is going on between Violet and me anyway. For now, we're just friends trying to figure it out."

Daisy studied him for half a second before setting the dishes in her hands down.

Hard.

"If you aren't planning on staying, then what the hell are you doing here? Because my sister doesn't need a new friend, especially a temporary one."

Startled by her aggressiveness, he rocked back on his heels. "Has anyone ever told you that you're a little scary?"

"All the time," she said. "But seriously, if you're just hanging around thinking my sister is just a way to pass the time, you should move on now. Because she is way better than a stepping stone. I'm not saying she's a saint, but she's pretty fucking close. So if you hurt her, I guarantee karma will follow you for eternity and bite you in the ass over and over again."

"I'm not planning on hurting your sister. I am just...I don't know, I just want to be around her."

"Hmm, fine. I'll give you the benefit of the doubt, but remember what I said. Karma on your ass forever."

VIOLET FINISHED BLOW-DRYING her hair and was fluffing the red mass as she stared in the mirror. When she'd washed her hair, she had indeed found batter clumped in the strands, and the thought that Dean might have actually seen it was making it hard to leave the bathroom.

Why was it that she was constantly at the losing end of their interactions? Melting down into a sob fest, getting reamed by her brother, and dealing with the general chaos of her life...How was he still here?

The real question is, why? What does he want? Because we both know that friendship is the last thing on your mind when he's around.

Which might be true, but Violet wasn't stupid. No matter what, she wasn't looking for someone else to care about, and he wasn't looking for a relationship. So essentially, there wouldn't be anything wrong with them hooking up as friends in theory, except...

Violet liked him. He was a good guy, and those were so hard to come by. If she let her guard down, she was going to get attached.

And when it was over, she'd have one more regret.

Yet, here you are, letting him stay to paint the porch.

Because despite her better judgment, she wanted to be around Dean. With so many stressors in her life, he was like this bright, warm light. She wanted to get closer and keep it forever.

The thought startled her. Where had that come from?

Writing it off as just her emotions getting away from her, she concentrated on getting dressed. She settled on a simple sleeveless shirt and jean shorts, since her phone said it was going to be close to a hundred and five degrees. She hadn't bothered with anything but her moisturizing face lotion and a little mascara; she'd just sweat it off anyway. Besides, it wasn't as if Dean hadn't seen her without makeup.

She walked out of her bedroom just as Daisy was heading to the front door in her Safeway uniform.

"Whoa, where you off to?"

"Got called into work, and since my last day isn't technically until Wednesday, I figured I'd go in. It's just six hours, so I'll be home around five."

"Okay. I'll probably make something easy for dinner," Violet said.

"Good with me." Violet followed her out the back door, since Dean was on the front porch painting. "Have you talked to Quinton yet?"

"Not yet. With packing and working and him doing… whatever he does, we haven't had a chance to meet up."

"Well, really, when you tell him—"

"Make sure there are witnesses with camera phones." Daisy waved at her as she jogged toward her car. "I got it. Don't worry."

Violet couldn't help it. With Casey at Alpha Dog and CPS watching her, all she did was worry.

"You clean up good," Dean teased as she came around the side of the house.

Violet laughed as she climbed up the unpainted porch steps. "Thanks. Can I help?"

"Sure, grab a brush. I was just trying to find a station on Pandora."

Violet picked up a paintbrush as the cords of "Jeremy" by Pearl Jam blared from his phone speaker. The song content pinched at her heart, considering Jeremy stood up in class and killed himself.

Was it ironic or just sad that it had been one of her mom's favorites?

"You like nineties rock?" she asked.

"Yeah, you?" he asked.

"My mom did. You know that song 'I'm Gonna Be (Five Hundred Miles)' by The Proclaimers? She used to march me around the house to that until I almost peed my pants laughing."

"She sounds like she was a great mom," he said.

"She was."

"You will be, too."

Violet froze midstroke. "I will be what?"

"A good mom. I mean, the way you are with your brother and sister, whatever hiccups they might have had, they are good kids. And they obviously adore you. I just mean that based on what I've seen, I think you're an amazing woman."

Her chest constricted, the sheer thought of kids of her own bringing on a nearly catatonic panic. For several moments, she couldn't speak, and then finally she blurted out, "I don't know about that."

She saw Dean swing her way out of the corner of her eye. "You don't?"

"Have you met my brother and sister?"

"But they're still good kids. Your sister got a scholarship. That's at least partly because of you."

"Still, I don't think it's in the cards for me. Not when there's a chance..." Her voice trailed off; she was unwilling to admit her fears aloud.

"A chance of what?" he asked.

A chance that someday I might just check out on the people who love me. Like she did.

"Nothing, it's just more family drama you don't need to know about." She dragged the brush across the railing roughly with her back to him, until he bumped her shoulder with his.

"I understand having fears and things you don't want other people to know about. I've been told that it's unhealthy, but honestly, I look at it as self-preservation."

Violet glanced his way in surprise. "Me, too. Probably why I've never had anyone in my life who lasted more than a few months." Why was she telling him this? "It's hard to get close to people when you can't let them see your darkest nooks and crannies."

"Considering what you've gone through, it's not surprising that it's hard to trust."

Violet wasn't sure how much he knew from her file, but even with the most basic information, how could he ever think she'd be a good mother, considering the examples she had?

People who have bad childhoods can overcome it and raise great kids.

"But if you ever do need anyone to talk to, I'm here."

"For now." She didn't mean to sound so bitter, but this whole situation was stupid, and she was just asking for heartbreak if she let it continue.

"Honestly, I have no idea if they'll ever let me go back, but I'm getting a little tired of avoiding you and pretending that I don't want to get to know you. So, I figured why bother fighting it? Let's be friends."

Friends, ha.

It was so laughable that she'd ever be able to be friends with him, not with the way he made her feel. Not with the way she wanted him. But she couldn't let herself get attached. If she grew to need him, it was going to be impossible to let him go.

"Sure, we can be friends for now." *Until you say good-bye.*

Chapter Eighteen

"Excellent, Casey!"

Dean cheered on Monday morning as Casey and Apollo completed a thirty-second down-stay. Casey was grinning ear to ear as several of the guys congratulated him, but when Dean approached him, the kid's smile slipped. Although Casey had definitely eased in with the other kids, he was still leery of the trainers. Dean had made space in Casey's schedule for time with Dr. Linda Stabler every day until his release, much to Casey's irritation, but if she could get through to him and get him to talk, Dean would let her have him all day long.

"You have done some awesome work. I'm proud of you."

"Gee, just what I've always dreamed of." Casey snickered, but none of the other boys joined in. In fact, they seemed to take a sudden interest in the grass, the sky, basically anywhere else but the two of them.

"All right, you're all dismissed. Good work today." As the guys took off, Dean said loudly, "Casey, you stay. Liam, can you take Apollo and Dilbert in while I talk to Casey?"

Liam grabbed Apollo's leash and took off as fast as his long legs would carry him. The puppy kept trying to look over his shoulder at his young master while Dilbert lumbered behind.

When Dean took a few steps toward Casey, he saw the flash of fear cross Casey's face, but before he could tell the kid he just wanted to talk, that mulish expression was back in place.

With a frustrated sigh, Dean just dove in. "Look, you want to be pissed off at the world, that's on you, but I don't want to hear you ever disrespect any of the instructors here, including me. Most of the kids who come through are grateful to be here instead of juvie, but if you aren't enjoying your stay, you've got one week left that you can finish there."

Casey's face started to tremble, and Dean noticed a definite sheen in his eyes, but the kid didn't back down. "I'll pack my stuff then."

Casey tried to escape, but Dean was done messing around. Grabbing Casey by the shoulders gently but firmly, he held the struggling kid in place while he bent his knees until he was eye level with Casey.

"Enough. I was just bluffing, damn it. You're not packing anything, but you *are* going to stop fighting me and realize that treating everyone who cares about you like the enemy isn't helping. Don't you think I've noticed that you haven't seen your sisters? They keep showing up here to visit you, and you don't even bother to come out."

"It's none of your fucking business!" Casey cried.

"You're my business whether you like it or not, and I want to make sure that you don't push away the only family you have—"

"I don't care! If she hadn't signed me up for fucking art classes, I'd have been fine! It's her fault! *Her fault*!"

Dean reeled back, surprised by the pure rage in Casey's molten red face and high-pitched scream. Dean wasn't even sure he knew what he was saying, but when one of Casey's fists swung out and caught Dean in the stomach, the air whooshed out.

And then it was as if Casey had eight arms swinging all at the same time.

Dean heard a shout but ignored it, wrapping his arms around Casey's thin body and pinning his arms to his side. Casey started to use his feet, but Dean dropped to the ground speaking in low, calm tones. Nonsense, really, but he'd seen Kline do it with one of the boys who had autism. The tight embrace had eventually calmed him, and Dean just hoped it would do the same thing for Casey.

Best was suddenly standing over them, bending down to intervene, and Dean shouted to be heard over Casey's yelling. "No, I've got him."

Best backed off as Casey's voice grew softer and hoarser. "Let me go. I hate you. I hate yo-ou." He choked on the last word, his body shaking as he began to cry, and Dean noticed that a crowd of kids had gathered at the edge of the field.

"Get them back inside," Dean said loudly to Best.

Best took off, and Dean realized he was burning up, slick with sweat from the heat and fight, but he held on as Casey started to relax, sucking in breath after breath between sobs.

"You're okay. No one is going to hurt you. You're okay."

Dean didn't release him for the longest time, wanting to make sure that the storm had passed. "If I let you go, are you going to turn into Rocky Balboa again?"

"No." The word was quiet and weak, but Dean took him at it as he released him. Sitting up, he waited until Casey joined him before he started talking.

"It is not my job to tell you how you should feel. I've never been where you are, and every time I try to think about it, it honestly makes me want to find whoever hurt you and pummel him to death."

"Because you like my sister?" The question had a bitter edge, and Dean shook his head.

"Because you are one of my men, a part of my squad. We're brothers, and nobody fucks with my brothers. I would want to kill the son of a bitch with my bare hands just on principle. I don't know what happened, and I would never press you on it, but what he did was wrong. It had nothing to do with you or your sister. The only one who deserves any of the blame is the person who you wanted to hurt today."

Casey didn't respond, so Dean kept talking.

"Look, I'm not going to lie, I may like your sister, but she's got nothing to do with you and me. I've got your back long after you leave Alpha Dog, because that is what we do here. We are there for each other and want to make sure that when you leave here, you have all the skills you need to make better choices. Do you get that?"

"People always want something," Casey said.

Dean wished that Casey and his sisters hadn't learned such a lesson, but the only thing he could do was try to prove them wrong. "My only angle is to make sure you get what you need so that you succeed once you're back out there. I don't want you to end up back in here or worse, but I can't tell you what is going to make things better. You have to decide what you can live with and what is going to help you heal."

"Thanks, Dr. Phil."

Dean grinned, glad he hadn't broken his spirits. "Hey, I am your elder by a few years. I know stuff."

"Can you teach me how to fight?"

Dean made a mental note to talk to Violet about it, but at this point, Casey was his primary concern. "I can teach you how to defend yourself."

"What, like self-defense? Isn't that for girls?"

"No, everyone should know self-defense. It gives you the maximum amount of power with the least amount of force. It would actually be good for all of you to learn, but for now, I'll start with you."

"Thanks," Casey said.

"I do have a question, though." Casey stiffened next to him, but Dean pressed on. "Do you really blame your sister?"

After a moment's hesitation, Casey said, "Kind of."

"Because she forced you to take art classes?"

Casey went on the defensive. "She didn't force me to do anything."

"But she told you that you had to go?"

"No, I wanted to take art classes, but we couldn't afford private lessons, so she found some cheap classes at the youth center."

Dean let him mull over that for a bit. "You can put the blame wherever you want, but if you ever want to find peace, then you need to face what happened head-on."

"I'm not ready to talk about it. I don't want to go to the cops or tell that shrink about it."

Dean laid his hand on Casey's shoulder and gave it a gentle pat. "You don't have to talk to Mrs. Stabler if you don't want to, but I'm sure your sister would listen. When you are ready."

Climbing to his feet, Dean held out his hand for Casey. "And if you think that you're getting away with smarting off, you're dreaming."

"Yes, sir."

"You're in charge of cleaning the bathroom for your unit until you're discharged next week." Casey opened his mouth, and Dean raised an eyebrow. "You want to object?"

For whatever reason, Casey snapped his mouth closed and shook his head. "No, sir."

"All right then, go on inside." Casey hesitated, and Dean waited for him to speak. "Something else?"

"Yeah, um . . . A couple of the guys said they went to my house this weekend to clean up the yard and paint. Is that true?"

Dean had expected Casey to be pissed about not being able to go, but he seemed more curious.

"Yeah, I noticed that it needed some work when I was over there talking to your sister about you, so I figured we'd count it toward some of the guy's community service."

"Thanks," Casey said.

"Don't mention it."

Casey hopped from one foot to the next. "And, just so you know, if my sister wants to date you, then it's okay with me."

"I appreciate your blessing," Dean said.

"Won't mean much if you don't do it right."

"Do what?"

"Violet doesn't get involved with guys. And the few I've found out about didn't last very long."

Dean folded his arms over his chest, amused. "Are you giving me dating advice?"

"I'm telling you how to not fuck up with my sister. I want her to be happy, and she seems to like you." Casey's pale face darkened in warning. "But if you hurt her, I'll destroy you."

If there's one thing to be said about Violet, she definitely brings out the protective instinct in people.

"Understood. What do you suggest first? Out of curiosity, of course."

Casey looked up thoughtfully, obviously taking his role as love guru seriously. "My sister hates horror movies, so don't take her to one at a theater. You're pretty safe with a chick flick or anything with Channing Tatum."

Strike the movies.

"Got it. She already mentioned her aversion to zombies."

"Oh, and she hates sushi and seafood."

"I'm not a fan of it either, so that works out well."

"You might want to grab a paper and pen and take notes," Casey said solemnly. "My sister is pretty particular."

"I tell you what. Does she like pizza?" Dean asked.

"Who doesn't?"

"Well, I'll start out by bringing her a pizza, and you make a list for me. Can't screw up too bad with pepperoni and cheese deep-dish, right?"

"Violet likes pineapple and Canadian bacon on thin crust."

"Check. And thanks for the tip."

"Sure thing," Casey said.

As Casey took off jogging across the lawn, Dean realized that he'd given Casey the same advice Martinez had given him. That he needed to deal with his issues and ask for help. How could he, a grown-ass man, ask a young kid to do what he couldn't?

There was a reason for that, it seemed. He was a damn hypocrite.

Violet left Alpha Dog, gripping the steering wheel as if she wanted to tear it apart. Today she'd been determined to get in and force Casey to talk to her, but Sergeant Kline had stopped her in the lobby and told her Casey was having a bad day. That it would probably be a good idea to let him be for a day or so.

Of course she'd had questions, but when she'd asked to talk to Dean, he'd been out of the office, and Kline hadn't offered any other explanation. Combine that with the flat tire she'd gotten on the way home, and she was in a piss-poor mood.

Violet turned down her street and pulled into the driveway. The only thing that was going to make her feel better was a hot shower and warm chocolate chip cookies.

She was trying to remember if she still had baking soda when she noticed a man in a charcoal gray suit sitting on the steps of the porch.

Who wears a heavy suit jacket in ninety-degree weather?

As he stood up, though, his frame stirred a familiarity in Violet that made her palms sweat buckets.

"Oh, God."

It was her dad. He was back, standing in their front yard after three years without a word.

Climbing out of her car, she tried to keep calm, studying the changes in him. He had cut his hair short and put on weight. He looked healthy and clean-cut, like a guy with an office job who drove back and forth to work in rush-hour traffic.

And so different from the man he'd been for them.

Blinding rage and the sting of betrayal boiled to the surface, making her question harsher than she intended. "What are you doing here?"

If he was surprised by her anger, he didn't show it. "Hello, Violet. It's good to see you," he said, ignoring her question.

"What are you doing here?"

He hesitated and seemed to be struggling to find the words. Her pulse hammered, and her blood pounded in her ears, drowning out all other sound. How the heck had he come to be here? How did he have the balls to just drop by?

Finally, he found his voice. "Well, I was actually hoping we could talk."

"About what?"

"Well, for starters, how have you been?"

Hysterical laughter bubbled up Violet's throat, nearly choking her. "Really? That's why you're here? To play some kind of catch-up game with me?"

"It's not a game, Violet—"

"No, it's not. You want to know how I am? I'm fine. I'm puzzled as to what in the holy hell you're doing, but I am great."

"Speaking of great, the house looks wonderful. You've really done a great job improving the place."

"A friend of mine did it. Not me. I wasn't going to put all of my hard-earned money into it just so you could show up and sell it out from under us."

"This isn't going the way I thought. Could we maybe just take a seat and talk? I won't ask to come in, but we could sit on the porch steps."

Violet didn't want to talk or sit or shoot the shit. In fact, if she stood out here much longer with him, staring into his clean-shaven face and clear dark eyes, she might just take a swing at him. How dare he show up here stone-cold sober. Was he actually here trying to prove something?

"Pass, but thanks for stopping by." Violet tried to step past him, but he grabbed her arm. Violet shook it violently and gritted out, "Take your hands off me."

"I know you're angry with me, and I want to explain. To make amends."

It would have been funny if it didn't make her really want to slap him. "You want to make amends? For what? For stealing our lunch money and blowing it on drugs? Or getting high and leaving me to raise your kids?" Violet's voice rose, and the neighbor's dogs started barking furiously, but she was beyond caring. "Or maybe you feel bad about attacking your son in the middle of the night when he was only eleven years old?"

He finally released her arm, but now Violet was seething and stepping into him aggressively. "Do you know he still has nightmares about you? Parents are supposed to make their kids feel safe, not scared."

"I know I made plenty of mistakes, but that is what I'm here to fix—"

"This is not something you can fix. We have no use for you." Violet spun away from him, heading for the porch steps.

"I hate to bring this up, but this house is in my name, and for better or worse, you, Daisy, and Casey are still my kids."

Violet faced him once more. "We might share DNA, but we don't belong to you. This house might technically be yours, but we aren't. If you want it back, we'll start looking for another place to live."

Her father ran his hands over the top of his head and released a frustrated laugh. "This is not how I wanted this to go."

"Then you really never knew me. After everything you did, you really thought you could just show up here and we'd be happy to see you? That's we'd just open our hearts and forgive you?" Violet didn't want him to know that she had worried, but she couldn't keep the telling tremble from her voice. "I thought you were dead."

"I know, and I'm sorry. I was so screwed up for a long time, Violet, and after you told me to go, I thought it would be better if I stayed gone."

"Then why are you here?"

"Because I've been sober for eighteen months, and for the first time in my life, I'm able to take care of you guys. I know it will take time to earn your trust, but I've changed."

Good for him. He's straightened out his life finally, and what? You're just supposed to let bygones be bygones?

"I appreciate that you've finally found God or inner strength or whatever, but it's too late. Daisy and I are both adults, and the last thing Casey needs is to have you triggering old wounds." Violet pointed to the road, in case she was being too subtle with him. "You can't repair something that never existed."

She'd almost made it inside when he called out, "I'm not giving up. Whether or not you think I deserve it, I will fight for the chance to know my kids."

Opening the front door, she tossed back over her shoulder, "If you'd ever been much of a father to begin with, you wouldn't need to get to know us now."

Closing the door on whatever else he wanted to say, Violet locked it and escaped into her bedroom, sliding down the back of the closed door with a sob. Hugging her knees to her chest, she just sat there, fighting long-buried memories.

How dare he do this now? How could he think that any of them would fall for this bullshit?

Hot tears seeped from her blurry eyes, and she wiped at her cheeks furiously. God, she was sure that she had shed all the tears she had for him, but look, there were more. Finally getting up, she went into the master bathroom and turned on the shower.

She undressed as the water heated up, her gaze flickering to where the tub had once stood. It had been a deep, spa-type tub that had come with the home. Her mother had loved it, languishing in the bath for hours. It was why Violet hadn't thought anything about how long she'd been in it the day they had found her.

When her dad had left and Violet had moved into the master bedroom, she'd come in here with a sledgehammer and shattered it to bits. Once she'd cleared away the rubble, she'd sold off everything of value her father hadn't taken and used it and some of her savings to cover up the space and put an old oak hutch where the tub had sat. She had hoped it would erase the very essence of her parents from the room, but they still haunted her.

Maybe she should let him have the house. They could make do with a studio apartment for a while, at least until she graduated in December. Once she had her diploma, she could look for a better-paying job. They would be fine.

Are you going to tell Daisy and Casey he's back?

She had to tell them, although she wouldn't be telling Casey much of anything if he didn't start speaking to her soon. Part of her was afraid that if Casey learned their dad was back and sober, he might actually want to live with him. That he'd leave her.

If he does, wouldn't that mean you were free?

Free from what? From having a family? People who needed her? If she didn't have Daisy and Casey to worry about, would she continue down the same path?

In the deepest, secret parts of her, she'd imagined something different, but only Daisy had an inkling of her desire. The thought of having her own eatery had always appealed to her, no matter how impractical it was, but she was a realist, and it never went any further than a mild fantasy. But if she only ever had to worry about herself now…

It was a train of thought she'd never entertained before, and even now, guilt ate at her. Was she selfish for wondering what life would be like if she didn't have these responsibilities?

God, how could she even consider any of this? Her father had only been sober for a minute; there was no way Casey would ever trust him enough to leave Violet.

You never know with kids. Even when they know their parents are losers, they still love them. Right?

Violet stepped into the shower, ignoring the little voice, and submerged herself in the burning stream. With any luck, the scalding water might take all her pain down the drain, too.

Chapter Nineteen

ON TUESDAY, DEAN opened the door to his therapist's office, the little bell announcing his arrival. Ever since the conversation with Casey, he'd been talking himself into telling Rita everything, including about the nightmares and lack of sleep. He'd been reading up on different treatments for his nightmares, and even if they were a symptom of PTSD, if he sought treatment, they couldn't keep him from active duty. At least, that's what several websites said.

Either way, it was time to practice what he preached.

"Dean, good to see you. Come on back."

Rita stood at the end of the hallway in a pencil skirt and blue blouse, a welcoming smile on her face. For some reason, knowing he'd be telling her the whole truth made him more nervous than every other time he'd visited.

"How are you doing?" Rita asked as she sat down in her chair.

"Honestly, I've been better. How are you?"

"I'm doing well." Rita grabbed her pad and pen, watching him over the tops of her glasses. "What do you mean that you've been better? Has something changed?"

"No, well actually, yeah." *It's now or never.* "I've been having trouble sleeping and I know I need some help with it." Dean's chest loosened at the admission. It felt good to actually tell someone.

"I see. Are you having trouble falling asleep or staying asleep?"

"Both, depending on the night."

"How long has this been going on?"

"On and off for six months or so."

Her pen stalled on the page. "Why are you telling me now?"

Dean was a little stunned by her question and stuttered, "I...Because I need help."

She set her pad and pen down and folded her hands in her lap. "But what changed? We've been meeting every week for well over six months, and you've avoided telling me about this. What is it about today that made you finally want to talk about it?"

Dean stared at her, trying to figure out what he thought she might want to hear before finally settling on the truth. "One of the kids at Alpha Dog is going through some bad stuff, and I told him he should talk to someone about it. Figured I'm kind of a hypocrite if I don't follow my own advice."

"Hmm, so you felt guilty?" she asked.

Guilty? Sure, he'd felt guilty every day for nine months, wondering why he lived and wishing he could go back and change what happened. If he could do it over again, he'd get up and get moving faster. Take the lead…

But if you had died that day, you wouldn't have met Violet.

And that thought gave him a whole new sense of regret.

"No, it wasn't about guilt. It was…It was about not being scared anymore." Taking a deep breath, he let it all out. "I have been so fucking scared since it happened, questioning myself and who I am. I've been scared that I can't be a soldier anymore, that people will always look at me and think, 'Oh yeah, he's the one who choked and let his squad die.' And it's so God damn stupid and selfish, because even if nobody ever trusts me to carry a gun at their back again, I'm doing something here. With the kids I help, the ones I train so that they can find a different path and overcome all the crappy homes, and parents, and just the shit that life throws at them. Instead, I come here, sit in this chair, and am terrified to tell the truth and have you end my career over there. When I'm not even sure that's what I want anymore."

"Really? For months all you've wanted is to be deployed again. Is it the job at Alpha Dog? Or something more?"

Dean hadn't really thought about what else had changed for him, but since he was being honest…

"There's a woman I met at a concert a little over a month ago. At first it was just a one-time thing, but I've seen her a couple of times since. Every time I tell myself that it's not fair or it's not what I want, I seek her out. I keep finding ways to see her, and touch her, and I just…Hell, I don't know what I want."

"Don't you?" Rita stared at him intensely before leaning forward. "Sitting here in this room once a week, Dean, I've gotten to know you. I knew that you were hiding something from me, but I want to share a couple things I've learned about you.

"You are not a coward. You were in shock, caught off guard by a violent and traumatic situation. Very few people would have reacted any differently, and from the reports I've read, there was nothing you could have done to save them. I know you won't believe that, but it's true.

"But I also understand that you are proud. Your father and a long line of grandfathers and uncles all served in the military. And I think that you're worried about how your father will feel if you get stuck behind a desk. Because it happened to him."

Dean remembered telling Rita about his dad, how he'd gotten orders to serve in Vietnam. His friend in basic had gotten a cushy job in New York. He'd begged his father to switch so he could see some action, and his dad had traded. He'd never told Dean that story, but Dean had overheard his parents talking about it one night. His dad had never wanted to go to war but hadn't wanted anyone to think he was a coward. He'd been relieved for the switch.

"You think I resent my father and that I've been trying to prove I'm better than him?"

"I didn't say that, but do you? When you think about what happened that day, do you compare yourself to him not wanting to go to war?"

Dean answered automatically. "No, I never hesitated. From the minute I signed up, I wanted to serve my country wherever they needed me."

"And this woman you can't seem to stay away from, does she need you?"

Dean laughed a little at the absurdity of the question. "Actually, she's told me over and over that she doesn't and that I'd just complicate her life."

"And what do you think?" she asked.

Dean thought about Violet hiding her tear-filled eyes from him. He pictured her run-down house and the way she had fought to keep him from helping her. How every time he'd held her, she'd melted the tiniest bit against him before steeling herself.

"I think she's afraid of needing me," he said.

"And how about you? Are you afraid of needing her, too? Maybe that's why you keep telling her you don't want to get involved." Turning the page on her yellow tablet, she started writing. "I'm going to give you a homework assignment. Two actually. The first is, I want you to take home these three questions and over the next week, really think about your answers." She ripped off the sheet and handed it to him as she stood and went to her large cabinet. She pulled a book from inside and handed it to him. It was one of those composition books with a black and white cover. "And I want you to write down every time you are feeling too anxious to sleep or you wake up from a nightmare. I'm also going to prescribe you something that should help you sleep better, but it is really important that moving forward we have complete honesty between us. All right?"

Dean read over the three questions she'd given him.

When I see myself in five years, how does my life look?

What do I need to do to be the best version of myself?

Name three things that make me happy.

"Dean?" His head jerked up as he realized that Rita had been talking to him.

"Yeah?"

"Do we have an understanding?" she asked.

"Yes. From now on, nothing but the truth."

VIOLET AND DAISY climbed into her car a little after two in the afternoon. Violet wanted to go by and see if Casey would let them in before she had to be at work and had asked Daisy to come along to talk. Violet hadn't told her sister yet that their father was back, partly because Daisy had been gone when she'd woken up this morning. Luckily, Violet had found their father's card tucked into the front door before Daisy had. She'd almost crumpled it up and thrown it away, but it wasn't fair to her brother and sister. They deserved to know that he wanted to see them.

But now, here they were all alone with a fifteen-minute drive, and yet Violet's tongue felt heavy and her mouth seemed too dry to speak.

"So, why the sudden invitation?" Daisy asked.

Clearing her throat, Violet concentrated on merging into the left lane of the freeway. "What do you mean?"

"I mean that you seem like you've got something you want to say to me, but you're not talking. You've got this whole creepy, foreboding silence going on, and it's freaking me out."

Just say it, you big wimp. "I came home yesterday and found Dad on the porch waiting for me."

After a beat, Daisy scoffed. "Well, at least we know he's not dead in some crack house. What did he want? Money?"

"No, he—" *God, why is this so painful to admit?* "He looked good. Really good. He's put on weight, and he was dressed in a suit. I mean, he didn't even wear a suit to Mom's funeral, and he shows up after three years asking for forgiveness wearing a fucking *suit*!" Violet's voice rose to a hysterical pitch on the last word, and suddenly, Daisy's hand reached out to squeeze her arm.

"Breathe. You look like you're about to hyperventilate, and I would rather not crash at sixty-five miles an hour."

Violet breathed in deeply and slowly while her sister kept the conversation going.

"I can't believe he showed up and just expected you to welcome him back with open arms. What an idiot."

Violet was a little surprised by her sister's calm, almost sardonic attitude. "How do you feel about him being back?"

"You mean, do I want to see him?" Violet glanced over at her, caught Daisy's thoughtful expression, and turned back to the road. "Fuck no, why would I? Honestly, I hardly remember what the man looks like; that's how much of an impact he's had on my life."

"He wasn't all bad." Violet didn't really know why she was defending him, but she knew she didn't want Daisy to regret writing him off. "Remember when he used to take us to Fairytale Town?"

"He only took us there to meet his dealer. It wasn't like he actually wanted to spend any time with us; we were his cover."

Violet had known that, of course, but had been hoping that Daisy didn't.

Exiting the freeway, Violet didn't know what else to say, so the last few minutes of the trip were silent until she parked.

"Are you going to tell Casey?" Daisy asked.

"If he'll let us in. I hate to admit it, but at this point, I'm afraid that he might rather live with Dad after everything he's been going through."

"Then he's a moron." Daisy got out of the car, and Violet let her wrap her arm around her shoulder as they walked inside. "Casey loves you and knows that you would do anything for him. There is no way he can say the same for Dad."

Violet appreciated the moral support, but after Casey had ignored her for the last week, she couldn't rule out the possibility that he was done with her. Maybe he did blame her for whatever had happened to him.

She and Daisy checked in with security, who radioed back to see if Casey was receiving visitors. When someone answered, the burly security guard grinned at them. "You're in luck. Visiting room three on your left. He'll be in shortly."

Violet nearly ran for the room, excited to see Casey finally. As they waited, Violet paced back and forth until the door opened and Casey stepped inside.

One week without seeing him, and Violet's gaze raked over him, searching for any changes she may have missed.

"Hi," he said.

"Hi is all you've got to say after ignoring us for a week?" Daisy said.

Casey's cheeks blossomed bright red. "Yeah, I'm sorry about that. Had a lot to think about."

"Don't tell me, tell Violet. She's the one who worries about you and loves you to pieces. I think you're a butt."

Violet saw his smile peek out, small but like a beacon of light. "You miss me."

"Yeah, keep dreaming, nerd."

Violet let them talk, watching the ease between them. Casey and Daisy always had a bond she couldn't touch, like regular siblings. They fought and teased and drove her crazy sometimes with their antics, but they loved each other.

Finally, Casey turned those green-gold eyes on her and swallowed. His gaze shifted to and away from hers several times before he finally whispered, "I'm sorry."

Violet didn't even care what for. Before he could say more, she wrapped him up in her arms, holding him close and ignoring his stiff shoulders.

"It's okay."

Slowly, Casey's arms wrapped around her waist and he relaxed against her. "No, it's not. I was blaming you for things that weren't your fault."

"I don't care, honestly. If it helps to place the blame on me—"

"No, Dean was right. I have to put the blame where it belongs."

Violet pulled back, staring down into his face searchingly. "Dean said that?"

"Yeah. He's a good guy, once you get past all that alpha-male soldier-boy stuff. He's not a total tool, if you were wondering."

"Are you trying to tell me something?" Violet asked.

"I'm just saying that if you like him, I wouldn't have a problem with you two hooking up."

Daisy burst into hysterical laughter, while Violet could feel her cheeks burning. "As glad as I am that you like Dean, there's something important I have to tell you."

Casey's expression turned guarded as he let Violet lead him over to sit down. "What's going on?"

"Our sperm donor popped up again," Daisy said.

"Daisy, damn it!"

"What? All I did was rip the Band-Aid off instead of treating him with kid gloves. He can handle it."

Violet wasn't so sure as she studied Casey's pale face and wide eyes. "Dad's back?'

"Yes. I saw him yesterday. He came by the house—"

"What did he want? Did he ask to see me?" Casey seemed to have gotten over his shock and was now buzzing with excitement.

"Yes, he mentioned wanting to get to know you, all of us again. He says he's been clean for a year in a half—"

"Ha." Daisy's sarcastic bark earned a cold glare from Violet.

"—and he wants to try to mend fences. What do you think?" Violet asked.

"We should at least give him a chance, right? You're always talking about love and second chances."

Except that Violet was pretty sure they were well over two chances, and she couldn't imagine what would happen if her dad fucked up again. Actually she could. It would end up just like before, with her picking up the pieces.

"If that's what you want, I can get in touch with him, but I'm concerned about you getting hurt."

A shadow crossed Casey's face, and he snapped, "I've already been hurt."

Daisy sprang to her defense with a snarl that sounded like it had come from an angry terrier. "Hey, she's just looking out for you, so stop biting her head off."

Casey's eyes closed for half a second and opened, meeting Violet's. "I'm sorry. I'm working on some anger issues."

"That's okay, honey, I get it. You have a lot going on with you."

"Do you really think Dad's better?"

His expression was so filled with hope that it ate at Violet, and a thread of anger weaved about, knotting in her stomach. "I don't know, but he looked good." And if he wasn't sober, he was not going to like how she dealt with him this time.

"I want to see him. Can you ask him to come here?"

Her heart squeezed, but she nodded. "Of course, Case." Knowing if she didn't get out of there, she might lose it, she said, "Hang on, I've got to go to the bathroom."

"Thanks for announcing," Daisy teased as Violet headed out the door toward the restrooms.

And bumped smack into Dean.

Violet lost her balance and started to stumble, but he caught her, pulling her close and pinning her hard against his body.

"Hi." She gazed up into his eyes, not even looking away when she felt a heavy weight leaning against her legs.

"Hey." His face was just a few inches from hers, and she had the crazy idea that his lips were actually moving closer.

Except something was pushing between them and against the front of her legs, and when she looked down, she found the black and white rear end and tail of Dean's dog. "Either your dog is jealous or he finds being squished between our legs comfortable."

"Most likely he's trying to get to your feet. He's got a thing for sleeping on them."

Sure enough, the moment that Dean took a step back, Dilbert flopped down on top of her feet, making her teeter a bit.

"Why is he lying on *my* feet?" she asked.

"Maybe because he knows you're prejudiced and he's trying to win you over?"

Violet tried hard to not be amused by the whole thing, but the dog had actually stretched out onto his side with his back to her legs.

Funny, how uneasy this dog had made her that first night at Dean's place.

"Excuse me?" Violet said, speaking to Dilbert, who lifted his head with a little moan. His brown eyes watched her almost expectantly. "What do you think you're doing?"

To answer her question, Dilbert actually rolled onto his back and started wiggling his entire body over her feet, his mouth open wide as if he was grinning at her.

Violet managed to get one of her feet out from under him with a laugh. "Your dog is a dork."

"I know. I'm glad to see you warming up to him," Dean said softly.

Violet's gaze connected with his once more, and she shrugged. "He's not really like the other pit bulls I've met."

"You shouldn't lump them all together. Any dog can be aggressive, but it doesn't mean that a whole breed is."

"I'll agree with that." Realizing that she'd completely forgotten about escaping to the bathroom, she said, "I should get back in there. Casey and Daisy are visiting, and I don't want to miss it."

"I'm glad he agreed to see you."

"Well, I got the impression I have you to thank for that," she said.

"No, I didn't do anything—"

Violet cut off whatever else he was going to say with an impulsive kiss right on his mouth. She pulled back with a jerk and covered her lips, amazed and horrified by what she'd done. In public.

Looking around, she was relieved that the only people she could see were the security guards, and they had their backs to them.

"I just...I am so sorry. I wanted to say thank you, and I didn't mean to do that. Not here."

She noticed the intense burning in Dean's gaze as he smiled down at her.

"Anytime you want to thank me, Violet, you go right ahead."

Violet groaned and shook her head. "It was just a thank-you. A one off. Don't let it go to your head."

"I've heard that before."

Violet stepped over a snoring Dilbert and walked past Dean to the bathroom, intending to escape without any more embarrassing maneuvers.

"Wait a second," he said behind her.

With a heavy sigh, Violet turned to face him. "You just couldn't let me escape with my dignity, could you?"

"No, actually, I wanted to ask your permission for something. Casey has asked for self-defense lessons, and I've agreed, pending your approval."

Violet's heart hurt for her brother. She hated that he didn't feel safe anymore, but the reality was that the world was filled with dangers. Not everyone faced them, but he had and he'd come through it.

But if this would help him, would lead him back to the kid he'd been before...

"Of course it's fine."

"I'll need you to sign a waiver."

Of course, because they couldn't do anything without some kind of legal document these days.

"Sure, I'll sign it."

"I'll bring it into the visiting room. Safer that way." He winked at her.

Violet placed her hands on her hips, playing a cockiness she didn't feel. "Why, because you think I can't keep my hands off you?"

"Or maybe I can't keep my hands off you."

Chapter Twenty

ONE WEEK LATER, the other boys in the unit made a circle around Dean and Casey while Dean demonstrated how Casey could throw a man twice his weight over his shoulder. When he'd approached the other instructors about incorporating a self-defense lesson into their daily routine, they had all been for it. Dean had e-mailed a permission and liability waiver to all of the parents, and anyone whose parents hadn't signed off was doing independent study.

Which was how Dean suddenly found himself flipped onto his back, staring up into the clear blue sky. Well, for half a second before Casey's head blocked his view, his smile a flash of white on his shadowed face.

Dean had decided to show the boys one defense move a day and let them practice it for twenty minutes. He'd expected a lot of excitement over it, but he hadn't expected Casey to master the move and take him down like a lumberjack on his second try. Self-defense aimed to use the least amount of strength for the maximum damage, but damn, the kid had skills.

Casey held his hand out to him, and Dean took it. Climbing to his feet, he rolled his shoulder and almost rubbed at it like an old man.

"Good job." Dean slapped his hand on Casey's back, pleased that the kid just grinned. "All right, listen up," Dean hollered. "Pick a partner and work on this move, and this move only, for five minutes. Then we'll go collect our dogs and get back to work."

Jogging over to the fence, Dean leaned back against it and watched, missing a familiar face. Liam had been discharged this morning and released to his new foster family; they were both veterinarians who lived in Folsom. Dean, along with Liam's social worker, had put feelers out to a few of the hospitals and shelters they worked with to get him the placement, although Liam hadn't gotten his hopes up, even after meeting them. But this morning, when he'd learned it was a done deal and they were picking him up, he'd actually cried.

Dean wished that all of these kids would get out of here and find something better waiting for them but knew it wouldn't work out that way for most of them.

Which brought Dean back to thinking about the three questions Rita had given him. If he wasn't here, who would fight for kids like Liam? Would whoever replaced him try to get other kids into a shelter or vet's office or help get them into advanced education? Would they go the extra mile for these kids or just sit behind a desk and wait for the next great advancement to come along?

"What are you thinking about so hard?" Best asked, coming up behind him. As he leaned on the fence next to him, Best waggled his eyebrows "Violet?"

"No, I was thinking about the kids. Things we can do to improve Alpha Dog, you know?"

"Cool, sounds good. Want to discuss it over some beers at Mick's tonight? Martinez bitched out, but Kline is down."

Normally, Dean would have appreciated the distraction, but he'd actually been planning to text Violet to see if he could bring over pizza and a movie.

"I'm going to pass tonight. I've got a lot of stuff to do—"

"Don't insult me by making up some excuse. If you have plans with your girlfriend, just say so," Best said.

"She's not my girlfriend, so I can't say that." *Yet.*

"But you want her to be." Best pretended like he was holding something in his hand and made kissy faces at it. "Oh, Violet, how I want you."

Quick as the Flash, Dean grabbed Best's arms and twisted them behind his back, pressing him down over the four-foot fence.

"Ow, shit, man, I was just kidding."

"She's not a punch line, she's someone's sister. Show some fucking respect." Dean released him and noticed that all of his guys were staring at them.

"Have you mastered it yet?" he yelled.

"No, sir," they answered in chorus.

"Then get back to it."

They did. Dean concentrated on what they were doing, ignoring Best, who was grumbling next to him.

"That hurt, man."

"Stop being a douche bag, and I won't hurt you anymore."

Dean caught Best's grin from out of his peripheral vision. "You've changed."

"How so?"

"You're not as dark and gloomy, but you're more intense. Focused."

"Maybe I'm finally accepting that this is my life."

"And yet, you don't sound bitter about it. A month ago, you would have been all caustic and surly."

That was before Violet. And Casey. And Daisy.

It was before he'd really started to appreciate where he was in his life and accept that this might be right where he was needed.

"I seem to recall you saying I was a 'bucket of dicks.'"

"Yeah, well, you were. Now you're just an asshole."

"Thanks, buddy."

Dean pulled out his phone and started to dial Violet, raising his eyebrow as Best continued to stand there. "You want to watch them for a minute while I step away to make a phone call?"

"Why not? I don't have to leave for a while."

"Where are you off to?"

"Gotta look at some new dogs at one of the shelters. They've got five for me to temperament test, or they'll be euthanized."

"I don't know how you do it. How you choose which ones live and die."

"The test chooses, not me. And if I didn't test them, then they'd all die. We can only do what is within our power." Still, Best sounded pissed off.

"Sorry, man, I wasn't trying to tick you off."

Best waved him on. "Never mind. Go make your phone call."

Dean walked a little ways away and tried calling but got her voicemail. At the beep, he said, "Hey, Violet, I was calling to see if it would be okay for me to bring a pizza by and maybe watch a movie with you. Call or text me."

Dean came back to stand beside Best, disappointed.

Then he thought of something.

"Would it be creepy to show up at a woman's house with pizza and a movie if you couldn't get ahold of her?"

"Probably." Then, Best shot him a wink. "Of course, I've never had a woman not answer my phone call."

VIOLET WAS EXHAUSTED. Wiped. Completely sapped of the strength needed to even change her clothes before she flopped down on the couch. She'd ended up working a double shift at the restaurant when one of the other waitresses called in. Although the tips had been excellent tonight, her feet and back were killing her.

On top of that, her phone had taken a dive into the dishwater this morning when she was talking to Tracy. She'd taken it apart and stuffed it in a bag of rice, but all day she'd felt naked without it.

Reaching under the couch for her laptop, she settled into the cushions to watch the fifth season of *Sons of Anarchy.* Just as the episode started, there was a knock at the door.

Groaning, she called, "Who are you?"

"It's Dean."

Violet's heart did a little leap of excitement, and she would have jumped up from her position if she wasn't so tired. What was he doing here? Since her impromptu kiss at Alpha Dog, they had been texting and he'd sent an e-mail with a permission slip, but other than that, nothing.

"Come on in."

The door opened, and Dean looked over the back of the couch at her. "You okay?"

"Long day." With a teasing grin, she added, "Is this dropping by unannounced going to continue to be a thing with you?"

"Ah well, I called, but you didn't answer, so I brought dinner anyway. If that helps make up for the long day and my rudeness." He held up a pizza box, and the smell was heavenly.

"It helps a lot." She sat up on the couch with her laptop. "I dropped my phone in dirty dishwater this morning, and it said on the Internet to put it in a bag of rice for twelve hours."

"Well, glad it wasn't just you avoiding me."

Violet laughed. "Wait a second. You thought I was avoiding you, and you still came over?"

"What can I say, I'm a risk-taker." Dean came around the couch, and she saw Dilbert lumbering around beside him, his tail wagging rapidly.

"Why is that dog in my house?"

"He's been feeling a little left out, so I figured I'd bring him with me. After the way you two bonded the other day, I didn't think you'd mind."

The dog did seem pretty mellow, even a little dorky. "I guess it's all right, but if he shits in this house, you are cleaning it up."

"Fair enough."

Violet slid her laptop back under the couch and sat with her feet tucked up underneath her. Dean sat down next to her and put the pizza on the coffee table.

"Go lie down," Dean said to Dilbert.

Dilbert flopped down on the ground right below where Violet was sitting. "Your dog has some kind of weird obsession with me."

"It's 'cause he's got good taste."

Violet's cheeks burned. "Thank you, I think."

She took a bite of the pizza and debated opening up the *what's-going-on-between-us?* talk. He had said that they could just be friends, but they sure didn't feel like just friends. And if he was still planning on leaving, there was really no point in even being that.

"So, do you know when you're getting reassigned?"

Dean paused midchew and swallowed. "I'm not sure I am."

"What do you mean?" she asked.

"Nothing, just some things have changed recently, and I'm not sure I want to go back anymore."

"How come you were taken out of the field?"

"Because when you're the only guy in your unit to walk away from a suicide bomber, they get worried about your mental health."

Violet nearly choked at his casual delivery. "Oh, my God! *Why* would you want to go back?"

His expression told her she'd asked the wrong question, but geez, she couldn't understand why anyone would make it through something so terrifying and want to jump right back into the fight.

"If every soldier backed down after a near miss, we wouldn't have an army."

Dean's logic was right on point, and it left her cold thinking about him putting himself in harm's way every day. She'd always known that it was dangerous, she watched the news, but it was different when it was someone you knew.

Someone you care about.

"Point taken."

They ate in silence for a while as she revved up her follow-up question. "So, your plan is to go back overseas, then?"

"It was. My plan was to move up through the ranks and put in my time until I retire."

"You said that things have changed, though?" Violet wasn't sure if her heart was pounding with fear or excitement at the thought that he might say he'd changed his mind because of her.

"Yeah. Just recently, I've started to realize that I actually like what I'm doing at Alpha Dog and I'm afraid if I leave, the guy who replaces me might not fight as hard for these kids to have a future."

He really is such a good guy. "Can't you rise through the ranks without going back?"

"Me wanting to go back had more to do with my own insecurities as a soldier. Proving to everyone that I can still do my job and that they were wrong to sideline me."

"This is about wounded pride? Really?"

"At first, maybe a little. Now, I'm just trying to focus on what I really want, and not some kind of misplaced duty."

Violet didn't want to tell him that things happened for a reason, although she firmly believed that and always had.

"Well, if it were me, I would rather stay here and work with kids. Not get shot at in the desert."

Dean leaned toward her and brushed his fingers across her cheek. "Are you saying you want me to stay?"

Violet's breathing sped up as those digits glided to the back of her neck and began kneading. And then she melted into a groaning puddle of mush and completely forgot what they were talking about.

"Oh..."

"Sore neck?"

"Sore everywhere."

"I can fix that," he said. Turning her around on the couch so that her back was to him, he ran his hand over her, his fingers digging into her muscles. At first it hurt so bad she almost told him to stop, and then slowly the knotted muscles started to unravel. Leaning forward until her forehead rested on the arm of the couch, she groaned as his rough palms slipped up under her white collared shirt, and he worked on her lower back.

And just like that, he stopped. "Violet?"

"Mmmm?" She stretched up and turned on the couch. "That was amazing."

"I thought for a second you passed out," he said.

"No, just becoming putty in your hands." Climbing to her feet, she picked up the pizza box to take it into the kitchen, but his hand caught her wrist.

"Is that right? That's all it takes to make you completely pliable?"

The conversation was quickly heading into a more-than-friends direction, but wasn't that exactly what she wanted to know? If they were really friends or if this was actually some kind of game? Because at this point, she was so confused by their ever-changing status that she wasn't sure what she wanted anymore.

You know you want him, right? Isn't that enough for now? Why does everything need to be figured out tonight?

Because she didn't want to fall for him and have him walk out like everyone else in her life.

"Is that what you want?" She spoke softly, their faces so close that she could lean forward just a bit and brush his lips with hers. "For me to just let you take care of me? To make me feel better?"

"It sounds kind of romantic, right? I swoop in and save the damsel in distress, and despite her efforts to escape, fate keeps throwing us together?"

Did he think she was kidding? She didn't need rescuing, and she didn't want him thinking he was some kind of savior.

He released her wrist, and she set the pizza down. When she faced him once more, her hands were planted firmly on her hips.

"You're ridiculous, you know that, right? I never said I needed you to save me. In fact, I believe I've told you the opposite over and over."

Suddenly, he tugged her down onto his lap and, before she could squirm away, tangled his fingers in her hair. "Maybe I'm the one who needs saving."

She stared into his eyes, captivated by their intensity. "From what?"

"From turning back into an angry, bitter asshole." Grazing her lips with his, he whispered, "Haven't you noticed I'm a better man around you?"

"Better? If a pestering, overbearing guy with a penchant for surprise drop-bys is better than..."

He kissed her, softly drawing on her lips until her stomach clenched with longing and she was gripping his biceps.

"Do you want me to go?" He nipped at her bottom lip. "If you aren't glad to see me, I'll walk out that door and you can keep the pizza."

Her body was practically vibrating with desire, and he was asking her if she wanted him to leave? It was probably the smart move, but Violet didn't feel like being smart.

She just wanted to be with Dean.

Violet cupped the back of his neck and brought his mouth back to hers. "Don't go."

As their lips clashed in another kiss, this one was less coaxing. It was filled with the pent-up wanting they'd both been holding back, and as his tongue pushed between her lips, she opened to him, wrapping her arms around his shoulders. Violet was swiftly swept up in him, the scrape of his rough palm against the sensitive skin of her neck as his hands sought the front of her blouse. The press of his leg against her throbbing center, aching to get closer.

His mouth began leaving feathery light kisses along her jaw as he slipped each button from its hole, spreading her shirt with his hands.

"I could still smell the sweet scent of your skin in my bed, and it drove me insane. Even after I washed the sheets, it was as if you had left a piece of yourself behind to tease me."

His words were sweet, romantic, and she wanted more of it. More of Dean. She was so tired of denying herself, of keeping him at a distance. Tomorrow she could worry. Tonight, she just wanted to feel what it was like to be with Dean. Not the guy at the concert, the gorgeous one-night stand she'd planned to never see again. She wanted Dean as she knew him now; the man who painted porches and cared too much and made her feel like she was alive for the first time.

Violet closed her eyes, tilting her head back as his lips traveled over her chest. When he pulled her breast from the cup of her bra and sucked the peak of her nipple into his mouth, she cried out, jerking against him, trying to soothe her arousal only to intensify it.

And then she was suddenly on her back, with Dean hovering over her on the couch. His hands covered her breasts, squeezing and manipulating them as his lips and tongue swept down the middle of her stomach. It was like being pulled in so many different directions she was afraid that any moment she would burst into a thousand pieces.

His hot breath warmed her through her slacks as he placed his mouth at the apex of her thighs, eliciting frustrated moans of desire as she raised her hips.

Dilbert broke out in a round of ferocious barks, startling her out of the moment.

"Shut up, Dil," Dean murmured.

Violet closed her eyes, sinking once more into the abyss of pleasure, until she finally heard it. Raised voices. Angry shouts.

And Daisy's scream.

Sitting up so fast her knee connected with Dean's jaw, she hardly had time to apologize as she buttoned her shirt crookedly. All she could think of was getting out that door and rushing to her sister's aid.

"Daisy!" Violet shouted as she practically jumped over the couch. Throwing the door open, she was greeted with a sight that made her blood hit subzero.

Daisy lay on the ground in their front yard with Quinton standing over her. As the bastard drew back his leg to kick her sister, Violet ran down the steps in a blur of speed to bowl the bastard over. As they tumbled to the ground in a tangle of limbs, Violet lashed out like a mad woman. Biting, scratching, kicking.

"Fucking crazy bitch!"

Quinton managed to climb on top of her and draw his fist back. Violet brought her nails up, raking down his face as he swung.

The explosion of pain in her cheek made her head spin, but before she could get her bearings, Quinton was gone. Violet crawled to her knees, seeing double as Dean slammed Quinton into the ground and twisted his arms up behind his back.

"Stay down, asshole, or I'll break your fucking arm."

The voice was Dean's, but it was darker, more guttural. Another sound drew her attention, and she crawled toward Daisy's sobs, pulling her sister into her arms and cradling her.

"It's okay, baby. It's okay."

Violet closed her eyes against the spinning world. She heard Dean tell someone to call 911 and opened her eyes to find people on her lawn. A few she recognized, neighbors she'd seen but never spoken to.

It could have been several minutes or several hours, she wasn't quite sure, but her head finally started to clear as police sirens screamed up their street. Daisy clung to Violet as if hanging on for dear life as uniforms spilled into the yard around them.

And then strong arms wrapped around her and Daisy, protecting them from the world. Dean's hands were running over her face, her hair…even her arms.

"I've got you," Dean whispered.

Violet would have smiled, but the muscles of her cheek were on fire. "My hero."

Chapter Twenty-One

DEAN DROVE VIOLET and Daisy home from the hospital, but neither said much. Daisy sat in the back with Dilbert, staring out the window while Violet rode up front, holding a cold pack to the left side of her face. Every time Dean saw her swollen, bruised cheek, he wanted to walk into the police station and get five minutes alone with the bastard.

But Dean had missed his chance to exact painful revenge on Daisy's ex-boyfriend, and besides, he didn't really think kicking the shit out of the worm would have made him feel any better.

Daisy had several cracked ribs, but those would heal in four to six weeks. Dean was more concerned about the psychological trauma she must have suffered.

Dean and Violet had been in the room with Daisy as she recounted what happened before they'd arrived. Daisy had met Quinton earlier in the parking lot of her work. She'd just planned on stopping in and grabbing a few things, figuring it was a pretty public place to break things off. When she'd told him that she didn't think she was up for a long-distance relationship, he had talked about moving with her to Oregon. Unable to get around it, she'd been honest and told him that she didn't want any kind of relationship with him. Period.

At first, he pleaded with her not to leave him, but when she told him nothing he said would change her mind, he'd started cussing and screaming at her. She'd rushed inside, and one of her coworkers had run interference until he left.

She hadn't realized he was following her until he pulled up behind her in the driveway.

His verbal abuse had escalated until she'd tried to walk away, and then he slapped her across the face. She's swung at him with her purse, but he'd knocked her to the ground and kicked her. And kept kicking her until Violet attacked him.

Dean had seen abusive relationships before. Hell, he'd seen a man knock a woman out with one hit. But he hadn't been prepared for the blinding rage that swept through his body when he saw Quinton strike Violet.

Dean reached across the console and laced his fingers through hers.

"You okay?"

"Yes, for the hundredth time." There was no bite of irritation in her tone, just a bone-deep exhaustion that gave a slight slur to her words. He knew Violet was already tired from work, but after the stress and the adrenaline, he wasn't sure how she was still awake.

Dean pulled into their driveway and went around to get their doors. Daisy was moving slowly, although that could have been because of the pain meds she was on. He helped Violet down, and she put her arm gently around her sister's waist.

"I'll make sure you get in all right," he said.

Violet just nodded as the two of them hobbled in front of him. Dean didn't try to interfere, except to reach past them to get the door.

They didn't even try to go up the stairs to Daisy's room, and Violet instead led her into her bedroom. Dean stood in the doorway as she pulled back the covers and had Daisy sit down on the bed. She took off one shoe at a time, undressing her the way you would a sleepy toddler, and a rush of warmth spread through him. How could she possibly think she wasn't meant to be a mom?

When Violet finally got Daisy situated, she walked softly across the room to where Dean stood and silently slipped her arms around him, leaning her good cheek against his chest.

He didn't ask if she was okay again, just held her in his arms and kissed the top of her head as they stood in the shadows.

"I could have lost her tonight," Violet whispered.

"But you didn't. You were there for her."

"I knew he was bad news, though, and still I did nothing. I didn't press her to end it or—"

"Hey, come on. She wised up and broke it off, but if you hadn't let her realize on her own that he was wrong for her, it might have pushed her to him."

"Sounds like you have experience with that," she murmured.

"I have younger sisters, and I've hated all of their boyfriends, except for Dotty's husband, but he's barely tolerable." He'd been trying to make a joke, but she didn't laugh. "The minute I said something, it was like they couldn't get enough of the douche bag."

"How did your sister get the name Dotty, anyway?"

"It was short for Doris."

"Oh, God, poor thing. Why would your mother do that?" she asked.

"She named us after the stars of some of her favorite movies. Mom used to sneak off to this theater in Queens that played all these old movies from the fifties and sixties. It was her favorite pastime before she married my dad. So I was Dean, for Dean Martin; Freddy was for Fred Astaire; Dotty for Doris Day; Audrey for Audrey Hepburn; Natalie for Natalie Wood; and James for James Dean."

Violet laughed, her breath puffing against his chest warmly. "What did your dad say?"

"Not much. I think he'd have named us all Hairball if it would have made her happy."

"You're lucky. My father was a jerk, even before my mom died. Before the drugs got really bad. My mother used to cry a lot, and when I asked what was wrong, she would always tell me it was nothing."

Dean led her over to the couch and pulled her up against his side as they sat.

"She never talked about it, never yelled back or stood up for herself. She'd just cry." She sat up and wiped at her wet cheeks with a laugh. "I hate crying, but I'm just like her. Any little thing and I turn into a water fountain."

"There is nothing wrong with crying. Everybody does it," he said.

"Really? Even you, Mr. Tough Guy?"

Dean swallowed, stroking his hand over her cheek. "I'm not so tough."

Violet covered his hand on her face. "Why do you say that? You are so brave."

Dean shook his head. "You are brave. Running out there and tackling that guy..." He kissed her forehead and gave her what he hoped was a fierce look. "Don't ever do that again, by the way. It took ten years off my life seeing that guy winding up to hit you."

"I had to. She's my sister. You can't tell me that if one of your brothers in arms was in trouble, you wouldn't do everything you could to save him."

Dean shook his head grimly. "I can tell you for a fact that I didn't."

Violet turned her head and kissed his palm. "You can tell me, if you want. If you think it would help."

Dean laughed bitterly. "I don't know if it will help, but you should know who you're getting." What a week for him. Telling Rita about his nightmares, and now he was about to tell Violet about *that day*. Would she look at him differently? Rita had said that he was in shock, that what had happened wasn't his fault, but he still wasn't sure. But he trusted Violet. And if he wanted to get closer to her, he was going to have to share the hardest parts of himself.

"The day my unit was killed, I cried. We were just doing a basic patrol of the area, and it was hot. So hot. And the sun was fucking blinding. I was covering the rear. Suddenly, Kent, who was on point, starts shouting about a kid. That there was a kid with a bomb."

"Oh, God," she whispered.

"And then there's this boom, and I'm flying through the air. I end up on my back with the wind knocked out of me, one of my men pinning me to the ground. I can't move, and there's this drumbeat in my ears, muffling everything else. But as that fades, I can hear screaming and calls for help. I finally managed to get..." he paused, swallowing hard. It was hard to say his name aloud. "Private Joel Hendrickson's body off me. I roll onto my side and see that my guys are everywhere, some still alive. Some in pieces. I freeze."

Violet's arms wrapped around his shoulders, and she held him hard against her. "It must have been terrifying."

"Yeah, it was. I finally got it together and called it in, but most of the guys were gone before help arrived. And that night, when it finally hit me, I cried. I cried like a damn baby."

Her arms held him tighter, and it felt so damn good to have her there, surrounding him, comforting him, that for a moment he gave in. He took the care she offered and basked in it.

Finally, laughing bitterly at himself, he pulled away enough to kiss her lips. "I'm supposed to be the one taking care of you."

When Violet put her hand to his cheek, he leaned into her touch.

"We can take care of each other," she whispered. "Will you stay and hold me?"

He kissed her so softly it was like the brush of a butterfly's wing.

"As long as you need me to."

VIOLET LAY IN the warmth of Dean's arms on the couch, listening to his heavy breathing. The early morning light streamed in through the curtains. How long had she slept? An hour? She listened for any stirrings from her open bedroom door, but Daisy was sleeping soundly. It was only Violet who couldn't quiet her mind.

Dean's words haunted her. *As long as you need me to.* She'd almost said *forever. I need you to stay with me forever.*

But it wasn't fair to ask, so she'd stayed silent.

The worst part was that the closer they got, the more she wanted to tell him all of it. When he'd talked about his unit, she'd wanted to share, to unburden her own pain, but saying her fears out loud was harder than she'd ever imagined.

How do you tell someone about your mother's suicide? That you found her bathing in a tub of red water, gashes on her wrist that she'd made with a razor. How do you explain that the image is always there, the peaceful look on your mother's face now that she was free?

Free of you.

And no matter how hard she tried, Violet couldn't shake the fear that she was just like her. That when life got to be too much, she would just check out. Leave the people who loved her behind to pick up the pieces.

It was why she'd chosen a psychology major and taken the job at the hotline. She'd wanted to help people with no one to turn to, but lately it had almost seemed like torture going in there and listening to them tell her how hopeless they felt.

And then the calls from the women with children, who regretted ever having them...Was that how her mother had felt? Had they just been a mistake to her?

Since meeting Dean, though, she'd been questioning everything and realized how unhappy she was. Her jobs, her major...All the things she'd chosen for herself didn't make her feel complete.

The only times she'd been happy at all in the last few years were when Casey, Daisy, and she did things as a family, without any of the drama. Or times she spent with Tracy, during their one-on-one chats or girls' nights. Baking. Cooking. Creating food always gave her a sense of peaceful bliss.

And Dean. When she was with Dean, even when he was driving her crazy, the warmth in her heart could only be described as joy.

The only issue with Dean was he always seemed to be around when she was feeling weak. He'd discovered so many of her secrets in just a few weeks; no one besides Tracy had ever known so much about her. And he was still here, wrapped around her back like a security blanket. Giving her the false promise that as long as he was with her, she was safe and sound.

A loud ringtone blared behind her, and Dean stirred. His lips brushed the back of her neck as his arms tightened. "I've got to go to work."

"Okay," she said. But when she tried to get up, he pulled her back down.

"I really, really don't want to leave."

His admission warmed her from the inside out. "But you have to."

"Yeah. In the army they don't fire you. They throw you in the stockade."

"Isn't that like jail?" She kept her mouth turned from his, positive that her breath was definitely lethal.

"Yep." He climbed up over the top of her, grinning as he stared into her eyes. "I love the way you look in the morning."

"What, like a mess?"

He took her closed mouth with a smacking kiss. "A beautiful mess."

"Just because you add flattering words does not change the fact that you called me a mess."

"You called yourself a mess. I just didn't disagree."

Violet climbed to her feet and winced at the pinch in her back. "Sleeping on the couch was a bad idea."

"Is this you angling for another back rub?" he asked as he slid his shoes on.

"Well, if you're offering..."

Laughing, he finished tying his shoes and stood up. "Tell you what. You teach me how to make an amazing meal, and I'll give you a deep-tissue massage that will turn your bones to jelly."

"That's a tall order you're trying to serve me. How do I know you can deliver?"

"Hey, I've only ever had your breakfast. How do I know you can really cook?" he asked.

"Well, I guess I can show you my skills tonight. Casey is getting out today. Anything in particular you want to eat?"

"I'll eat anything you put in front of me."

"Yes, I remember your fridge contents. How about Dr. Pepper pulled-pork tacos? It's Casey's favorite," she said.

"I'm drooling already, but are you sure you wouldn't like to be alone with him?"

"Actually, I was hoping maybe you'd bring him home for me. I'm afraid to leave Daisy."

He seemed surprised but pleased. "Sure, I can do that. What do you want me to tell him?"

"Just that Daisy was hurt but she's okay, and I'll explain everything later."

"All right." He grabbed Dilbert's leash from the floor, and when the dog stood up, he immediately leaned against Violet's legs, and she jumped.

The soft, short hairs of his fur tickled her palm as she found his ear, rubbing it in her hand tentatively. Dilbert leaned harder into the love, moaning, and Violet laughed.

"See, I told you that you were going to like my dog. He's a lot like me."

"Pushy? Tenacious? A pain in my—"

"You know, I was gonna kiss you, but now you're just hurting my feelings," he said. Then, with a shrug, he laid one on her anyway. "What the hell, right?"

Before she could respond, he was heading for the door, with Dilbert reluctantly following. Just before he stepped outside, he tossed her a tired smile. "I'll see you tonight."

As the door closed with a click, Violet realized that she wanted to keep hearing that.

Chapter Twenty-Two

VIOLET WOKE UP hours later to the sounds of grunts and groans coming from the stairs. Sitting up on the couch, she found Daisy trying to carry a box downstairs, but her face was beaded with sweat and laced with pain.

"Are you crazy?" Violet shouted.

Daisy put down the box, breathing hard. "I have to pack up. I start school on Monday."

"You little idiot, you took a beating last night." Violet got up and grabbed the box from the floor, thankful that it wasn't as heavy as it looked. "You are supposed to be taking it easy."

"What am I supposed to do this weekend then? I'm driving my car while you're in the U-Haul, so I have to be able to carry this stuff."

Violet hadn't even thought about that, but one problem at a time. "No, no, you aren't driving. You aren't doing anything except sitting your ass down on that couch."

"Don't be ridiculous, Vi!" Although, she did sit on the couch as Violet suggested.

"I am not ridiculous. You cannot drive and move yourself alone." But if Violet drove her up, who would drive the U-Haul? Her list for potential moving partners was short, so she'd start with the obvious choice. "I'll call Tracy. One of us can drive you while the other hauls your stuff."

Violet went into the kitchen to grab the house phone, since her cell was still in a bag of rice, and dialed Tracy, even as Daisy hollered, "You are being spazztastic."

"I am not."

Tracy answered on the second ring. "Well, where the hell have you been?"

Hanging with a hot soldier and getting into fights with psychos in my front yard. The usual. "Sorry, it has been drama-rama over here, let me tell you."

"Do tell."

But Violet did not want to get into it right now, especially since she had to get the pulled pork started. "I will, I promise, but you wouldn't happen to have the weekend off, would you?"

"I don't. I work all day Saturday, and then I'm going with my mom on Sunday to visit Nana for her birthday. Do you wanna go with me?"

Violet wanted to groan aloud. As much as she loved spending hours with Tracy's family, listening to Tracy and her mom bicker was something she could do without. Good thing she had an excuse. "I can't. I have to move Daisy up to college this weekend, and I really needed you to drive the moving truck."

"Moving truck? I thought Daisy was driving up on her own," Tracy said.

"Yeah, that was the plan." Violet knew that if Tracy found out from someone else and not her, she would be pissed, so she continued, "Until Quinton attacked her last night, cracking a few of her ribs."

"The fuck!" Violet yanked the phone away from her ear as Tracy screamed, "And why am I just hearing about this now?"

"Because I just woke up, and you're the first person I called."

"Okay, I am slightly appeased." Violet rolled her eyes at Tracy's magnanimous forgiveness. "But why didn't you call last night? I would have taken her to the hospital or police station. You did have that son of a bitch arrested, right?"

Ah, and here came the other bombshell. This time, she was prepared as she pulled the phone from her ear. "Yeah, someone called the cops, and Dean restrained him after he hit me—"

"Hold up, hold up, hold the fuck up!" Even from a foot away, Violet could hear Tracy's shout. "First of all, Dean your *one-night buddy* from over a month ago?"

"Yeah, that's the one." Violet put the phone on speaker and set it on the counter. She grabbed a package of Pop-Tarts from the cupboard, realizing that she was too hungry to cook.

"Okay, we'll come back to that. Now, where is that piece of shit being held so I can break both his kneecaps? He's not getting away with hitting one of my girls."

Violet loved that Tracy treated Daisy as just another friend, instead of her little sister. "What are you going to do, storm into the police station and demand five minutes alone with him handcuffed to a chair?" Violet started the coffeepot, considering it. "I guess the idea does have merit."

"I am serious, Vi. That man is living on borrowed time. He better hope he doesn't get bail, or he's going to disappear before he even meets his jailhouse butt boyfriend."

"Tracy, really, Daisy's fine. I've just got to figure out how to juggle all of this alone while she heals," Violet said.

"I'm sorry, hon." Tracy's sly laughter suddenly exploded from the phone. "Maybe you don't have to do it alone. What's *Dean* doing this weekend?"

Violet shook her head, though she knew that Tracy couldn't see her. She hadn't even put Dean onto the list yet, mostly because helping her move her sister was a big favor to ask. "I am not going to ask Dean to drive seven hours up and another seven hours down to help me move my sister. That's a job for best friends and husbands, not...whatever we are."

"And what are you, exactly? Because in the last six weeks, I haven't heard boo from you about him besides seeing him at Alpha Dog and this morning."

With a heavy sigh, Violet poured her coffee and considered how to answer. "Let's see. So far, we've hooked up for one wild night of sex, and he's painted my house and saved me from a psychopath. You define it."

"Well, let's see. Is he good in bed?"

More like amazing.

"We only had the one night."

"And...Scale from one to ten, where did it rank?"

"Twenty."

"Daaaamn. I took home the wrong friend."

Violet almost snorted her coffee. "What, Tyler didn't rock your world?"

"Oh, no, the boy was good, but it just wasn't...Sex is just sex unless it means something, you know?"

Violet hadn't known...not until Dean. From the moment they had met, there had been something about their attraction that stayed with her. Haunting her and growing more intense with every touch.

"Okay, so we've established he is a sexy good time, but the house painting...Now that is a man who isn't afraid to get his hands dirty. Plus, any man who does manual labor for you is husband material."

Husband? "Whoa, whoa, let's take this down a notch. There is no talk of husbands or marriage or baby carriage!"

"Well, to be fair, you brought up the baby carriage, which makes me think you've been having your own thoughts."

"New topic."

"Fine, fine, but him painting your house is huge. Men do not cook or do chores for women they aren't serious about."

"So you think he's serious, even if he's been telling me he isn't?" Violet's heart did the tango, dipping and swooping around in her chest with excitement.

If she was happy about the potential seriousness of Dean's intentions, did that mean she wanted serious? She'd been saying she had no room for him, but he already seemed to fit. With her. In her house. Her sister and brother liked him...

"Hello, are you listening to me?" Tracy hollered.

"Sorry, making breakfast." Violet opened the package of Pop-Tarts and bit into one, speaking around the pastry. "You were saying?"

"Yes, I was. Now, as I was saying, men never know what they want until they meet the right woman."

"That's a little sexist, don't you think?"

"No, it's the truth. Every man says he wants to keep things light and casual until he meets a girl who makes him want to take out the trash, watch chick flicks, and even paint porches."

"Anything else?"

"Are you chewing in my ear?" Tracy asked.

Violet stopped chewing and tried to speak but ended up sucking some Pop-Tart down the wrong tube. She barely made it to the sink before she spewed the rest of the Pop-Tart out.

In a strained, raspy voice she wheezed, "Of course not."

"I know you're lying but I'm going to let it go, even though you know how disgusting I think that is."

"Fine, I'm done. What were you going to say?"

"I was just going to tell you that a man who will protect you with his life is something every woman wants, and if I were you, I would not let him go."

Violet considered Tracy's opinions, but even if all of those things were true and Dean was looking for something more, she hadn't quite sorted through all her feelings on the matter. "Still, I'm not going to take advantage of the guy."

"Well then who are you going to get to drive the U-Haul?"

Violet wasn't sure.

When she hung up, promising to call Tracy back later, she just started calling everyone in her phone. Between calls she prepped the pork butt, then chopped onions and peppers until her eyes watered with frustrated tears. A half an hour later, she still had nothing. Nobody. Not a single person Violet or Daisy knew could help out this weekend.

Daisy limped into the kitchen just as Violet poured her second cup of coffee. "How goes the search for a second driver?"

Violet shot her an irritated glance. "It's not."

"Guess we're just going to go back to plan A, which is me driving myself, huh?"

Violet glared at her as she put the Dutch oven filled with the Dr. Pepper pulled-pork ingredients into the oven. When she'd suggested this recipe, she had forgotten that it took hours to prepare, but there was no help for it now. She'd just let Dean cut up all of the produce when he got there.

"I will figure something out. In the meantime, how about you go lie down and stop irritating me?"

"You know, you're not being very nice to your poor, injured sister." Daisy gave her the saddest pout she had ever seen, and Violet threw an oven mitt at her.

"I have been a freaking saint! Now get out of here while I figure out what to do."

Daisy grumbled as she left the room, and Violet was glad for the quiet. She needed to think, and the only thing that helped stimulate her brain was making something.

Violet grabbed her phone parts from the bag of rice and put them back together, saying a little prayer that it would still work. The last thing she wanted to do was pay a hundred-dollar deductible for a new phone.

Yes! The phone turned on, and as she ran her thumb across the screen and clicked on several apps, it seemed fine.

She pulled up her Pinterest recipe board, zeroing in on chunky cheesecake brownies. Rummaging through her cupboards, she found everything she needed, luckily. She hoped that they were as delicious as they sounded, because she definitely needed a win here.

As she began mixing the ingredients, she weighed her options. Maybe she could just bring Daisy her car in a few weeks. It wasn't like she should be driving anyway. What if she got into an accident with those cracked ribs?

What's the harm in asking Dean? It's not like you'd be alone with him. Casey will be there.

The problem was, she *wanted* to be alone with him. Last night, despite all the chaos, she'd enjoyed getting caught up in Dean again. There was so much to him, more than she'd ever guessed from their first meeting, and she wanted to know everything.

But had he changed his mind about what he wanted? Was he simply attracted to her? Fond of her? If he got the okay tomorrow to go back overseas, would he jump at the chance without any regrets? They were questions she wasn't sure she had the right to ask, especially since she had pushed hard for something casual, nothing serious or complicated.

Pretty sure that ship sailed a while ago, don't you think?

Maybe for her, but what about him? Did he think about her first thing in the morning the way she did about him? Did he daydream about her touch, his body warming with joy the way hers did? Because she couldn't seem to stop it from happening, this giddy, ecstatic happiness that had possessed her normally reasonable self. He'd done this to her.

And she was deathly afraid that when he left, she'd never experience it again.

DEAN GATHERED UP his laptop bag just after five, pausing to snap Dilbert's leash onto his collar before heading toward the B barracks. He'd told Casey earlier that he'd be giving him a ride home because his sister had been hurt, and although he'd wanted to know everything, Dean had merely told him what Violet had said. Casey hadn't seemed to mind that Dean would be the one giving him a ride, which cheered him.

Dean knocked on the barrack door. "You ready to go, Casey?"

"Yeah, I'm coming."

A few moments later, Casey came out of the barracks holding onto Apollo's leash, followed by his bunkmate, Henry. Dean could tell Casey had been crying but said nothing as Casey bent down and scratched the dog behind the ear.

"Take care of him, okay?" Casey handed the leash off to Henry, who flashed him a reassuring smile.

"I will." Henry squeezed Casey's shoulder when he stood up with a smile. "Stay out of trouble."

"I'll do my best."

Casey hiked his duffle over his shoulder and walked past Dean.

When they reached the front area of the program, Dean asked, "You happy to be going home?"

"Yeah, I am. I missed Violet's cooking," Casey said sheepishly.

"Well, she told me she's making some kind of Dr. Pepper thing you love."

"Pulled-pork tacos? Yum!"

"We're this way," Dean said.

He hit the unlock button for his truck and loaded Dilbert into the back. When he climbed in, Casey was already belted and ready to go.

"This is a nice truck." Casey ran his hand over the dash admiringly.

"It's fun, too. I take it up to the mountains to fish and snowboard when I can." Dean backed out of his parking space and turned onto the street toward the freeway.

"I've never been snowboarding…or fishing."

"We'll all have to go sometime. Do you think your sister would like to go?" Dean asked.

"I doubt she'd fish. She might try snowboarding, but she's kind of a klutz."

Dean chuckled as he took the Raley Boulevard exit and made a left. "You don't say?"

"Sure, she can trip standing still," he said.

"I'm not going to repeat that, for your safety and mine," Dean said.

"Oh, she knows. Brings it up constantly."

As Dean pulled down Casey's street and slowed to a crawl in front of his house, the kid's eyes bugged out.

"Wow, it looks so different."

"Better, right? Think you can help your sister keep up with the yard?" Dean phrased it as a question, hoping that Casey wouldn't take it as criticism.

Casey didn't seem to, eyeing the yard thoughtfully. "What will I need to keep it up?"

"Some gloves, a lawn mower, and a weed whacker," Dean said.

"Okay."

Dean parked the truck in the driveway and killed the engine. "You don't have any of those things, do you?"

"We have a lawn mower in the back shed, but I don't think it runs. Our weed whacker disappeared along with some tools years ago, and we just figured Dad took them."

"Do you ever miss him?" Dean asked.

Casey's face shuttered. "Wasn't much to miss. He was either high or off trying to score." Casey cleared his throat. "He's back, you know?"

Dean was surprised that Violet hadn't said anything. "When? Have you seen him?"

"Not yet. Violet said he wants to see me, though."

"How do you feel about that?"

"I don't know. On one hand, I want to give him a chance because he's my dad, but all I remember of him was this scary guy who used to yell at us to be quiet. And I hardly remember my mom. The only real parent I've ever had is Violet."

Dean debated whether or not he should ask Violet about her dad but decided that if she wanted to tell him, she would in her own time. "You should tell her that."

"Tell her what?" Casey asked.

"That you love her and she's done a good job. Because I've got to be honest, I don't think your sister thinks very highly of herself. I think she worries you'd have been better off with a foster family."

Casey said nothing as he stared mutinously out the window. Finally, he muttered quietly, "That's stupid."

"Just repeating what I heard." Dean climbed out of the truck and shut the door with a thud. Opening the back door, he took Dilbert's leash and waited as the dog hopped down. When he came around the front of the truck, Casey jumped out of the passenger side and fell into step with them as they crossed the walkway.

"Does she really think I'd have rather gone into the system?" he asked.

Dean glanced at him thoughtfully, debating on how best to answer. "I think she is afraid that she might have acted selfishly and that if she'd let you go, you might not have gotten into trouble. In my opinion, I think you're a good kid and that the graffiti was an isolated incident. An outlet for your frustration. Maybe even a call for help."

"Geez, man, now you sound like my psychiatrist. I like art, that's it. I wanted to paint something on the school that people would look at and wonder who had done it, and I'd know it was me."

"Why don't you just go to your principal and see about creating a mural? We had them when I was in school," Dean said.

"Only seniors are chosen to do murals," Casey said.

"Then when you're a senior, you can do it. Until then, you need to find some legal ways to explore your artistic side," Dean said.

Casey paused on the porch, clenching and unclenching his fists. "I tried doing that. Violet set me up with art classes, remember?"

The bitter tone in Casey's voice drew a question from Dean. "So, why did you stop going?"

Casey finally met his gaze, and Dean could tell he wanted to tell him something.

Just then the door swung open, and Violet squealed when she saw them. "I thought I heard your truck!"

She went to Casey first, who accepted his sister's hug with a resigned look on his face, a far cry from the way he'd pushed her away only a month ago.

Violet pulled away and waved them inside. "Come on, I've got food all ready." She paused as she looked down at Dilbert with a frown. "You again."

"Still hate dogs, huh, sis?" Casey took Dilbert's leash from Dean and led him inside past Violet.

Alone for a minute, Dean pulled Violet toward him and gave her a long, slow kiss. "Hey."

"Hi." The word was spoken as softly as a sigh, and he didn't let go of her hand, just rubbed his thumb across the skin.

"How is Daisy?"

"She's resting."

"Well, I haven't told Casey anything."

"I better get in there then, before he starts hollering for Daisy and wakes her up."

He let her pull away and followed her into the house. She looked adorable in a pair of jeans and a simple pale blue peasant blouse. Her hair was pulled back loosely in a ponytail, and he wanted to reach out and use it to tug her gently back into his arms.

"Daisy?" Casey called.

"Case, shh, she's resting," Violet said.

"Resting? Daisy doesn't rest." Casey's small face appeared paler than normal, and his voice trembled as he asked, "It's really bad, isn't it?"

"No, sweetie. It isn't good, but she's going to be fine. Believe me, it could have been worse."

"Are you going to tell me what happened?" Casey asked.

Dean watched as Violet made Casey sit down at the dining room table, scooting her chair around so she was basically sitting next to him. As she told him about the events of the night before, Casey became increasingly agitated, and she continued to run her hand over his shoulder and head, reassuring him that Daisy would be fine. Her entire demeanor was that of a concerned parent comforting her distraught child.

Because that was essentially what Casey and Daisy were to Violet. Dean wasn't sure why this was really just occurring to him, but Violet treated her younger brother and sister less like irritating younger siblings and more like beloved offspring. The actual title of who they were to each other didn't matter as much as the fact that they belonged to Violet and she to them. She had risked a lot to hang onto her family. She was loyal, compassionate, steady as an oak, and would protect her loved ones with the ferociousness of a tiger mom.

She was everything Dean wanted in his future wife.

Only Violet was here and now. And Dean had a hard time imagining there was anyone else who would ever challenge him or enchant him the way Violet did.

Chapter Twenty-Three

VIOLET WALKED INTO her bedroom to check on Daisy before dinner and found her sitting up in bed, holding her phone.

"What is it?" Violet asked.

"He won't stop texting me," Daisy said grimly.

Violet knew exactly who she was talking about. The police department had warned her that Quinton would probably make bail, so they'd filed for a temporary restraining order. It was supposed to include calls and text messages, so Violet held her hand out for the phone. "You don't need to read them. Tomorrow we'll get you a new number, and in just a few days, you'll be a state away, starting a new life."

"What if he follows me? What if he doesn't stop?" Daisy's voice was filled with high-pitched panic and tears. "I should have listened to you. You told me he was bad news, and I insisted—"

"Daisy, listen to me. You did what so many women can't. You got out. You told him it was over, and you are moving on with your life. You are strong and courageous and amazing. Whatever power trip he might try, you took back control the minute you chose to take care of yourself first."

"But you never would have put yourself in that position," Daisy said.

"Maybe not, but I've made plenty of bad decisions, handled things all wrong. That's just life, sweetie. If we don't fall down, how are we going to get back up?"

"Did you get that from a self-help book or something?"

"Actually, I think it was an Internet meme." Violet heard the door creak behind her and turned to see Casey. "Someone else wants to see you."

Daisy glanced around Violet, a wide smile spreading across her face. "Case!"

Violet got up, and Casey took her place, giving Daisy a gentle hug. She left the room just as Casey mentioned something about cutting Quinton's balls off, and as she read through the text messages, she had a hard time not siding with her brother on this one.

It's not over, bitch.

Violet gripped the cell phone and walked into the kitchen to find Dean cutting up the produce for the tacos.

She had no idea what expression she wore, but it must have scared Dean, because he immediately set the knife down and gathered her against him. "Hey, what's wrong?"

"I don't know how to protect her," Violet whispered.

"Daisy? She's going to be fine—"

"You know as well as I do that a restraining order is just a piece of paper." She pushed away to show him the texts from the unknown number. "He's harassing her. What if he decides to follow her to Oregon? Stalk her? I mean, I might just be paranoid, but it happens every day."

Dean's large hands ran down her arms, and although his touch helped, it couldn't fully chase her fears away.

"It's not going to happen to Daisy, okay?" His lips brushed her forehead, warming her skin, and she sighed, closing her eyes. When his mouth covered hers, she held onto his arms, sinking into the hard length of his body.

Finally, she broke the kiss, breathing hard. "Are you trying to distract me?"

"A little. Is it working?" he asked.

"Yes, but if we don't stop, I'm afraid we're going to get interrupted and potentially scar Casey and Daisy for life."

"I guess I'll just have to forgo the pleasure of this"—he kissed her once more before releasing her—"and fill the void with food."

"Wow, I'm a little insulted that I am so easily replaced," she teased.

"Oh, it's not easy, but the way I see it, I'm starving. The meat smells incredible, and even *if* you wanted a piece of me here and now, I couldn't give a peak performance without proper nourishment."

"Counting your chickens a little early, don't you think? A kiss is just a kiss."

"But it took your mind off your sister's ex-boyfriend, so I'd say it did the trick." Picking up the knife again, he asked, "What else do you want chopped up for these tacos?"

"A couple of tomatoes from the crisper." Violet put on her oven mitts and pulled the meat from the oven, where she'd been keeping it warm.

"What's a crisper?" he asked.

"Good God, did your mother teach you nothing?" She laughed as she came up behind him and pointed to the drawers at the bottom of the fridge.

"Hey, if you'd called it the drawer or even the tomb of rotten lettuce, I'd have known exactly what you were talking about," he said.

She kissed his shoulder, patting it as she walked away. "Of course you would have."

Violet pulled the lid off of the taco meat and scooped a chunk onto the fork. Holding her hand under it so it didn't drip on the floor, she blew on it before offering it to him. "Try it."

He opened his mouth and wrapped his lips around the fork. Violet swelled with pride as he chewed and moaned, closing his eyes.

"God, that is awesome."

"Why, thank you." She started to turn away, but he grabbed her hand, shocking her as he ran his tongue along the length of her palm, catching every stray drop of juice. The muscles at the juncture of her thighs clenched, imagining him using that tongue right where it ached the most.

"Hey, where's the food?" Daisy's voice rang out louder than necessary from the other side of the door, and Violet groaned.

"Yeah, what are you trying to do, starve us? Abuse!" Casey chimed in.

Taking the plunge, Violet said, "So, this might be a bad time to ask, but are you busy this weekend?"

Dean lowered her hand but kept ahold of it. "What did you have in mind?"

"Well, I need someone to drive the U-Haul while I drive Daisy's car up to Oregon State U on Saturday. I wouldn't have asked, but unfortunately, everyone else is busy. You could look at it as a mini vacation, though you'll probably have Casey riding with you, talking your ear off. And then on the way home, I'd be there, too."

"Huh."

"What does 'huh' mean?" she asked.

"Hello, we are dying!" Daisy called in a singsongy voice.

"Hang on!" she yelled. "So?"

"Well, I was just deciding whether or not I should overlook the fact that I'm your last choice."

"Oh, come on. I didn't want to ask you to do it because I didn't want to overstep whatever this is," she said.

"So I can save you from short, annoying dudes and psychos, but I'm not the guy you think of to help you move?"

Violet caught his grin and scowled. "I can't believe you are messing with me right now."

"Oh, come on, it's kind of funny. I mean, I bet that we could fit everything your sister owns in the back of my truck, and yet you didn't even think about using me for my vehicle." He ran his finger down her nose and tapped the end. "I think that means you might like me."

"Oh, yeah? How do you figure that?" she asked.

"'Cause you were afraid if you asked, it might scare me off. Am I right?"

Violet pursed her lips. "That would be presumptuous on my part, especially considering that this isn't supposed to be anything serious, right?"

Dean's hand cupped her cheek as his dark gaze held hers. "I might have been wrong."

"About what?" She held her breath, waiting for him to say what she hoped he would.

"That casual is all I could give you. That we could be just friends who occasionally kiss and make out."

"Oh, yeah? What could we be then?"

Forever.

His lips stole across hers as he whispered, "Everything."

He couldn't have said anything more perfect, in Violet's opinion. Kissing him back, she ignored the door being flung open and the disgusted sounds from her sister and brother.

"Ugh, we're never going to get to eat now."

SEVERAL HOURS LATER, Dean picked Best and Kline up from Best's place. Dean had left Dilbert with Casey and was relieved that Violet had seemed okay with the dog. She had asked him where he was going, and he'd merely told her he needed to take care of something. The less she knew about what he was up to, the better.

He'd sent Best and Kline a text that he needed their help with something, and without asking any questions, they'd said okay.

Now it was time to give them an out.

Kline climbed into the backseat of the truck, and Best grabbed shotgun.

"What's up?" Best asked.

Dean hadn't told any of his friends about last night, wanting to keep Violet's personal business private, but after reading Quinton's text messages, Dean knew that there was only one way to deal with the son of a bitch.

"Last night, Violet's little sister's ex-boyfriend attacked her and Violet," Dean began. "He was arrested, but he's out on bail and won't leave Daisy alone. I want to make sure he gets the message."

"Dude, we can't touch him. If we do, he'll rat us out, and it will not only screw us, but the program," Best said.

"I'm not going to touch him. We're just going to have a chat."

Dean caught Kline's hard expression from the backseat as he nodded. "I'm in."

Best groaned and ran his hand over his shaved blond head. "Yeah, I'm in, too, but if we get fucked, I'm gonna be pissed."

It was barely nine as Dean rolled up in front of Quinton's house. He'd asked Daisy for Quinton's address when they'd been cleaning up the dishes, and she had given it to him freely. From the look on her face as she'd written it down, he had a feeling whatever love she'd had for Quinton had been stomped into the ground last night.

Inside the house, the shades were drawn, but there were several shadows passing in front of the lit windows.

Dean rolled down his car window, listening to music blaring from inside.

"Sounds like a party," Best said.

"Does it make me old that my first reaction is to say it's a Tuesday?" asked Kline, the youngest of them all at twenty-six.

Dean climbed out of the truck without answering. Best muttered, "Shit," before his passenger door slammed, and Dean heard the heavy fall of their footsteps behind him.

"So, what's the plan?" Kline asked.

"We're going to walk in, and as soon as I'm sure he understands where I'm at, we'll leave."

"And if that doesn't work?" Best asked.

"It will work." It had to work, because he wasn't going to let this asshole worry Violet or Daisy for another day. They deserved to be safe and happy.

And he was going to make sure that happened.

He turned the knob on the front door and walked right in. A few people looked up curiously, but the majority of them were too caught up in whatever they were smoking or drinking to give a fuck who they were. Dean singled out a skinny tweaker standing at the edge of the room and stalked toward him.

"You know where Quinton is?" Dean asked.

The tweaker's eyes widened at the three of them, and he looked like he was about to piss himself. "He's in the back bedroom."

"Alone?" Dean asked.

"No, with a woman."

Figures the piece of shit would be screwing another girl while he fucks with Daisy.

They headed down the hallway to the last door, trying the knob. When he found it locked, Dean knocked forcefully.

"Take a hint, fucker, we're busy."

Dean clenched his jaw, resisting the impulse to break the door down, and knocked again, shaking the wood frame. He could hear movement on the other side of the door before it was thrown open, and Quinton stood there, all puffed up.

"What the...?" Dean saw recognition dawn in Quinton's eyes a second before he tried to slam the door on Dean.

Swiftly, Dean barreled into the room with Best and Kline behind him, knocking Quinton back into the room. Screaming erupted from the bed, and Dean glared at the hysterical blonde clutching the sheet to her chest.

"Shut up, we're not going to hurt you," Best snapped.

"You assholes are trespassing." Quinton pulled his phone from his pants, holding it up. "I'm calling the cops."

Kline stepped forward and snatched the phone out of his hand. "No, you won't, because half your party guests are loaded and in possession. If the cops show up, you'll be pissing off a lot of people."

Kline handed Dean the phone, and he started scrolling through it, searching for the texts. Finding the first one, he stopped and read aloud. "'I am going to make you sorry, bitch.'"

Dean looked up at Quinton, who had turned sheet white.

"I'm really curious…Exactly how are you going to make her pay? You going to beat her up some more?" Dean turned to the woman on the bed and said, "Did you know you were in bed with a guy who put his ex-girlfriend in the hospital?"

"Shut up," Quinton said.

"Oh yeah, and not only did he get arrested for it, he violated the restraining order in less than twenty-four hours by texting her threats. Is that really the guy you want to be jumping into bed with?" Dean asked.

The girl stood with the sheet and started gathering her clothes from the floor.

"He's full of shit—"

Dean placed his forearm across Quinton's neck and backed him into the wall. The woman screamed again and ran for the door.

"Hey, buddy, I thought you weren't going to lay a hand on him," Best said.

"I'm not." Dean waited until Quinton's face was beet red and released him. Quinton fell to the ground, sucking in air. "I thought that woman was going to attack him, so I was just moving him out of the way."

"You're dead, mother—"

Dean squatted down. "Before you finish that sentence and hurt my feelings, let me tell you exactly what is going to happen here. You're going to forget about Daisy Douglas and move on. If you so much as breathe in her direction, it will be my new mission to destroy you in every way possible. That means tipping off the police to possible criminal activity. Right now you're looking at assault on Daisy and her sister, but one call, and maybe the cops find enough crank to tack on a dime or more to your sentence. Do you really think you're going to get off?

"If the assault charges go to trial, the jury is going to take one look at the Douglas sisters, at the pictures of their injuries, and they are going to convict you for the pathetic piece of shit that you are."

Dean noticed Quinton's trembling form and went in for the kill. "Or you could save yourself the maximum on two assault charges, menacing, and whatever else the judge throws at you, and take a plea deal. If you're lucky, you might get probation. You can go on being a worthless member of society again in a few years instead of twenty."

Grabbing the front of Quinton's shirt, he hauled him to his knees and stood up. "Or you can go after Daisy again and take your chances. Then again, you might end up at a prison where I know a few guards. Maybe they take a little longer to save you when another inmate jumps you for being an asshole. It would be a terrible shame to get your ass kicked daily with no protection, all over a girl who doesn't even want your sorry ass."

Quinton nodded, his eyes the size of silver dollars.

"Is that yes, it would suck, or yes, you'll stay away from Daisy?"

"I'll stay away," Quinton said softly.

"Good. Remember, you send one more text... You even look at her when you pass her on the street, and—"

Dean released him, and he crumpled to the floor, so Dean didn't bother finishing the threat. The guy had gotten the message.

As they walked into the deserted living room, Best said, "I guess the party's over."

"Was it something we said?" Kline joked.

Dean didn't join in on their laughter, too busy thinking about Violet. Was she sitting up, worried about Quinton trying something else?

The three of them climbed into the car, and as Dean started it, Best spoke up, dead serious. "I gotta tell you, man, you scared the hell out of me for a minute there. It definitely gave me second thoughts about every time I've given you shit."

"Good, then maybe it will stick with him," Dean said.

After Dean dropped the guys off, he called Violet, hoping she was still up.

"Hello?" she said.

"You don't have to worry about Quinton. He's not going to bother Daisy anymore."

He could hear Violet draw a big, shaky breath on the other end. "Are you sure?"

"Yeah, I'm sure."

The quiet on the line lasted so long, he finally asked, "You still there?"

"Yeah, I'm here, but I don't know what to say. You could have gotten in trouble or hurt or—"

"I did it so you and Daisy wouldn't have to be afraid anymore. Because I want you to feel safe. Always."

Dean didn't say the words that had been rattling around in his head all day, three little words that might change everything between them, for better or worse. Instead, he remained silent. If things went the way he was hoping, they'd have plenty of time to get there.

Dean thought he heard a sniffle and then a very watery, "Thank you."

"Anytime. Anything else I can do for you?"

"Come back."

Dean put the truck into gear and stepped on the gas. "On my way."

Chapter Twenty-Four

Violet climbed the stairs to Daisy's dorm room for what seemed like the hundredth time on Saturday. Dean had been right about being able to fit everything into the back of his truck and the rest in Daisy's car. The ride had been pleasant, with Violet and Daisy in one car and Casey and Dean in his truck. They'd left Sacramento at six in the morning, and after stopping for lunch, they'd made it to the university just before three.

Nearly two hours later, Violet collapsed on Daisy's bed with the last box in her arms, breathing hard. "Just so you know, the next time we move you, your place better be on the ground floor."

Daisy was lying on the floor in a heap. "There will never be a next time. I'm going to live in these dorms forever."

Dean came into the room and sat next to Violet on the bed, his hand going to the back of her neck. When he started rubbing gently, she groaned and leaned into his hand.

"Me next," Daisy said.

"Get your own," Violet growled.

Casey bounded into the room with Daisy's desk lamp and a bundle of energy Violet found exhausting. "How much caffeine did you give him?" she asked Dean.

Dean shook his head. "None, I swear. He's been like this all day."

"I wonder when your roommate's going to get here, Dais. Think she'll be pissed you took the left side?" Casey bounced on the other bed a few times and finally lay down. "Huh, this is pretty comfortable."

Violet was too caught up in the amazing touch of Dean's hand as he worked on the tense muscles of her neck and shoulders. She couldn't blame the entirety of her tension on the drive or the hauling of boxes.

For the last four nights, Dean had stayed over, and although she knew that part of it was to make her feel more secure, she had been sure that after his sweet declarations, they were going to... well, for lack of a better term, *do it*.

Instead, he'd been the perfect gentlemen. They'd kissed, of course, but he'd actually taken the couch instead of sharing Daisy's bed with Violet. At first, she'd thought it was adorable having him downstairs making sure Daisy was comfortable and that he didn't step on Casey's toes, but now she just wanted him to stop pussy-footing around and take her like a man.

"Hey, Dais, if your roommate doesn't show up, can I stay here with you tonight?" Casey asked suddenly.

Violet's eyes flew open, and she could have sworn she saw something pass between her brother and sister.

"Sure, we can have a movie marathon," Daisy said.

"You guys don't want to go exploring?" Violet asked.

The two of them looked at each other and shook their heads simultaneously. "Nah."

"We'll just walk to the store and grab some kettle corn, Oreos, Doritos...you know, binge on junk food," Daisy said.

"Do you want us to go with you? We could grab dinner," Violet said.

Casey shook his head at her. "Why don't you guys go get some dinner and take in the sights? We can meet here in the morning and grab some Denny's or something before we head back home."

Violet wasn't completely dense. They were setting her up to be alone with Dean, and while she appreciated the gesture, it felt a little skeevy.

Before she could open her mouth, though, Dean grabbed her hand and stood. "Then I guess we'll leave you crazy kids to it."

Violet glanced up at Dean, who had a definite devilish gleam in his eye.

But she was so torn. On one hand, she'd been desperate to get Dean alone all week, but this was the last night she'd get to spend with her sister for months. She was going to miss her.

As if reading her thoughts, Daisy climbed to her feet and hugged Violet hard. Putting her mouth against her ear, she whispered so softly that Violet strained to hear.

"I love you, but if you do not get out of here with Dean, I am going to do something embarrassing."

Violet didn't need to know what her sister had planned. If they wanted her to go, she'd go, but not before she did a little embarrassing of her own.

"I am so proud of you." Violet released Dean's hand to squeeze her little sister, kissing her cheek.

"Thank you. For everything," Daisy said.

Violet blinked at the sting of tears in her eyes and pulled away. "I'll have my cell on if you need anything."

"We won't. See you tomorrow," Daisy said.

Violet shot her siblings a glare as she and Dean left the room.

"I can't believe they chased us off like we were the lame old people no one wants around," she groused.

Dean took her hand once more and brought it to his lips. "I think it was more their way of paying you back for making them so happy."

"What do you mean?" she asked.

He stopped with her in the stairwell, pressing her against the wall with his body. "I mean, they love you and want you to come back tomorrow deliriously ecstatic."

"And how are we going to manage that?" she asked.

"Well, I thought we could start by getting dinner," he said.

"Like a... Like a date?"

"Yeah, that's the idea."

Violet considered playing coy, pretending that she hadn't been dying for this moment. Did she have her reservations? Yes, of course, but right now they were being browbeaten into submission by the cheerfully insane part of her that was only sure of one thing…

That she had fallen completely and irrevocably in love with Dean Sparks.

And she desperately wanted to push away all the worry and fear of the future and just *be*.

"Okay, I'd love to go on a date with you," she said.

"Good, because we've got reservations in two hours." He pushed away from the wall and took off down the stairs with her hand in his, her sore legs screaming in pain as she tried to catch up.

"You made a reservation? Wait, you planned this?" Realization dawned on her, and she burst out laughing. "How much did you give Casey to go along with your plan?"

"Fifty bucks," Dean said.

"Sounds about right. Was Daisy in on it, too?" They exited the stairwell and went out the building toward the parking lot.

"Yeah, but your sister wasn't as cheap. She did pack you something extra to wear, though, so I consider it worth it."

Violet could just imagine what her sister had picked out for her; probably something short, tight, and leather, knowing Violet would hate it on sight.

"So, the first order of business is to go to the hotel and change." As he unlocked his truck, he released her hand and grinned at her over the hood. "I don't know about you, but I could really use a shower."

Violet pictured the two of them in the shower getting dirty as they cleaned up, and her heart kicked into a rapid tempo.

"Well, climb in, Vi. Time's a-wasting."

Violet started as he used her nickname—usually reserved for friends and family—for the first time, then climbed into his truck slowly, her body humming with joy.

AN HOUR AND twenty minutes later, Dean walked out of his hotel room with a smirk. Violet had been less than thrilled when he'd insisted on separate hotel rooms, but he'd planned this night out perfectly and wanted it to start with the feel of an actual date.

He went to the door next to his and knocked. They still had forty minutes until the reservation, but he didn't want to get lost and miss it. Daisy had found an intimate little French restaurant that boasted a romantic atmosphere. And considering this was the first time he'd ever put so much effort into making a woman happy, he hoped Violet liked it. Otherwise he was going to feel like an idiot.

Dean knocked again, nervously impatient as he pulled on his suit jacket.

Finally, the door opened, and Violet stepped out.

Staring at her with his mouth hanging open, he took in the simple black heels that made her long, pale legs look incredible, especially when paired with a dress in deep, royal purple that hugged every curve and stopped midthigh. The strapless bodice showed off her smooth shoulders and arms, while that long mane of red hair was twisted up into a loose knot. Her eyelids were darkened with purple and gray, bringing out flecks of black and gold in her brown eyes he'd never noticed before.

And her mouth...good God. Her mouth was a lush, wet invitation to sample its sweetness.

"It's too much, isn't it?" she asked suddenly.

"What?"

"The whole thing. The makeup, the dress. I overdid it."

Dean shook his head. "No. Not. At. All."

Violet's face brightened, and the wariness and uncertainty that had been written all over it melted away.

"Really?"

"Yeah."

Dean held out his hand to Violet, and the two of them headed down the hotel hallway. He helped her into the elevator, and as they traveled down alone, he had to fight the urge to push her back into the wall and slide his hand up that tight, short skirt.

They exited the elevator and crossed the lobby. Dean noticed a few men follow Violet with their eyes until they caught Dean's gaze and quickly looked away.

"Are you sure I look all right? You're awfully quiet."

"I'm just waiting for one of these guys to try to snatch you away from me," he said, only half joking.

"What?" Violet's laughter rang out as they crossed the parking lot to his truck, and he couldn't resist that saucy mouth anymore.

Spinning her into his body, he cupped the back of her neck and devoured her lips, running his tongue across the sweet surface. It would be so easy to just toss her up and over his shoulder and head right back up to his hotel room, strip off that tiny purple dress and make her come apart under his hands and mouth.

But he had planned this night to show her that he wasn't just interested in a temporary thing anymore.

With her, he wanted everything.

Dean broke the kiss and reached past her to get her door. "Hop in."

"Are you sure?" Her husky tone made his eyes nearly cross with lust.

"No, which is why you should do it. Because if we spend any more time in this parking lot, we might never make it out."

She giggled as she climbed inside. His mouth went dry as her skirt rode up over her thighs, flashing black lacy panties that made him want to reach up and run his hand across the rough pattern.

Dean closed her door, placing his hands flat against the door and breathing hard. Man, he hadn't been this wound up on a date since he was fourteen. Back then it was hormones, but now, it was all Violet.

Dean got into the truck and buckled up. As he entered the address into his GPS, Violet's hand crept over and started massaging his thigh above his knee, working its way up.

"Violet…"

"Yes, Dean?"

"If you don't behave, I will not be responsible for what happens next."

She pulled her hand back, and he concentrated on getting them to the restaurant. He'd never imagined that their date would be this torturous, but things just became more painful as the night progressed. Even after they were seated in a corner booth, she slid all the way around until she was plastered against his side.

"Dean?"

"Yeah?"

"Breathe," she said.

He let out a breath, even as she picked up his arm and put it around her shoulders. "It's chilly in here, isn't it?"

Dean couldn't agree, since he seemed to be sweating buckets, but he pulled her closer. "Better?"

"Very much."

Dean frowned as he read through the menu descriptions, searching for a simple steak. When the waiter finally came around to take their order, he looked at Dean like he was a cockroach when he asked if they had anything without a fancy sauce on it.

When the server walked away with their order, Violet giggled. "You, sir, are an uncultured swine."

"To be honest, Daisy chose this place. I would have probably picked that bar and grill we passed down the road."

"Me, too," she whispered loudly.

Dean's eyebrows shot up, and he grinned. "We still could."

"Yes, we could." She held up the dessert menu to him. "But I was kind of looking forward to sharing one of these sinfully rich desserts with you."

"Then we'll stay. Tonight, it's all about what you want," he said.

"Okay, not that I mind this new and definitely improved attitude where you cater to my every whim, but it's just not you. So are you going to explain what we're doing here?" she asked.

I'm trying to show you what you mean to me.

"I just wanted to do something nice," he said.

"You have done plenty of nice things. You've painted and cleaned up my house. You saved me and my sister from a violent bastard. You have watched over all of us and been so good to Casey...Honestly, I don't know if I can ever repay you for everything you've done."

"I didn't do any of that so you would owe me something," Dean said, affronted.

"I know, which is what makes you even more special. You are a good guy."

"Only because I want to make you happy."

Dean never looked away from her face, even as she brought his hand up to her mouth. "I want to make you happy, too."

Chapter Twenty-Five

As they walked back through the lobby to the hotel elevator an hour and a half later, Violet was as jittery as a virgin on prom night. She knew what was going to happen, and even though they had been there before, part of her was afraid she had built everything up in her mind. Perhaps sex with Dean wouldn't be as good as she remembered, or maybe she would be the disappointing one.

Dean pressed the third-floor button, and the elevator doors closed. Violet glanced his way shyly as he tugged on her hand, and just as the doors opened again, he swung her up into his arms.

"Not this again!" Violet laughed.

Dean ignored her as he stepped out and passed by an elderly couple who smiled at them.

"Good evening," Dean said.

"Good evening," they responded.

When they were out of earshot, Violet hissed, "You know, you're being a bit too obvious about what you plan on doing to me."

"What do you mean? I was just going to carry you to your room and tuck you in—"

"You better be joking! I wore my sexy underwear just for you, and it is *not* comfortable," she said.

"I saw." Dean grinned as he dropped her to her feet and slid his key into the card reader. "And the first thing that came to mind was pulling it off with my teeth."

Violet didn't wait for him to try to pick her up again. Pushing the door open, she grabbed him by his suit jacket and jerked him into the room after her.

The door shut behind them with a loud click, and darkness shrouded them as they fused together. Hands roamed unsteadily as they struggled with buttons, buckles. Shoes dropped in their wake as they sought the bed blindly.

Violet unzipped the side of her dress and peeled it off, stepping out in only the lace underwear. The skim of his rough hands against her waist was like exquisite sandpaper, stimulating her nerves even as his thumbs hooked into her panties.

And then she sensed his movement as he knelt in front of her, his mouth worshiping her stomach, hips, and thighs. She sighed as he dragged her panties down, exposing her to his seeking mouth and tongue. It was so different from the first time he'd loved her, maybe because the lights had been on and it had been driven by raw need and passion.

This was different. This was slow and sweet. His fingers gently spread her as his mouth found her clit, pressing against the little button and thoroughly teasing it.

Dean moved her until she felt the bed behind her and wordlessly lay back, her feet still touching the floor. The rustle of clothes and their heavy breathing were the only sounds as Violet reached for him, finally finding the warm muscle of his shoulder as he came over her.

They seemed to be making music with just their bodies, and it was the most beautiful thing Violet had ever experienced. The rasp of his stubble on her skin. The catch of her moan as his hand found her once more and the cries that followed as she came, soaring and lifting off the bed. The distinct crinkle of the condom wrapper and finally Dean's deep groan as he pushed inside her aching body.

And as she moved along with Dean, her arms and legs wrapping around him, Violet realized she never wanted the music to end.

DEAN THRUST IN long sure strokes, wrapped in the warmth of Violet's body. He was holding back. He wanted this to be good, so good she would finally understand what he'd been trying to convey without words.

That this was love and he never wanted to let her go.

Violet's lips found his neck and shoulder, sucking, and his balls tightened, his dick jerking inside her as he drew closer to the finish.

Shifting up, he dragged his length across the hidden point inside her and felt her muscles quiver around his cock. Repeating the motion again, he concentrated on every tell, ignoring his body's screaming need for release as he sought to finish her off one more time.

Finally, she let go, pressing up and grinding against him before he followed her down with a shout, his body shaking as he came hard.

When their breathing finally started to slow, Dean got up wordlessly and disposed of the condom, his mind full of things he wanted to say to her. But as he climbed under the covers, words failed him. Pulling her against him, he tucked the blankets around them and stroked the skin of her shoulder.

"Dean?"

"Hmmm?"

"Do we need to talk about what this is?" she asked.

Kissing her forehead, he was surprised that the thought of dissecting their relationship wasn't as terrifying at it would have been just three weeks ago.

Because you love her, idiot.

"Would it make you feel better if we did?" he asked.

"I don't really know. If the conversation doesn't go the way I'm hoping it will, it might make me feel worse."

Dean pulled her up until she was sprawled across his chest and searched for her lips in the dark, giving her a long, deep kiss.

When he broke it, he whispered. "As long as what you want is to be with me, then I think we're good."

He felt Violet's smile as she turned and kissed the palm cupping her cheek.

"Yeah, we're good."

Chapter Twenty-Six

On Monday morning, Violet listened to the sound of Dean's even breathing as she played with the hair on his chest. They'd driven home yesterday with Casey, who had fallen asleep in the backseat for the last four hours of the trip while the two of them had held hands in the front. Something had definitely changed between them, although they hadn't talked about it specifically. It was subtle; suddenly, Violet knew it was okay to wrap her arms around Dean at lunch yesterday. She hadn't asked, hadn't worried that he would think she was pushing him. Just like when he'd put his hand on her knee as they drove.

Kissing her way across his chest, she felt him wake under the press of her mouth.

"Good morning."

She smiled up at him before continuing her kisses. "Morning. Your alarm went off."

"It did?" He reached over for his phone and groaned. "I haven't done that since I was a teenager."

"Must have been exhausted from the long drive."

"Or something else."

Violet's cheeks burned as she remembered doing that *something else* to him, running her lips up and down his length until he'd lost control. It wasn't even something he'd asked for; she'd wanted to do it. She'd never done it without the guy prodding her into it, but last night, just the feel of Dean in her mouth and at her mercy had been hot and heady, and she'd loved every minute of it.

And when he'd returned the favor, well, she'd enjoyed that, too.

"We probably don't have time for *something else* now, do we?" she asked.

"No, I have a meeting at ten at the base."

A sudden knock at the front door startled them, especially when Dilbert stood up at the end of the bed and released a loud woof.

Violet sat up with a groan. "Who would come knocking at eight in the morning?"

"One of Casey's friends? Maybe they heard he got out and wanted to say hi?" Dean asked.

"What teenaged boy do you know who likes getting up before noon?" Violet grabbed her pajamas off the floor and slipped them on, trepidation settling in the pit of her stomach. No one good ever came knocking early in the morning, and suddenly, she was picturing a police officer notifying her that Daisy was hurt, or maybe CPS was back…

By the time she reached the front door, her hand was shaking. As she pulled it open, she found a guy with a bicycle helmet on smiling at her.

"Violet Douglas?"

"Yes, can I help you?"

"Here you go." The guy held out an envelope to her, and she took it.

"What is this?"

"You've been served. Have a good day."

Served? Like court papers served?

In a panic, Violet ripped into the envelope and pulled out the folded papers. Her knees threatened to collapse under her weight as her eyes scanned the court document.

She didn't even hear Dean come up beside her. "What is it?"

Her chest was so tight she could hardly breathe, let alone speak. For the first time in years she had been happy, had pushed everything to the back of her mind as she'd gotten caught up in Dean.

Just like the first time they'd met.

Now, here they were again: Violet's world crumbling around her because she'd ignored a problem, and Dean standing next to her, witnessing it.

"My…my father. He wants his parental rights reinstated."

"I didn't know he was back."

Violet's gaze shot up. "I didn't know I had to tell you."

"You don't have to tell me. I'm just a little surprised you didn't, especially if you were worried about this. Did you have his rights terminated?"

"When I petitioned to be their guardian, I had to prove him unfit. Between the three of us, and his criminal record, the judge ruled in my favor, but..."

"But what, Violet?"

Her father was taking her to court. He was trying to take Casey from her.

Her breathing shallow and fast, she started to sway.

Dean scooped her up and closed the door with his foot. He carried her to the couch and sat down with her in his lap, stroking her hair and murmuring. Violet buried her face in his neck, soaking up the comfort he offered.

"It's going to be okay. You'll see. You have done a fantastic job with Casey—"

Violet jerked back with a laugh. "You mean letting him get arrested?"

"Every kid has issues, even those with two parents."

"But we're not talking about them. Who knows what he'll tell them about—" Violet snapped her mouth shut.

"About what?"

Violet had only ever told Tracy the truth about the night her father had attacked Casey, as she was afraid of the memories. Of the fear and the rage that had coursed through her body, of wondering if she'd had one more bullet, if he hadn't stopped hurting Casey...would she have killed her own father?

He opened up to you. If he loves you, he'll understand.

"I know you've read Casey's file, so you know what my mother did and that I found her." Just talking about it conjured up the image, and she winced. "And that I raised Daisy and Casey while my dad got high all the time." Dean nodded encouragingly, and Violet took a deep breath. "But we lied when we told the courts that he just took off. I...I threatened him."

"What do you mean?" Dean asked.

Violet closed her eyes, afraid to look at him. "I pointed a loaded gun at my father and told him to leave and never come back."

Dean sucked in his breath, but moments passed without a word from him. Finally, she opened her eyes, but she couldn't tell what he was thinking by the unreadable expression on his face.

"Why would you do that?"

The question didn't sound accusatory, but it still rubbed Violet raw. "Because he had Casey pinned down on the bed, terrifying him. He was high and looking for money for another fix, and he started choking Casey. I ran and got my gun, and I...I put a hole in the wall above him to make him get off, but he just sat there, telling me I wouldn't do it. So I told him I would. And I meant it." Violet wiped her hands down her face, tracing the trails of tears down her cheeks. "I would have shot my dad to save my brother. And if I had it to do over, I would do it again.

"But now he's back, and he wants to pretend like none of it ever happened. Wants a fresh start and to get to know us, and I just...I don't know how to do this. I don't know how to deal with this. Either way, I lose. If I fight him and he tells them I threatened him, I'll lose Casey, and if I just give in, I lose him anyway. I don't know what to do."

"If you've seen your dad, maybe you can talk to him? Come to some kind of agreement where he can have supervised visits with Casey. Maybe he'll drop the suit if you give him a chance."

A wash of irritation flooded Violet. After everything Casey had been through, how could Dean be so cavalier about Casey's well-being? "My brother has already been at the mercy of two monsters. If I voluntarily let him back into our lives and he hurts him again, then it's all on me. It will be like making a deal with the devil."

"Okay, I understand everything you're saying, but if your dad really has changed, shouldn't you at least try?"

"No, because addicts get sober all the time, but most of them relapse. What if I let him into our lives and one day I find out he slips up and puts Casey in danger? I can't do that, not voluntarily."

"But just because a lot of addicts fall back into the habit doesn't mean your dad will. Don't you think that people deserve second chances?"

"This wouldn't be a second chance; this would be his millionth chance." Violet pulled out of Dean's arms, but he held tight. "Why are you on his side? You don't know him or everything he did to us." Struggling to get off him, she snapped, "I don't know why I even told you."

Dean's dark eyes bored into hers. "I thought you told me because you trusted me. And maybe you wanted my help."

Violet yanked away, needing the distance from him. How could she have been so wrong to think he would understand? "No, for the last time, I don't need your help. I don't need you to take care of me or paint my house or rescue me anymore." Violet didn't want to be shouting all of these things, but it was like she couldn't stop. Every time her life started to take a turn for the better, another obstacle would pop up. She'd been happy, finally. Let herself believe that she could have a normal, joyful existence with love and a family, but she'd been right all along.

Happy endings really were just a fantasy.

"Please, just go. I need...I need some time to think."

"About us or your dad?"

"I don't know."

"Got it." Laughing bitterly, he started to walk toward her bedroom, then stopped. "You know, I thought that this whole pushing people away thing was over. After this weekend, and everything I've done—"

"Do you want a fucking medal? Is that it? Do you want me to be simpering and forever grateful to you? I just had a three-ton weight dropped right back on my shoulders, and you're whining at me about your hurt feelings?"

Dean shook his head, and the pain in his eyes was so intense that she almost took a step toward him, but she couldn't take care of him. Handling another heart just wasn't in the cards for her.

"No, I was saying that I thought for a second that there was something real here, something worth staying for."

Swallowing hard, she drove the nail into the coffin. "Well, I guess you were wrong."

"I guess so. Dilbert." The dog slunk out of the bedroom to Dean's side, and Violet turned away as he slammed out of the house, wrapping her arms around her body.

It was the right thing to do, better for everyone. She had been crazy to think that this would all work out.

She heard a squeak from above and looked up just as Casey came down the stairs, stopping at the edge of the living room. "What is wrong with you?"

That was the question, wasn't it? If only she had a good answer. "It's none of your business—"

"You are my sister, and you are messing up the best thing that has ever happened to you. Even I'm smart enough to know that."

Casey went back upstairs, and Violet sank into the couch. He was right. She had lashed out defensively and stupidly jumped down Dean's throat because she was terrified.

Why the hell was she ever worried about Dean hurting her? It turned out she could sabotage her happiness all on her own.

DEAN HAD A hard time sitting still for his meeting with General Reynolds, especially when all he wanted to do was go for a run or take a few turns in a sparring ring. Anything to fight through the cyclone of emotions circling inside him.

"Hello, Sergeant Sparks." General Reynolds smiled beneath his salt and pepper mustache. "How are you doing?"

Dean stood and saluted him. Instead of telling him the truth, he lied. "Doing well, sir."

"That's good." As the general sat down, so did Dean. "I wanted to have this meeting because I know you've been requesting to get back into the field for some time and we have a spot open with a team leaving at the end of the month."

Dean sat stunned as the general kept talking, unable to get his mind to shut up. Still reeling from the blowup with Violet, he had no idea where they stood. And now, here was the opportunity to get back out there after all this time, and it was the last thing he wanted.

Rita's questions raced through his head. In five years, he wanted to see Alpha Dog expanding and helping more kids and dogs. He wanted to create a better system for the kids who left the program, better placements for the ones who didn't have families.

Forget about Alpha Dog. What about you?

As clear as day, he pictured living in a nice house with a big backyard and coming home from work to Violet in the kitchen. Violet laughing at something Casey said while balancing a red-headed little girl on her hip.

His kid.

He hadn't meant to push so hard about her dad. Why had he tried to fix it? He should have just sat back and been her sounding board, but he'd had to play devil's advocate. He knew enough from dealing with his mother and sisters not to do it, and yet, seeing Violet so miserable had made him want to solve all her problems. All he had been doing since meeting her was trying to fix everything wrong in her life, while she kept repeating she didn't want or need his help.

But he hadn't listened, had just continued to push. Now he might have lost her.

Realizing that he hadn't been listening to anything else the general had said, he caught only the last bit.

"I hate to lose you because you have done a great job running the Alpha Dog pilot program, but if you're still interested—"

"Actually, sir, with all due respect, I'm not." It was blunter than he'd intended, but there it was. Even if his future with Violet was gone, he knew what he wanted, finally.

The general's bushy eyebrows rose up. "You're not?"

"No, sir. I'm not." Feeling as if he should elaborate, Dean continued, "Once I realized that the only reason I wanted to go on tour again was to prove that I wasn't done, I actually started thinking about my life now. And I'm happy, sir. I enjoy working with the kids and the dogs. I like making a difference to them. I like having a purpose and knowing that they are getting the best from me."

Leaning back in his chair, the general grinned broadly. "Well, I'm actually glad to hear it. It would have been a bitch replacing you." The general stood and held out his hand. "Keep up the good work."

Dean took his hand. "Thank you, sir."

As Dean left the general's office and the base, he was tempted to call Violet. Although she had definitely been out of line and flown off the handle, he shouldn't have slammed out of there like that.

Still, he waited. The conversation they needed to have was one that shouldn't happen over the phone.

He pulled into Alpha Dog and was surprised to find Casey standing out in front, waiting.

Dean climbed out of his car. "Does your sister know you're here?"

"Yeah, she dropped me off. I told her I wanted to see Apollo, and she said she'd come back and get me."

"So what are you doing out here instead of visiting Apollo?"

"I wanted to talk to you about this morning."

Dean shook his head. "Casey, I don't know what you heard, but this is between me and Violet."

"You know she didn't mean it, though, right? That she was just being an idiot because that's what she does? She overreacts and then regrets what she does after. It's her MO." Casey cast him a pleading look. "Just don't give up on her yet, okay?"

"I'm not doing anything, Casey. I think we both just need time to cool off."

Casey's phone rang, and he jerked it out of his pocket, looking at the caller ID before answering. "What's up, dude?"

Casey's face lost all its color, and Dean stepped toward him, afraid he'd collapse.

"You did? Holy shit." Casey swallowed and nodded, his eyes huge. "Yeah, yeah man. I'm coming now."

As Casey dropped the phone from his ear, Dean asked, "What's going on?"

Casey's eyes were massively wide, nearly taking up his whole face. "My friend Jose. He's down at the police station."

"Is he in trouble?"

"No, the...the guy who...The art teacher at the youth center's been arrested. Jose recorded him with his phone confessing." Casey started dialing on his phone. "I gotta call Violet. I need to get down there."

Dean took Casey's arm and led him toward the truck. "I'll drive you. Your sister can meet us there."

"Don't you have to work?"

"I'm the boss. I'll get someone to cover for me."

Chapter Twenty-Seven

VIOLET SAT ACROSS from her father at the IHOP in Natomas, nursing a cup of coffee. His dark eyes, once bloodshot and wild, were clear and sharp as they stared back at her from across the booth. It was unsettling to say the least. In twenty-four years, this was the first time she could actually see how her mother might have fallen for him. His square jaw was clean-shaven, and his once dark hair had flecks of gray throughout, but he was still handsome.

After she'd dropped Casey off at Alpha Dog, slightly relieved she hadn't seen Dean's truck, she'd taken Dean's advice and called her father. He'd agreed to meet her, but now that they were sitting face to face, she had a hard time coming up with something to say. Luckily, he spoke first.

"I take it you got the papers."

"Yes, I got them." She took a sip, ignoring the way the cup shook in her hands. She shouldn't be this nervous.

She had been the adult, the one to stay and handle her responsibilities. So why did this Jack Douglas make her feel like a rebellious daughter trying to punish him?

"I want you to know that I had already filed the papers before I saw you. I wasn't trying to hurt you."

A flash of anger burned in her chest. "You're going to take Casey from me. I call that trying to hurt me."

"No, that's not what I'm doing. I am trying to get my rights back. It has nothing to do with taking Casey or hurting you. I just want to be able to see him." Running his hand along his jaw, he emitted a laugh filled with bitterness. "Believe me, I understand why you would think that. I've been an asshole for most of your life, so why would you believe me?" His earnest expression held her spellbound as he pleaded, "I have been trying to deal with everything that was wrong with me, everything that made me turn to drugs in the first place, but it is a process. Nothing I say is going to make you see me for the man I am now, but I would just like to prove to you that I have changed."

How could he expect her to believe that he had been able to eradicate twenty-four years of behavior in a mere year and a half? "So you're telling me that you weren't doing this whole thing to get custody? That you weren't going to tell people I forced you to leave?"

When he reached across to take her hand, she moved back. Violet saw the hurt in his expression before it was gone, but he couldn't have expected this would be easy.

"Violet, the events of that night are shaky, but I don't blame you for anything. I was an out-of-control mess. I know that. All I want is a second chance. I'm not telling the court anything except that I left you guys because I was afraid I might hurt you if I didn't get help."

Deep down, she wanted to believe him, but after her explosion with Dean, she wasn't in much of a positive frame of mind. "Why? Why would you do that?"

"Regardless of what you may think of me, Violet, I'm weak, but I am not a monster. In my right mind, I would never hurt any of you."

The little girl inside who had always hoped he'd get better wanted to believe him. "I don't know if I could ever trust you."

"That's why I am here. To try. That's all I'm asking. For you to just try."

Try. She tried every day to be the best for Casey and Daisy. She tried to better herself and their situations. She'd tried to let Dean in and be happy, but it seemed like every time she tried, shit went south.

Before she could tell him any of that, though, her phone rang. "Sorry." Glancing down at the screen, she saw Casey's smiling face. "Sorry, I need to get this. It's Casey."

"Of course, go ahead," her dad said.

Violet answered. "Are you okay?"

"We're headed to the police station; can you meet us there?"

What the hell had happened now? "Who? Are you okay? What is going on?"

"Dean's driving me. I'll explain when you get there."

Violet stared at the phone as Casey hung up, then panic took over. Jumping to her feet, Violet said, "I'm sorry, I have to go."

"Is something wrong with Casey?"

"He's going to the police station but won't tell me why."

Her father threw down some money. "I'll follow you."

Violet almost argued, almost told him that she could handle it, but paused. It had taken a lot for him to come back here and face his kids. He could have stayed away and started over elsewhere, but he was here. Trying.

Dean had tried to tell her that people changed. She owed it to herself to see if he was right.

"Fine."

Her father's face brightened, and he raced ahead to open the door for her.

And at least when you get to the station, you won't have to face Dean alone.

When Violet arrived at the police station fifteen minutes later, she and her father were brought back to a holding room where Casey and Dean sat. As they stood up, Violet avoided Dean's gaze awkwardly, a blush burning her cheeks.

"What is going on?" Violet asked, grabbing Casey to her in a bear hug.

Casey stared past Violet at his father. "Dad?"

"Hey, Case. Wow, you got big."

"I'm short," Casey said.

Their father smiled softly. "So was I, until I was eighteen."

Violet's chest pinched when Casey returned his smile. "Really?"

As much as Violet wanted Casey to have this moment with their dad, they were inside a police station and she was dying to find out why. "Why are we here, Case? Did something happen with your sentence?"

"No, no I—" He glanced over at Dean and their dad. "Can I talk to Violet alone?"

Dean clapped him on the shoulder. "I'll be right outside."

Violet stared at him, wishing she could say something, anything, but she didn't want to talk in front of Casey or her father.

"I'm Jack Douglas."

"Dean Sparks. I'm a friend of your daughter and son."

Whatever else was said between them was lost to her as they left the room. Violet sat down next to Casey at the table. "What is going on?"

Violet could feel Casey shaking next to her, and the fear squeezing her stomach into knots intensified.

"I'm going to tell them what happened to me," he said.

That one statement hit Violet in the gut like a sucker punch. "You are?" He nodded slowly, and she wrapped her arm around his shoulder. "What changed your mind?"

"Jose. He's been wanting me to come forward with him, but I told him it would be our word against his."

Violet's heart slammed in her chest. "Whose?"

"The art teacher at the youth center, Mr. Davis."

Mr. Davis. The tall, lanky art teacher had been so kind when she'd gone down to the youth center to sign Casey up last year. So normal. How could she not have known he was a monster?

"Mr. Davis is the one who attacked you?"

Casey nodded, a tear falling down his pale cheek, and Violet beat down the violent urge to find Mr. Davis and make sure he never touched another kid again.

"He...He asked me to stay after class one afternoon for some extra help, and I was excited, you know? I thought he was a good teacher, but then he tried to give me a beer from this mini fridge under his desk. At first, I thought it was cool of him, but then he sat down next to me. He...He put his hand on my leg and tried to go higher. I knew something was off, so I ran." Sniffing, he added, "I told Jose about it, and he said I was lucky. He didn't run."

His meaning sunk in, and Violet hugged him harder. "Oh my God."

"But Jose told him he was going to the police. That there were other kids, too, that they'd all found each other and he was going to jail. Jose recorded the whole thing, even Mr. Davis offering him money to keep quiet."

"Jose is really smart," Violet said, softly.

"And brave. A lot braver than me."

"You did the right thing." Violet kissed the top of Casey's head. "You're here now, and I'm so proud of you. That's all that matters."

AN HOUR LATER, Dean and Violet's dad waited in the lobby while Casey gave his statement. Violet had stayed in there with him, and although Dean and Jack had tried to make conversation while they waited, most of the time they were silent.

Finally, Casey came through the door with Violet close behind, her face red and swollen from crying, but Dean thought she still looked absolutely beautiful. He'd wanted to hug her, hold her to him and tell her everything was going to be fine, but when she hardly looked his way, he kept his distance.

Casey stopped a few feet in front of his father. "Violet told me that you want to get to know me."

"That's right."

"Wanna drive me home?" Violet started to protest, but Casey cut her off. "I'll be fine, Violet. I'll see you at home."

Dean could tell that Violet wasn't happy about it. He was tempted to tell her that Casey would be fine, but he held his tongue. They followed Casey and Jack to the parking garage silently, listening to them talking.

Finally, Dean asked, "What floor are you on?"

"Three. You?"

"Two."

"Oh."

They climbed the stairs together, and Dean, who couldn't stand the awkward silence any longer, said the first thing that came to mind.

"I was offered a chance to go back overseas today."

Violet glanced at him, but he couldn't tell what she was thinking. "Wow, so you got what you wanted."

Had she not been listening to him the last week? "I told you, it's not what I want anymore."

"Yeah, but that was... Well, I'm happy for you."

"I turned it down."

Dean stopped on level two, and Violet, a few feet above him, swallowed. "I hope you didn't do that for me."

The words couldn't have cut him deeper if she'd used a knife. What the hell did that mean? Did that mean that she was done with him? It was over just like that?

"Of course not. I did it because I love Alpha Dog."

"Good."

"Okay."

Violet opened her mouth, and his spirits soared as he waited for her to say something, anything.

Instead, she gave him a nod. "I've got to get going. Good luck, Dean."

Unable to believe she was just walking away, Dean refused to break in front of her. "Good-bye, Violet."

And then he watched the love of his life walk up the steps and disappear like they'd never been anything more than a fling.

Chapter Twenty-Eight

Two Weeks Later

DEAN HAD JUST finished taping up Casey's birthday gift when Best walked into the room.

"Hey, we're all riding over together. You want to join us?"

"No thanks. I'm going to stay." Placing the finished gift on the edge of his desk, he tapped it twice. "Can you take this with you, though? I'll call him and take him out later, but I've just got a lot of shit to do."

Best stared at the present in disgust. "Fuck, no, I am not taking that gift and letting you puss out."

Dean knew what Best meant. He thought that Dean was afraid to see Violet, but he wasn't. He was over it. He'd made up his mind to stay for him, not her, and if she was willing to let him go, then he could do the same.

He was just really busy.

Dean glared at Best. "Mind your own fucking business."

"Not when you mope around here like some lovesick ogre, growling and roaring at everyone. You yelled at Dilbert the other day just for being Dilbert!" Pointing his finger at Dean, he continued, "Whatever happened between you and Violet, you need to sack up and deal with it, because this is not healthy. I mean, you were bad before you met her, but at least you were tolerable. You're so miserable, you're bringing down everyone else around you."

"Then you better get out of here before I contaminate you, too."

"Fine, I guess if you're not interested in Violet, I'll have a go—"

Before he knew what he was doing, Dean was around the desk and had Best pinned to the door by his throat. "Finish that sentence and it will be your last."

Banging on the other side of the door made Dean release Best, who coughed and wheezed.

"I was just... trying to get you to admit... that you love her."

Of course he loved her, he would always love her, but love wasn't always enough. "Like I said, leave it alone."

Best shook his head. "You know, I never thought you were a coward. At least, not until today." Dean bristled, but Best stood his ground. "Casey told me that Violet cries all the time, if that helps make up your mind. Maybe whatever you thought was over was just two stupid, stubborn people mucking it up because they have their heads up their asses."

Clenching his fists, Dean took a menacing step toward his friend. "I swear to God, if you don't get out of here—"

"I'm gone. Enjoy your own company then."

Best left, and Dean sat down at his desk, staring at Casey's gift.

For two weeks, he'd nearly called Violet, holding his thumb over her smiling face on his phone, but every time he'd stopped. Convinced himself that it wouldn't do any good. That she didn't feel the same way.

But Casey said she'd been crying.

Grabbing his keys and Casey's gift, he headed for his truck. He could do this, for Casey's sake. He could see her. Talk to her.

Tell her he missed her.

No, he wasn't going to do that. Wasn't going to put himself out there again just to get his heart stomped on.

But if she's crying…

It's not because of him. She'd made that clear.

FOR TWO WEEKS, Violet hadn't been able to stop crying. Luckily most of her classes were online, so no one had to see her. Except for at work, where they all seemed to back away when she'd start to tear up. She'd managed to hold most of her shit together, but it was especially hard at night, alone in the dark…

God, she missed him.

Why couldn't she just tell him that? Just show up at his door or at Alpha Dog and tell him she loved him.

Except that she'd blown it, big time. She'd had the chance to tell him how she felt when he'd told her he was staying. Instead, she'd made it sound as if she didn't care, as if his leaving wouldn't have affected her at all.

What an amazing liar she was, even to herself.

He was never going to forgive her, and what was the point of putting herself out there if there was no hope?

"Everything looks great," Tracy said beside her, pulling her out of her self-pity.

Violet looked around the backyard, at the bright blue tablecloths and Star Wars cake she'd made for Casey's fifteenth birthday party. A bunch of his friends from Alpha Dog were there, including Liam, whom Violet had heard so much about. Jose and a few kids from school were also there, standing around talking.

Her dad was manning the grill, smiling and joking with everyone who approached him. Their relationship was still hard, still awkward, but that was something only time could heal.

Unlike her broken heart, which seemed to get worse instead of better.

Violet was just laying out the utensils when Casey hollered, "Dean!"

Her heart froze while the rest of her spun around so fast, she nearly crashed into Tracy.

"Simmer down, you don't want him to think you're desperate."

Violet ignored the dig as her eyes devoured him. He looked exactly the same, except his expression was just as closed off as the first day they'd met.

What did you expect? That you would tell him it's over and he'd be excited to see you?

She watched him hand Casey a wrapped package, and then Casey said something that had made him look around. When his gaze found hers, she had the crazy urge to run to him.

Instead her feet seemed glued to the grass as Casey walked away with his present and Dean made his way toward her.

"Hey, you are squeezing my hand!" Tracy hissed.

Violet released her hold on Tracy, hadn't even realized she'd reached out for her. "You are not being supportive."

"Why, because I won't let you crush my hand or because I am about to leave you alone with the man you still love?"

"Tracy, I swear—"

But she was already gone, and Dean was now in front of her.

"Hello, Violet."

She swallowed and pasted on what she hoped was a welcoming smile. "Hi, Dean."

"How are you?" he asked.

Miserable. "I'm fine, how are you?"

"Good."

Well, this isn't awkward at all.

A thousand things Violet wanted to say raced through her mind. How she'd missed him. That she was sorry and wished she'd handled things differently.

That she still loved him so much it had been hard to think of him without hurting.

Instead, she said, "Thank you so much for coming. I know it means a lot to Casey."

And me.

"Of course I'd come for Casey"—he hesitated—"but I can't stay. I just wanted to say hi."

Disappointment sat like chalk on her tongue, the bitter taste in her mouth turning her stomach. "Oh, well, sure. I'm glad you did."

"I just..." Violet watched his throat work as he struggled and finally shook his head. "Yeah, I can't do this."

He spun away from Violet and walked around the side of the house. Violet could feel dozens of eyes on her, and her face burned as he disappeared.

Go after him. What are you waiting for?

But she couldn't seem to make her feet work, until someone literally pushed her from behind. Violet stumbled and glared over her shoulder at her little brother.

"Why did you push me?"

"Because you're just standing there like an idiot when you should be running after him."

Sure, she'd been thinking it, but it was another matter to have her brother call her on it.

"Seriously, Vi, if you don't hurry, he's going to be gone, and you need him. Hell, I need him...to distract you so you'll stop making me watch those crappy movies you like."

Violet choked on a laugh, knowing her brother was right. Not about how crappy her movies were, but the other thing.

She needed Dean.

Racing after him, she hit the front walkway as he was climbing into his truck.

"Dean! Wait!"

He paused, and as he looked around, she noted his exasperated expression and ignored it.

"I'm sorry. For how I left things—"

"No, I'm sorry, I shouldn't have just shown up here like this."

"But I'm glad you did—"

"Look, Violet—"

"No." She rounded the tailgate and stood in front of him, breathing hard. "I don't want to look anymore. I don't want to search for reasons why things won't work out between us. Since the moment we met, we have put everything else before being with each other, and I'm done. We've been thrown back into each other's path again and again, and I don't want to miss my last chance."

While she caught her breath, he shook his head. "Or the universe is trying to tell us that we're one of those couples who care about each other but can't be together."

"No, I don't believe that. I think that the reason that it hasn't worked is because we were both afraid and holding back. I know I was. I was afraid that if I let you in, you were going to be another person I put before everything I wanted, but I realized that no one was getting in the way of me living but me. And I can't live without you."

"You seem to be doing all right," he said.

Tears rolled down her cheeks as she laughed bitterly. "I'm not living, Dean. I had no idea what if felt like to be alive until you. I can be without you, I can go to work and school and be with my family, but it's not complete. For the longest time, I didn't know who I was, but I do now. I'm someone who loves to cook, and maybe I will open a restaurant one day, or maybe it will just remain a passion. I hate working at the hotline, and after the new year, I'll be looking for something else. I don't want to dwell on the past and continuously worry about my future. Instead of concentrating on all the drama, I want to be grateful for all that's right in my world. Raising Casey and Daisy was the hardest thing I'd ever done until now, and you know, I don't regret a second of it, even the bad times. I'd do it again, because they are a part of me. Just like you. Even if you get in that truck and I never see you again, that missing piece will go with you and I'll never be complete."

Dean's hard expression eased a bit, and his mouth kicked up at the corner, a small smile, but it gave Violet a mountain of hope.

"Did you just tell me that I complete you?"

"In so many words, yes."

Dean put his hands on the side of his truck bed and leaned over, sighing. "You could have told me this at any time, but you waited until I showed up here. Why?"

"It was easier to stay away. I know I've screwed up, but I've never known how to ask for help. I know how to fight, I know how to keep people at a distance, but this is my first bout into love, so I'm bound to make a shit storm of mistakes. I'm just hoping that you'll forgive me for them."

Violet waited, holding her breath as Dean remained silent.

Finally, he stood up once more and faced her, arms crossed over his chest. "It wasn't all you."

"What?"

He took a step toward her, and despite his guarded stance, she could feel the distance between them evaporating.

"I let you push me away. I knew what you were doing, and I didn't fight. I rolled over and conceded defeat, when I should have broken down your door and told you that without you, I'm just a miserable, angry asshole. I should have come back every day and told you how much I missed you. And that when I turned down the chance to go back overseas, I lied when I said it had nothing to do with you. I realized that I'd wanted to go back for the wrong reasons. It wasn't going to erase what happened or bring back the friends I lost.

"The week before we fought, my psychiatrist asked me three questions. What does my life look like in five years, what do I need to be the best version of myself, and what are three things that make me happy?" His hand came up to cup her cheek, and she covered it with hers as he finished. "The answer to every question was you. Yes, Alpha Dog and the guys, Casey, Daisy, and Dilbert were all there, but you were the center of everything. The only future I wanted included us, but I thought that you didn't need me the way I needed you."

Violet threw herself against him, trusting him to catch her. "Oh my God, I do. I do. I am so sorry. So sorry."

"I am, too." The warmth of his breath and kiss in her hair made her squeeze harder.

"Can we start over?" she whispered.

Dean pulled back, framing her face with his hands. "No way. You and I have gone through some shit, and as many mistakes as we've made, we need those. They're going to remind us to do better. To be better."

"But we just can't pick up where we left off," Violet said.

"Why not?"

Without waiting for her response, Dean kissed her, and she pressed back, never wanting to lose this feeling again. To be without Dean. Holding tight to his waist, she would have protested, but the love she saw shining down at her eased her worry.

With one last brush of his lips, she sensed the promise in this moment. That they had something real and wonderful and would never take it for granted again.

Then Dean smiled down at her, and she suddenly got it.

Fresh starts were for the weak, for people who couldn't face their mistakes.

But together, they could take on anything.

And they would.

Epilogue

Four Years Later

Dean Sparks stood in the crowded hallway next to his wife, waiting impatiently for the unveiling to begin.

"Why are you muttering like that?" Violet asked.

"I'm not muttering." Was he? He hadn't even been aware he was doing it, but they had been standing there for fifteen minutes at least, and he knew that Violet had to be uncomfortable. After all, she was carrying about twenty-five pounds of extra weight in front of her body.

As Dean searched for a place to seat his very pregnant wife, he thought he saw her wince.

"What was that?"

"Nothing, it's just Braxton-Hicks," shc said.

"Are you sure?" Violet was just over eight months, but he had heard stories from his sisters and his friends. Plus, there was that video of the woman giving birth while the husband was driving.

Dean shuddered, a cold sweat breaking out all over his body just thinking about it.

Suddenly, the crowd exploded in applause as Casey came around the corner and stood in front of a large white sheet. Looking at him now, Dean couldn't believe he was the same kid he'd first met. Now nearly six feet tall and still growing, it seemed, Casey smiled out at the crowd. Dean remembered how Casey had once dreamed of doing a mural for his school, and now he was about to present his second one. The school had asked him to do another before he left for NYU, and he had spent all summer painting, showing none of them what he was working on.

Casey's high school principal stepped out to make the introductions, just as Jack Douglas and his wife, Sandy, pushed through to stand next to them. "Sorry we're late, but traffic was awful."

"It's okay, it is just starting." Dean watched Violet give her father a tentative hug before greeting Sandy warmly. It seemed that no matter what Jack tried to do to make up for all those bad years, Violet never quite seemed at ease with him. Dean was sorry for that but proud of her for trying. It was all any of them could do.

"Where the hell is Daisy?" Violet griped.

Daisy appeared between them. "I'm here, Vulcan hearing and all. Sorry, but that line to the bathroom was fucking ridiculous."

Dean coughed, hiding his laughter as Violet glared mutinously at her sister. He could almost hear Violet trying to tell Daisy to watch her language, but she didn't bother saying it aloud. If Daisy was incorrigible at eighteen, there was no changing her at twenty-two.

"Thank you all for coming," the principal said. "Today, I have the pleasure of introducing one of the finest artists to ever grace these halls. We asked him to paint something special to reflect our community before he leaves us for NYU in a few weeks. Please welcome Casey Douglas."

More clapping as Casey waited, and once it was quiet again, he spoke loud and clear. "Thank you for coming. This particular piece was inspired by my past to prove that no matter how dark the time, we can't give up. We must continue to search for the best within ourselves and the world around us. I was lucky to have my family and friends to get me through. Some kids don't have that kind of support, but I hope that this at least will give them hope."

"And so, without further ado, here is *Violets in the Sun*."

Violet gasped as Casey pulled down the sheet to reveal a bright purple field of violets and a blast of sunshine highlighting their colors. On either side of the mural was darkness with the hint of shapes, and there were mountains in the background. The mountains were lit up with oranges, pinks, and yellows, and atop one was a single figure reaching toward the sky.

There were collective sounds of approval before more thunderous clapping, which echoed through the hallway.

Dean leaned over Daisy, careful to not let Jack hear, and spoke in Violet's ear. "If you were ever worried that kid doesn't love you, I think we can put that to bed."

Violet flinched, and Dean turned toward her just as her skin turned sheet white.

"Violet, what's wrong?"

She reached out and gripped his arm, her eyes wide. Daisy moved out of the way as Violet said loudly, "We have to go."

Alarm shot through Dean like electroshock. "What is wrong? Are you okay?"

"I think"—she swallowed—"my water just broke."

IF SOMEONE HAD told Violet five years ago that she would be lying in a hospital room in the labor and delivery ward, holding her daughter, she would have laughed in their faces. Never in a million years could she have imagined her life turning out like this. The fears and doubts were still there, at the back of her mind, but they no longer plagued her every day. She had spent the last four years discovering who she was, and she was eternally grateful for the man standing next to her for supporting her.

Dean leaned over and kissed her forehead, smiling down at the little wrinkly bundle in the pink blanket. "She's the prettiest thing I've ever seen."

"I think so, too."

A knock on the door nearly made Violet groan. For hours, friends and family had been streaming in to say their congratulations, and although she appreciated having them, she was exhausted and dying to sleep.

Casey and Daisy peeked inside, and Violet was relieved it was them.

"Hey."

"We come bearing gifts from Meredith. She says she needs you, and the place is falling apart," Casey said, holding up a pink pastry box from The Sweet Spot Eatery.

Violet had started working at the little restaurant and bakery just after Dean and she had celebrated their sixth-month anniversary. It had been the move to solidify her dream of one day owning her own shop, but for now she was content to come in early and bake all the delectable treats that graced the dessert case. Meredith had hinted lately about making Violet a partner, but it was a big decision, one she still wasn't sure she was ready for. Time would tell.

Casey and Daisy came to stand next to the bed. Daisy wrinkled her nose. "Babies are ugly."

"She is not!" Dean practically roared, startling the baby in Violet's arms.

"Geez, don't be so touchy. I meant ugly in a way a pug is ugly, you know, so ugly they're cute."

Casey laughed as Dean's face turned molten red, and Violet sighed. "Do you have to torment him? I am too tired to referee."

"That's what little sisters are for," Daisy said.

This seemed to mollify Dean, who grunted at Daisy.

Casey reached out his arms, surprisingly. "Can I hold her?"

Violet handed off her daughter to her new uncle, tears blurring her vision as she watched Casey smile tenderly down at her.

"What's her name?"

Violet swallowed. "We were thinking about Hope."

Casey trailed a finger over Hope's cheek. "I think that's perfect."

Dean's phone rang, and he stepped out of the room to take it.

"I think I'm going to go grab a cup of coffee, see if maybe I can score a hot doctor's number," Daisy said, shimmying her hips out the door.

Violet shook her head. "Isn't she dating a med student already?"

"Not anymore, apparently," Casey said.

As Violet watched Casey move around the room with Hope, she sniffled. "I'm going to miss you when you leave."

Casey glanced up to meet her gaze, a puzzled expression on his handsome face. "I'm going to be home in a few months for Thanksgiving."

"I know, but the house won't be the same without you."

"You mean, you're going to miss me and my friends eating all of your food and trampling all over your clean house?"

"Of course I will." In truth, Violet had always known that Casey and Daisy would go off to college and start their own lives someday, and there had been a time when she'd looked forward to it. But today, it all felt too soon. Everything was changing so fast. "I remember the day Mom brought you home from the hospital. You had soft red hair and alien fingers. I just can't believe that—"

"Okay, enough, you are just suffering from a wash of hormones or something." Casey sat down next to her and handed her back her daughter. "You do not need to stress and worry about me. I'm going to be fine, and I guarantee that you will be so busy, you will probably forget my name half the time."

"You're stupid," Violet said. "I'm going to miss you so much, I'll probably call you a dozen times a day and show up at your dorm, embarrassing you in front of all your cool new friends."

Casey squeezed her shoulder with a smile. "You never embarrass me, Vi...except when you do that thing where you try to sing and it just sounds like fighting cats—"

She would have smacked him, but her arms and heart were too full. "You're a brat."

"I am what you made me."

A lump burned at the back of her throat. "Then I did really good."

Dean chose that moment to return, glancing between them curiously. "That was my mom. She's laid over in Denver but will be here soon."

"Well, I've got some more packing to do, and you need to rest. New babies are brutal, I hear." Casey winked at them as he left the room, and Dean chuckled.

"I'm gonna miss that kid."

"Me, too." Violet leaned her head back against the pillow and gazed up at him. "I'm so tired."

"Here, I'll put her in the crib and let you get some rest."

Violet loved the way Dean carried Hope, as if she would shatter in his arms at any moment. As he laid her in the plastic crib, Violet scooted over on the bed. "Come up here."

With an eyebrow raised doubtfully, he shook his head. "There's not enough room."

"We'll snuggle. Come on, I need you."

And that was all she had to say. Slowly and carefully, Dean crawled up into the bed next to her and wrapped his arms around her.

"Happy?" he asked.

"Not the word I'd use."

"And what word would you use?"

"It hasn't been invented yet."

She felt his lips stretch into a smile against her forehead. "I love you, Violet."

As Violet drifted off to sleep, she murmured, "I love you, too. Forever."

To My Readers,

Every twelve minutes, a death by suicide occurs in the United States. These deaths leave behind devastated loved ones, and often with one lingering question; why? If you or someone you know, are experiencing suicidal thoughts, please reach out to a loved one or contact the National Suicide Prevention Lifeline at 1-(800) 273-8255. Please remember, you are not alone.

Acknowledgments

This is my eleventh published work, and through this whole crazy process, there have been so many amazing people who have stood by me and helped me through. First off, I want to thank my awesome editor, Chelsey Emmelhainz, who gives me all the right notes and encouragement. I want to thank my amazing agent, Sarah Younger, for putting up with me, even during my crazy times. To my parents, family, and friends who support and encourage me, especially my husband and our children: Thank you! To my author friends, who understand the ups and downs and struggles, I love you and thank you for all of your listening ears and advice. Thank you to my Rockers for their unwavering awesomeness! I love your guts. To Katherine from the K9 Connection Program: Thank you for the e-book and answering my questions!

Look for the next book in

Codi Gary's Men in Uniform series,

Hero of Mine

Coming August 2016 from Avon Impulse.

About the Author

An obsessive bookworm, **CODI GARY** likes to write sexy contemporary romances with humor, grand gestures, and blush-worthy moments. When she's not writing, she can be found reading her favorite authors, squealing over her must-watch shows, and playing with her children. She lives in Idaho with her family.

Discover great authors, exclusive offers, and more at hc.com.

Give in to your Impulses . . .
Continue reading for excerpts from
our newest Avon Impulse books.
Available now wherever ebooks are sold.

CHANGE OF HEART

by T.J. Kline

MONTANA HEARTS: TRUE COUNTRY HERO

by Darlene Panzera

ONCE AND FOR ALL

An American Valor Novel

by Cheryl Etchison

An Excerpt from

CHANGE OF HEART

By T.J. Kline

Bad luck has plagued Leah McCarran most of her life, until the tide turns and she lands her new dream job as a therapist at Heart Fire Ranch. But when her car breaks down and she finds herself stranded, the playboy who shows up to her rescue makes Leah wonder if her luck just went from bad to worse.

Leah McCarran couldn't believe her luck as she popped the hood of her classic GTO and glanced behind her, down the deserted stretch of highway in the Northern California foothills. Steam poured from her radiator, and there wasn't a single car in sight.

She blew back a strand of her caramel-colored hair as the curl fell into her eye and caught on her mascaraed eyelashes. Even those felt like they were melting into solid clumps on her eyes. It was sweltering for mid-May, and, of course, her car decided to take a dump on the side of the highway today. She fanned herself with one hand as she looked down at the overheated engine. It probably wouldn't have been nearly this big a deal if her cell phone hadn't just taken a crap, too. To top off her miserable day, she'd spilled her iced coffee all over the damn thing getting out of the car and likely destroyed it once and for all.

This wasn't the way she'd hoped to start her new job or her new life at Heart Fire Ranch.

Walking back to the driver's side of the car, Leah had no clue what to do now. Luckily, her boss wasn't expecting her until this evening, and she'd had the foresight, knowing her penchant for bad luck, to leave early. But until some Good Samaritan decided to drive by *and* stop for her, she was S.O.L. She kicked the tire as she walked by. As if trying to deny her even that small measure of satisfaction, the sole of her worn combat boot caught in the tread, nearly making her fall over.

"Son of a—"

Leah caught herself against the side of the car, willing the tears of frustration to subside, back into the vault where they belonged. That was one thing she'd learned as a child: tears meant weakness.

And showing weakness was asking for more pain.

She bent over into the car, looking for something to mop up the sticky mess the coffee was making on the restored leather interior of her car. She reached for the denim shirt she'd been wearing over her tank top before she'd left Chowchilla this morning, before the air had turned from chilled to hell-on-earth-hot.

"Shit," she muttered. Trying to sop up coffee with denim was like trying to mop a floor with a broom: it did absolutely no good.

"Hot damn! That is the most incredible thing I've seen all day."

The crunch of tires pulling off the asphalt of the highway was a welcome sound, but the awe she heard in the husky voice was enough to send a chill down her spine. Leah threw the shirt down onto the coffee-soaked floorboard. Standing up, she spun on the heel of her boot, her fists clenching at her sides as she tried to control the instinct to punch a man in the mouth.

"Excuse me? Do you really have so little class?"

"Oh, shit! No, that's not . . ." She watched as the man unfolded himself from a late model Challenger and shut the door, jogging across the empty two-lane highway to her side. "I'm sorry, I meant the car."

Leah crossed her arms under her breasts and arched a single, disbelieving brow. "Sure, you did."

A blush flooded his dark caramel skin. "I swear I meant the car. Not that you're not . . . I mean . . . crap." He cursed again. "Let me try this again. Do you need some help?"

An Excerpt from

MONTANA HEARTS: TRUE COUNTRY HERO

By Darlene Panzera

For Jace Aldridge, the chase is half the fun. The famous rodeo rider has spent most of life chasing down steers and championship rodeo belts, but after an accident in the arena, his career is put on temporary hold. When he's offered a chance to stay at Collins Country Cabins, Jace jumps at the opportunity to spend more time with the beautiful but wary Delaney Collins.

The cowboy winked at her. Delaney Collins lowered her camera lens and glanced around twice to make sure, but no one else behind the roping chute was looking his direction. Heat flooded her cheeks as he followed up the wink with a grin, and a multitude of wary warnings sounded off in her heart. The last thing she'd wanted was to catch the rodeo circuit star's interest. She pretended to adjust the settings, then raised the camera to her eye once again, determined to fulfill her duty and take the required photos of the handsome dark-haired devil.

Except he wouldn't stand still. He climbed off his buckskin horse, handed the reins to a nearby gatekeeper, gave a young kid in the stands a high five, and then walked straight toward her.

Delaney tightened her hold on the camera, wishing she could stay hidden behind the lens, and considered several different ways to slip away unnoticed. But she knew she couldn't avoid him forever. Not when it was her job to shadow the guy and capture the highlights from his steer-wrestling runs. Maybe he only wanted to check in to make sure she was getting the right shots?

Most cowboys like Jace Aldridge had large egos to match their championship-sized belt buckles, one reason she usually avoided these events and preferred capturing images of plants and animals. But when the lead photographer for *True Montana Magazine* called in sick before the event and they needed a fill-in, Delaney had been both honored and excited to accept the position. Perhaps after the magazine viewed her work, they'd hire her for more photo ops. Then she wouldn't have to rely solely on the profits from her share of her family's guest ranch to support herself.

She swallowed hard as the stocky, dark-haired figure, whose image continuously graced the cover of every western periodical, smiled, his eyes on her—yes, definitely her—as he drew near.

He stretched out his hand. "Jace Aldridge."

She stared at his chapped knuckles. Beside her, Sammy Jo gave her arm a discreet nudge, urging her to accept his handshake. After all, it would be impolite to refuse. Even if, in addition to riding rodeo, he was a hunter, an adversary of the animals she and her wildlife rescue group regularly sought to save.

Lifting her gaze to meet his, she replied, "Delaney Collins."

"Nice to meet you," Jace said, his rich, baritone voice smooth and . . . dangerously distracting. His hand gave hers a warm squeeze, and although he glanced toward Sammy Jo to include her in his greeting, it was clear who held his real interest. "Are you with the press?"

Delaney glanced down at the Canon EOS 7D with its high-definition 20.2 megapixel zoom lens hanging down from the strap around her neck. "Yes. I'm taking photos for *True Montana*."

The edges of his mouth curved into another smile. "I haven't seen you around before."

"I—I'm not around much, but Sammy Jo here," she said, motioning toward her friend to divert his attention, "used to race barrels. You must know her. Sammy Jo Macpherson?"

Jace gave her friend a brief nod. "I believe we've met."

"Del's a great photographer," Sammy Jo said, bouncing the attention back to her.

Jace grinned. "I bet."

"It's the lens," Delaney said, averting her gaze, and Sammy Jo shot her a disgruntled look as if to say, *Smarten up, this guy's in to you. Don't blow it!*

Except she had no desire to get involved in a relationship right now. And definitely not one *with a hunter*. She needed to focus on her two-and-a-half-year-old daughter, Meghan, and help her family's guest ranch bring in enough money to support them.

An Excerpt from

ONCE AND FOR ALL

An American Valor Novel

By Cheryl Etchison

Staff Sergeant Danny MacGregor has always said military and matrimony don't mix, but if there's one person he would break all his rules for, it's Bree—his first friend, first love, first everything.

Bree Dunbar has battled cancer, twice. What she wants most is a fresh start. By some miracle her wish is granted, but it comes with one major string attached—the man who broke her heart ten years before.

The rules for this marriage of convenience are simple: when she's ready to stand on her own two feet, she'll walk away and he'll let her go. Only, things don't always go according to plan . . .

She pulled into the garage of her parents' home and stared in the rearview mirror at the house across the street where Danny used to live. The same one where he was now staying. She had no idea how much longer he'd be in town, but odds weren't in her favor he would just leave her be. She'd thrown down the gauntlet and Daniel Patrick MacGregor had never been one to back down from a challenge.

Hitting the garage remote, the house slowly disappeared from view as the door lowered to the ground. Bree headed inside, her mother greeting her at the back door as she opened it.

"Can I help you carry some things in?" she asked while drying her hands on a dish towel.

"Nothing to bring in."

Bree scooted past her mother, not yet ready to rehash the morning's events.

"I thought you were going to the store?"

"I'll go back later."

She grabbed the ibuprofen from the cabinet by the sink, the dull ache behind her eyes now reaching epic proportions. After swallowing two small tablets with a single drink of water, she headed for her bedroom.

"Is everything okay, sweetheart? You look flushed."

"Fine," she said, ducking out of her mother's reach. Twenty-eight years old and her mother still wanted to check her temperature with the back of her hand.

"Are you sure? You're not running a fever, are you? Your immune system still isn't where it needs to be. You need to be careful—"

"I'm fine, Mom. I swear. Just going to lie down for a bit."

Bree darted upstairs, escaping to the relative peace and quiet of her bedroom. She closed the door behind her, sighing in relief to see her mother wasn't hot on her heels.

She loved her dearly and wouldn't have survived chemo treatments without her, but sometimes her mother's care and concern was too much. Suffocating. And despite her best intentions, she was always reminding Bree that she'd been very sick, when all Bree wanted to do was put it behind her.

For now, she'd settle for crawling into bed and trying to forget the morning ever happened. As she closed the blinds, a familiar old truck pulled into the driveway across the street. The door flung open, and booted feet hit the concrete. Instinctively she jumped back from the window, not wanting Danny to think she'd been standing there, watching, waiting all this time for him to return home.

Bree held her breath and with the tips of her fingers lifted a single wooden slat so she could peek out. The old truck's passenger door sat open wide, but there was no sign of either brother. The screen door swung open and Danny bounded down the porch steps, reaching the truck in four long strides. He grabbed the last few grocery bags from the floorboard and shoved the door closed with his elbow. On his way back into the house he suddenly stopped and turned to look across the street. At her house. At her bedroom window.

Despite peering through a tiny gap no wider than an inch, she knew he could somehow see her. She could feel his gaze locked on hers. But he didn't drop the grocery bags on the front porch or storm across the street toward her. Instead, he just stood there. His expression completely unreadable.

Surely he wouldn't march across the street and start things up again right now? He wouldn't dare.

Oh, but he would.

Maybe he expected her to do something. Wave. Stick out her tongue. Flip him the bird. Instead, like a deer caught in a hunter's sight, she stood frozen, unable to will herself away from the window. Then he did the very last thing she expected him to do.

He smiled.

A smile so wide, so bright, she hadn't seen the likes of one in over a decade. Although she didn't want to admit it, she'd missed that smile desperately and her heart squeezed painfully in her chest. Finally, Danny looked away, breaking eye contact, releasing her from his spell. As he turned to go inside, he shook his head, apparently unable to believe it himself.

For a long time after he went inside, Bree stood there looking out the window. And the more she replayed it in her mind, the more she began to wonder if she'd imagined the entire thing.

Only one thing was for certain—things between them were far from over.

stared the door closed with his other. On his way back into the house he suddenly stopped and turned to look across the street. At her house. At her bedroom window.

Despite peering through a tiny gap no wider than a finch, she knew he could somehow see her. She grabbed [illegible] gaze locked on hers. And he didn't drop the grocery bags on the front porch or [illegible] the street toward her. Instead, he just stood there. His expression completely unreadable.

Surely he wouldn't march across the street and start [illegible] right now? He wouldn't dare.

Or would he?

Maybe he expected her to do something. Wave. Stick out her tongue. [illegible] the bed. Instead, like a deer caught in a hunter's sight, she saw [illegible] couldn't [illegible] herself away from the window. Then he did the very last thing she expected him to do.

He smiled.

A smile so wide, so bright, she hadn't seen the likes of one in over a decade. Although she didn't want to admit it, she'd missed that smile desperately and her heart squeezed painfully in her chest. Finally, Danny looked away, breaking eye contact, releasing her from the spell. As he turned to go inside, [illegible] her knees [illegible].

[illegible] there [illegible] And [illegible] she [illegible] and the [illegible] to wonder if she'd imagined the whole thing.

Only one thing was for certain—things between them were far from over.